By JORDAN GILLESPIE

Harmonious Hearts 2015

NEW STATE
Accuracy

As Frisk Gillespie
Harmonious Hearts 2016
Harmonious Hearts 2017

Published by HARMONY INK PRESS
www.harmonyinkpress.com

JORDAN GILLESPIE

ACCURACY

Harmony Ink

Published by
HARMONY INK PRESS

5032 Capital Circle SW, Suite 2, PMB# 279, Tallahassee, FL 32305-7886 USA
publisher@harmonyinkpress.com • www.harmonyinkpress.com

Trade Paperback ISBN: 978-1-64405-803-9
Digital ISBN: 978-1-64405-802-2
Library of Congress Control Number: 2019949979
Trade Paperback published January 2020
v. 1.0

Printed in the United States of America
(∞)
This paper meets the requirements of
ANSI/NISO Z39.48-1992 (Permanence of Paper).

To Malena, who believed in my writing when I couldn't.

CHAPTER ONE

"BETA GROUP Five, ready your weapons."

Clicks could be heard throughout the room as guns were taken off safety.

"Take aim."

Fifteen pairs of arms rose as one to lock on to their targets. There was a brief pause.

"Fire."

The weapons discharged, and muffled cries of pain could be heard. The cries eventually died out and left only heavy breathing from the shooters.

"Safety on."

The fifteen shooters all clicked on the safety of their guns and lowered them.

"All clear. Next round in ten minutes."

When they were given the all clear, the shooters relaxed and stepped back from the shooting line. They spread out into their usual groups where they chatted among themselves, for the most part ignoring the grisly sight they had created on the far wall of the training room. One young woman did not step back right away, nor did she make any effort to avert her eyes. Her gaze remained locked to her target, to the blood seeping from the wound she had placed squarely in the abdomen. Only when the cleaners opened the handcuffs that held his arms above his head and pulled him down onto the ground did she finally turn away.

"Lai, you shouldn't do that."

Lailani looked up when she heard her nickname. Her best friend, Jaime Martinez, walked toward her at a quick pace. He didn't stop next to her but rather turned around and pulled her along with him to the far wall, as far as they could get from the fifteen dead bodies.

"You know it upsets you," Jaime said as they reached the wall. Lai glanced around to be sure no eyes were on them.

"And it doesn't upset you?" she asked with a raised eyebrow. Jaime sighed and ran his hands through his messy black hair.

"It upsets everyone," he replied. "You know that."

"Do I?" she hissed. She nodded to a group of four of their peers where they stood laughing with each other. "Do they seem upset?"

"No," he conceded.

Lai nodded and glanced back up at him. "Exactly. More of us should care."

"Come on, *asere*, you know live target practice is part of our training."

Lai sighed but said nothing. She took her attention off her friend and gazed across the room. She took extra care to keep the dead bodies out of her field of vision.

"I wasn't thinking about killing people when I signed up for this," she said after a moment. She eyed the thirteen other members of her training squad and tried not to think too harshly of them. She, too, after all, had just executed a man. Who was she to think she was better than any of them because it gave her a queasy stomach?

"I don't like it any more than you do, but these people were already on death row," Jaime reminded her.

"Or had a life sentence," Lai countered.

Jaime shrugged. "Same thing."

"Only because we made it that way."

"Why are you arguing with me? I don't enjoy doing this."

Lai sighed again. "Sorry. I was thinking about what Oscar told me last week."

Jaime frowned and lowered his voice even further. "Be careful talking about that, Lailani. Oscar had a breakdown. We don't know if anything he said is true."

"It could be," Lai replied, matching his volume. "And if it is, then none of us should be doing this."

Before Jaime could reply, all heads turned as the doors opened and armed guards hauled fifteen more prisoners into the room. Each had their head covered with a cloth bag and their hands handcuffed in front of them. The handcuffs were then connected to a long chain that went up to a collar around their necks and down to shackles on their ankles. Lai gave them a quick assessment. From the additional guards, the extra restraints, and the way each was clenching and unclenching their fists in anger, Lai figured they were in for violent crimes, most likely rape or murder. That lightened her mood only slightly.

The prisoners were brought before a firing station where blood and bits of organs were splayed on the walls. During target practice the walls were never cleaned. The bodies were simply removed for disposal to save time. After the session was finished, the students would go to their next session and the cleaners would bring in the bleach and other harsh chemicals to wipe away the traces of death from the room.

The prisoners were each stood before a station. The handcuffs were undone, only to have the people's arms held out to their sides and connected to the other handcuffs that dangled from the wall behind them. Their collars were removed, and their ankles were chained to the ground. One man tried to struggle as his wrists were cuffed to the walls and earned himself a firm elbow to the ribs. He groaned as the officers restrained him and left him on the wall. When all the officers had stepped back, what was left was fifteen people standing with their arms spread out at their sides, as if welcoming their impending deaths.

All but one officer left the room, save the four that always guarded the doors. The one that remained walked past the prisoners, pulling off the bags that covered their heads. Lai looked at each of the prisoners in turn. Twelve of them were men, three women, and all had eyes that burned with hatred as they stared at their executioners. Their instructor, Sergeant Washington, paid no attention to the people standing against the wall. She directed her attention to her students and spoke with a voice that commanded attention from all.

"For this exercise you will be practicing in a different way than usual," she told them. Lai frowned, and many students mumbled to each other in confusion until the sergeant raised her fist for silence. When she got it, she continued. "You will not be shooting to kill. You will be shooting to maim."

Shouts of hatred and defiance rose up from the prisoners chained to the wall. The sergeant finally turned her attention to them and fixed each with a blistering stare. Her eyes turned as dark as her skin. It took nearly two minutes for the shouts to die down. The sergeant let them go on until they faded on their own. When the last prisoner was silent, she turned to one of the guards standing by the door.

"Guard, fetch me fifteen gags."

The guard nodded once and disappeared through the door to get the gags. The shouts returned from the prisoners. They spat curses, some directed at the sergeant, but most were yelled to the students. Lai wished she could run out of the room and hide in her quarters. People had yelled before, but never like this. Most begged for their lives, a few cursed the students, but none had ever shouted such vile things at her. One man noticed her staring and fixed his beady eyes on her. His muscles bulged as he strained against his restraints and yelled to her what he would do if she got too close to him. She shuddered and turned to face the back wall. Jaime put a hand on her shoulder and squeezed. He leaned close to her and whispered in her ear.

"It's all right, *asere*. He can't hurt you," Jaime soothed.

Lai forced a smile. "I know. It just doesn't feel too pleasant to have a man tell you he would disembowel you if he weren't handcuffed."

Jaime glanced back over his shoulder to the prisoners. To his relief, the guard had come back and was putting the gags in the mouths of the screaming prisoners. As he did, their shouts became muffled.

"The one who was yelling at you is at my station," Jaime told her. "I'll make him regret saying those things."

Lai said nothing. She stared hard at the wall in front of her until the last shout ceased, and then turned back around. The man still glared.

"Students."

All eyes turned back to the sergeant. She stood grim-faced as she regarded them.

"It is one thing to know how to kill a person." Her gaze swept over each prisoner. "It is another to know how to shoot without killing them. There may come a time when you are required to subdue your target without ending their life. When that time comes, you need to know how and where to shoot so they do not bleed out before they can receive medical attention.

"You should each have six bullets left. I want you to empty your guns on these prisoners. Aim in places where a wound would allow them to survive but would slow them enough so they could be subdued if necessary."

"Sergeant Washington?" came a quiet voice from the side of the room. The sergeant's gaze fell on the student who had spoken. Lai stood on her toes to see over the heads and discovered it was Rylen, the most recent addition to the group, only having joined Beta Five three months earlier.

"Rylen?" The sergeant nodded for him to speak. Rylen eyed the prisoners with clear apprehension.

"Are we allowed to shoot them without killing them? I mean, isn't that torture?"

"This knowledge may save your life in the field one day" was the reply. Rylen did not seem entirely convinced.

"But just because they're prisoners doesn't mean they deserve to be in pain."

The sergeant paused for a moment before speaking. "Allow me to relieve you of your worries. This is perfectly legal. This training exercise has recently been implemented, and representatives of the American Republic have signed off on the practice. As for the moral dilemma you face, worry not. These prisoners are all serial murderers, and nine of them are rapists."

Lai's attention strayed back to the man who had threatened her with such a fate just moments before. His glare now seemed teasing to her.

"They are the lowest and vilest scum of the human race," the sergeant preached. "What you are about to do to them is little compared to what they put their victims through."

This seemed to quiet the worries of the students. Rylen nodded and stepped back. No one else voiced any concerns. Lai struggled to break the gaze of the man.

"To your stations," the sergeant commanded.

With little reluctance, the students all walked to their stations and stared at their targets. Jaime had to pull Lai along to make her follow. She did, and focused her attention on the woman in front of her. She spared no glance to Jaime's station beside her.

"Ready your weapons."

Lai pulled her gun from her belt and turned off the safety. The others did the same.

"Take aim."

She lifted her gun and aimed toward the woman's shoulder. She gave the quickest of glances to the woman's face and saw only hatred in her features. She wondered how many people this woman had killed, and vaguely wondered if she herself could be counted as a serial killer.

"Fire."

"Patawarin mo ako Diyos," Lai mumbled, a prayer in her native Tagalog language. She hesitated only the briefest moment before discharging her weapon.

CHAPTER TWO

"I CAN'T believe I killed mine."

Lai opened her eyes and rolled her head over on her pillow to look at her dorm mate who had spoken. The girl, Siobhan, was sitting on her own bed across the room with her head in her hands. Two others, Tamsin and Virginia, were sitting on either side of her as they offered her words of comfort and gentle back rubs. The rest kept to their own devices. Lai closed her eyes again and tried to ignore them but found her mind wandering back to the events of their training session earlier in the day.

Shoot to maim. It was an order the students had never been given before, but according to Sergeant Washington, they were likely to be given again. It was the first time since Lai had begun her training three years prior that protocol had been changed so drastically.

Lai had not killed her target. She had shot the woman six times, once in each shoulder, once in each calf, and twice in her left thigh. Even with the gag on Lai could tell she was screaming. They all were. Being shot once was bad enough, but six times was brutal. When the sergeant had called the all clear, she said the guards had orders to wait two minutes before intervening and giving medical assistance. If the prisoner did not die within those two minutes, they would have passed the exercise. Lai couldn't help herself; she had watched the woman she had shot for the full two minutes, watched her crying in pain, her struggles getting weaker as the wounds stole her energy. Just before the sergeant had called for the guards to take the prisoners to the medical station, Lai had stared into the woman's eyes again. The hatred in them was staggering.

Three of the fifteen prisoners had died before the two minutes were up. The students who killed their targets were Devlin, Vineet, and Siobhan, who was now sulking in her bed.

Lai sighed and opened her eyes again. She sat up and stretched her sore arms above her head. The movement caught the attention of her dorm mates.

"You've been quiet tonight, Lani," said Kieran from the bunk next to Lai's. Lai rolled her eyes.

"It's Lai," she mumbled.

"What's the matter, Lani," Kieran continued, "you don't like it when your target survives?"

"I don't like making them suffer," Lai replied. She closed her eyes for a moment and rubbed them with her palms, hard enough to make stars dance behind her eyelids. "At least when we kill them, they don't have to suffer."

"Why should we care if murderers and rapists suffer?" Kieran shot back. A few of the other girls voiced their agreement. Kieran smirked at the support and fell back on her bed, her head landing in the lap of her girlfriend, Deirdre.

"They're still people. I don't think anyone deserves to be in pain."

"So you don't think they're in pain when we kill them?" Deirdre asked.

Lai groaned. She was in no mood to argue with her dorm mates. "I think if you're a good shot, they won't have to be in pain for very long."

"She has a point." Virginia spoke up from where she sat beside Siobhan. All eyes turned toward her.

"Pray tell," Kieran said.

Virginia frowned at her. "When we kill them, we're doing them a favor. If they weren't dead, they would be in prison for the rest of their lives, like people used to be before the Republic took power. What kind of life would that be? I'd rather be dead than in prison for life."

"What does that have to do with being in pain?" Kieran asked.

"Like I said, killing them does them a favor. We're giving them pain for a moment rather than letting them live in misery. This exercise… it's different. We're causing them pain deliberately and then leaving them to suffer for two whole minutes."

"Two minutes is not that long."

"I'll bet it feels a lot longer when you've got six bullets in you."

At that Kieran had no biting remark. Lai held back a smile. It took a lot to shut that girl up. Lai let the silence continue for several seconds before she spoke again.

"Virginia said it. This felt wrong. I'm sure some of the guys would agree with me."

"Jaime would agree with anything you say," Kieran said. Deirdre gave her a sharp smack on her shoulder.

"What's that supposed to mean?" Lai asked with a pointed glance. Kieran returned the expression for a moment before a smirk appeared on her face.

"I only mean that boy would do anything for you. And I bet you'd do anything for him."

"Stop it, Kier, you know she's asexual," Deirdre chided.

Kieran shrugged.

"Jaime is my friend," Lai insisted truthfully. "That's all."

"We know that," Virginia agreed. "Kieran's just annoyed that you got a better score today."

"I am not even going to dignify that with a response," Kieran said.

Lai once again had to hold back her smile. *You just did*, Lai thought. She almost said it aloud but thought better of it. She really didn't want to argue. Instead she stood up and walked over to where Siobhan still sat, moping. It appeared the comforting words from Tamsin and Virginia had done little.

"Siobhan?" Lai said. Siobhan glanced up through her reddish-brown hair. Lai smiled kindly. "You did fine. That was the first time we've ever tried to shoot without killing. It wasn't easy."

"You did it easy enough," Siobhan whined in her distinct Irish accent.

"I got lucky," Lai insisted. She raised an eyebrow to Tamsin and Virginia. They got the message and stood up to head over to Tamsin's bed. Lai sat down next to Siobhan and put a hand on her arm.

"You still did better than both the boys did," Lai pointed out. That got a smile out of Siobhan. It was true; Vineet and Devlin's prisoners had both died in about thirty seconds. Siobhan's had taken a minute and a half. Even Naja and Claudia's, their other two dorm mates who were already fast asleep, had apparently died before they could get medical attention, though it still took longer than two minutes.

"You'll do better next time." Lai had to swallow back the bile in her throat as she said it. Telling someone she would do better at shooting a person wasn't the easiest thing for her to say. Still, she knew it would help comfort the girl.

"I hope you're right." Siobhan sighed. "If I don't, the sergeant will throw me back to basic training."

"Oh, come on. She wouldn't do that."

"But she might hold me back for a few months."

Lai conceded the point with a nod of her head. Sergeant Washington had been known to hold students back if it took them more than three tries at an exercise. Lai herself had never had that problem; she was arguably the most skilled shooter in her group.

"Hey, Lai."

She looked up when Tamsin called her name. The girl tipped her head to the analog clock on the wall above the door. Lai peered at it in the dim light. The time was quarter after ten.

Lai realized she was going to be late to her meeting with Jaime. She gave Siobhan's arm a squeeze and stood up quickly. She brushed a hand over Tamsin's arm on the way past.

"Thanks, Tam," she said.

Kieran sat up when she passed her bed, but she did not look over. "One day I'm going to tell the sergeant about these secret meetings of yours."

"No you won't," Lai said. She knew Kieran wouldn't tell, or Lai might just have to tattle about Kieran's late-night trysts with her girlfriend outside their dorm. Behind her, Kieran shrugged and settled back down.

Lai opened the door and slipped through without a sound. She carefully closed it behind her and glanced around, checking for patrolling guards. She had her route down to the minute, and her four-minute delay while arguing with her dorm mates would allow her no mistakes. She had to be extra cautious as she was less sure about her timing. If she were caught, she would be hauled down to the sergeant's office and given extra chores for a month. Curfew was strict at the academy.

Lai had been a student at Colonel Parks Academy since she was fifteen. She had been eager to begin her training as soon as she became old enough. Her stepfather had been thrilled. Her *ina*, her mother, had been less pleased but was never one to deny her daughter what she wanted. To Lai, becoming a protection officer was the noblest of causes. She would protect the innocent, cleanse society of those who attempted to break the peace, and defend the American Republic.

No one could fault Lai for thinking as she did. Since she had moved to the Republic six years prior to beginning her training, she had been indoctrinated from every angle as to the righteousness of the Republic. She was taught in school that before the revolution the former country had been in political chaos. The United States of America, as it was called, was divided on a great many issues. This caused much tension between officials, and decisions were hardly ever made, as everyone spent most of their time arguing over who had the better morals. It wasn't until one woman had stepped forward and declared that the country must join together under one law that would protect the people and stop the senseless argument between political parties that anything changed. Though there was discord for many years, eventually the majority of people came around to her cause and the American Republic was created to ensure the safety of all.

At least, that was how Lai had been taught. That was what she believed. Coming to train at the academy changed her perspective on a great many things.

For one, she began to question the system that condemned the majority of their prison population to death. Before the Republic, prisons had been overcrowded. After the Republic was formed, their new leader, President Emilia Theodore, signed a law that allowed any prisoner on death row or with a life sentence to be used as live target practice for the new protection officers. She reasoned that live targets would give the officers the necessary experience to protect those who deserved it. Lai had never questioned this practice until she was the one doing the executions.

She couldn't say with certainty that she still wanted to be a protection officer, and she had grown to hate the target practice. Even when the prisoners didn't scream and threaten her, it was difficult, and she had nightmares often enough of watching the people bleed out, the life going out of their eyes as she watched what she had done. A few times she had woken up screaming at the memories. That gave Kieran plenty of material to taunt her with.

Lai did her best to put those thoughts from her mind as she slipped through the halls to the meeting place. Her destination was the empty mess hall. The hall itself was not patrolled at night. Most guards were either stationed around the dorm rooms, the officers' rooms, or the weapons storage. No one worried about kids breaking into a room filled with empty tables. That made it the perfect place to meet Jaime.

While the students all had downtime, it was hard to find any privacy when there were always curious ears around. You were never free to speak your mind during the day, as there was an officer standing guard at most doors. Even speaking as they had done during their target practice was a risk. If Lai wanted to speak to her friend without fear, it had to be done in secret.

Only their dorm mates knew of the secret meetings, but they were unlikely to tell. Every student had secrets, and no one wanted to betray the trust of their peers lest their own secrets come to light. Kieran and Deirdre's activities were only the beginning of what Lai knew about her group members.

Lai ducked around a corner and flattened her back against the wall. Footsteps faded in the distance. She remained where she was until they silenced completely and then hurried to the end of the hall. She spun around that corner and continued to the end of the long hallway until she reached the doors of the mess hall. With a final glance behind her, she pushed open a door and stole inside.

She searched around the dark room and found Jaime seated on the table off to the side. He waved her over. She crossed the room and hopped up next to him.

"You're late," he said with a frown.

Lai sighed and leaned against him. "I know." She pouted "Siobhan was fussing about killing her target today."

"Poor Siobhan."

Lai ignored his sarcastic tone and closed her eyes.

"I miss Oscar," she whispered. She felt Jaime put his arm around her, and she settled into his embrace.

"So do I," he whispered back.

Oscar had been a member of Beta Five until the previous week when he did something Lai had never heard of before. He had broken into the records office. According to what he had told her, he found records of several groups of prisoners set to be executed in the next few days. There was information about each prisoner, including the crimes they had committed to get a death sentence. Oscar claimed that more than half a dozen of them had only committed minor felonies. He knew enough about the law to know that carjacking did not equal an execution. At least it shouldn't, but according to the records, it did.

Oscar was Lai and Jaime's other best friend. He had come to them one night during their secret meeting and been near tears as he relayed the information he had seen.

"They barely did anything," he had cried as he clutched Lai's arm hard enough to leave marks. "One woman, she got drunk and threatened an officer with a knife. But she didn't even hurt him. That's not a crime that gets you on our death row, but she was on it. What if they execute my brother next? He may have robbed someone, but he never hurt anybody."

He had been inconsolable. Jaime had suggested that he had been reading the wrong files, that perhaps these people were not to be used as target practice. Oscar had nearly screamed that he knew what he had seen. His dark skin had gleamed with sweat, and he panted heavily. The next morning he was much the same. Sergeant Washington had taken one look at him and sent him for a psychological assessment. By the end of the day, the doctor reported that Oscar had suffered from a mental breakdown due to stress and recommended he be removed from the training program. The sergeant had agreed.

Jaime still doubted what Oscar had seen, but Lai knew her friend. Jaime had only known the two of them since they joined the program together. Lai had known Oscar for nine years. He was the first friend she made when she moved from the Philippines. They had gone through grade school together and joined the academy at the same time. Lai had cried over the loss of her friend as if he were dead rather than in a hospital, as the sergeant had reported. It was only through Jaime's support, and the support of the other girls in her group, that she had held herself together to continue training. But for the past week, her mind had been haunted by thoughts of what Oscar had told her, that some prisoners were not guilty of crimes worth their lives.

"Oscar would want us to move on." Jaime's words broke Lai out of her thoughts.

She straightened up and wiped her eyes. "He would want us to keep digging into it," she argued.

Jaime let out a noisy breath. "That's a dangerous road to go down, *asere*. Oscar was getting into things we have no business being in."

"You don't think it's our business whether or not the people we execute deserve it?"

"I thought you didn't believe in the value of some lives over others."

Lai squeezed her eyes shut and leaned forward until her forehead touched her knees. "I don't. But the law does. You know what I mean, *letse!*"

"I was just reminding you of your morals."

"I think I lost those when I signed up to kill people."

"Hey."

Lai waited for him to continue speaking. When he didn't, she sat up straight and stared him square in the eye. He matched her gaze evenly.

"We do this so we can help people in the future. And we clear out the prisons. What's the point of having people serve a life sentence with no chance of parole? They'll only be miserable."

"You sound like Virginia," Lai said through clenched teeth. Jaime offered her a ghost of a smile.

"Virginia is a smart girl," Jaime replied.

Lai shook her head. "It wasn't like this in the Philippines. At home we didn't even have the death sentence. People served life in prison, and it wasn't the worst thing in the world."

Tears formed in the corners of her eyes. "*Aking ina* had a friend, a good friend, who killed someone and ended up with a life sentence. She brought me to visit him once. He was a nice man. He didn't love prison, but he said it was better than dying. He thanked God that he lived in a country where they couldn't kill him for his mistakes.

"Until I moved here, I thought that was the right way to do things. When we left home, when my mother married a Republic man, suddenly I was taught that a death sentence was the right thing, the just thing. So I believed it. Now I'm nearly an adult and I have no idea what to think."

Jaime made to put a hand on her shoulder, but she pulled away and stood up. She crossed her arms and refused to look at her friend.

"Oscar found a problem," she continued tearfully. "I believe him, Jaime. I believe he knows what he saw. The government is becoming too brazen. They're quietly going against their own laws because they know the people wouldn't stand for it, and we are carrying out their unjust wishes without even knowing it. What if that woman I shot today, the one I didn't kill.... What if the law would have spared her?"

"She was clearly a violent criminal, *asere*," Jaime said softly. "Just like the others today."

"Then another woman. A woman I shot two weeks ago begged for her life. I ignored her because I trusted the law had done its part. What if I was wrong to trust the law?"

When no reply came, Lai turned back around and threw her arms in the air. "What if there is no just law anymore, Jaime?"

Jaime did not meet her eyes. He stared at the ground and kicked his feet back and forth through the air. The glow of the security lights shone off the metal on his prosthetic right leg. Lai kept her gaze trained on him for a long twenty seconds until he finally met her eyes again.

"I don't know," he whispered. "Lailani, I just don't know anymore."

CHAPTER THREE

THE SHOTS rang out through the training room. Lai clicked the safety on her gun and holstered it, taking a few steps back from her station and keeping her gaze from the life she had just taken. She kept her focus firmly trained on the ground as she walked to the back wall to lean against it. Though she was looking down, she still knew it was Jaime who walked up next to her when she saw his familiar prosthetic leg. That was one good thing that had come out of the Republic, she reasoned. A technological revolution that changed prosthetics forever.

She had read in old medical texts that in the past, prosthetics were stiff and hard to move properly. President Theodore had a cousin with an amputated arm and had sought out the best engineers in the Republic to create better prosthetics for her cousin and anyone who might need one. The result was electronically powered limbs that moved as smoothly as regular ones. They had to be charged every two weeks, and charges were expensive, but they were strong and could last a lifetime. Jaime told her that when he had lost his leg, he was grateful not to be living in the old United States or he would never have passed the rigorous physical tests to get into the academy. The prosthetic he had as a child may have worked, but it paled in comparison to his current model supplied by the academy.

"Almost done for the month, *asere*," Jaime said as he leaned against the wall next to her. Lai nodded. He was referring to the fact that they only did live target practice one week out of every month. There were hundreds of training groups in the Republic, and there simply weren't enough prisoners to shoot five a day every day. Lai was glad it was Friday. That meant she wouldn't have to think about killing another person for a month.

"Almost done," she echoed. She glanced opposite them to see the cleaning crew had taken the last body away, though blood was still sprayed across the wall. She swallowed hard and ignored her discomfort. One more. She only had to kill one more person, and then they could get back to the parts of training she actually enjoyed.

Sergeant Washington stood tall as the students milled about. She gave Lai and Jaime a cursory glance and then focused her attention on Vineet and Tamsin, who were both waving their guns around without a care. Lai wondered if the sergeant had seen her put five more bullets than instructed into her gun. She had been distracted earlier, her thoughts still on the conversation she and Jaime had the previous night. In her distraction she had grabbed ten bullets to load into her gun instead of five. She only realized this when she had opened the chamber after the first round and seen the nine bullets. She knew if she said anything now, she would get in trouble for being reckless. She figured that when they were done training for the day, she could find a way to discreetly remove the extra bullets without anyone seeing.

The doors opened and Lai turned her attention to the line of prisoners being pulled through. She made note of each person as they were paraded along the wall to the stations. From what she could tell with the bags over their heads, they all appeared to be young, and none were especially muscular. They were cuffed in front, but there was no collar or ankle shackles. Lai figured they were young kids who killed someone on a whim, possibly even by accident, and were now going to pay for it with their own lives. She clenched her fists at her sides. She didn't like killing other kids.

"Students, to your stations," the sergeant commanded. The fifteen students all made their way over to their stations as the prisoners' arms were lifted above their heads and chained to the wall above them. Their ankles were then shackled as well to make escape impossible. Lai stopped at her station and took a closer look at her prisoner. She could see long blond hair spilling out from the bag over her head; it was greasy from the little care it had been given since she had been selected for target practice. Lai was not surprised. She seldom saw a well-kempt prisoner on the line.

At the sergeant's nod, an officer walked up to the first prisoner and started to lift the bags off their heads. Each kid—she had been correct; they all appeared to be under twenty—had a gag in their mouths. After the ruckus caused the previous day, every prisoner had been gagged before coming in. The bags came off each head until the officer reached her station, station thirteen, and pulled the bag from her next victim.

If she could have moved, Lai would have choked. It had been two years, two long years, but she knew right away. The hair was longer and messier, and she had never seen her wear orange, but Lai was sure of it. She knew this girl.

It was her cousin.

Lai couldn't make herself move, much less speak. Her cousin, Melanie, was staring at the ground. Lai kept her eyes locked on Mel's until the other girl glanced up. When she did, she started and her eyes went wide. She struggled momentarily and tried to say something from behind her gag. The officer gave her a kick to shut her up. Mel complied, but her gaze never left Lai's.

This can't be happening, Lai thought. She tried desperately to think of another explanation, but none came to her. If that hadn't been Mel, and only a girl who resembled her, she wouldn't have reacted the way she did when she saw Lai.

Seeing her cousin for the first time in two years caused memories to flow through Lai's mind. She remembered when she first met her new cousin after moving to the Republic. She had been terrified of the foreign country she was now going to call home. She was suddenly faced with a new man she was supposed to call her father. To add to the confusion, Lai had to learn a whole new language when she was nine years old.

Mel had been her first English teacher. Though only a year older, and hardly a skilled educator, Mel had been patient with Lai and put in her best effort to help her understand the nuances of such a complicated language. Lai's mother had hired her a tutor to teach her the bulk of it, but Mel had been invaluable when it came to truly understanding. Lai had never forgotten how Mel had been her friend and mentor in her strange new world.

When Lai left for the academy three years earlier, she and Mel tried their hardest to keep in contact, but it was difficult when Lai was training over two thousand miles away. Add in the fact that Mel had been less than pleased at Lai's career choice, and the two had lost contact two years ago.

Seeing Mel in front of her again, it was as if they had never been apart.

None of the other students seemed aware of what had just happened between the two girls. The sergeant told them to ready their weapons. She instinctively unholstered her gun and removed the safety, though she did not lift it when ordered. She paid little attention to what was happening around her. She barely even flinched when fourteen weapons discharged around her. It wasn't until her name was shouted by the sergeant that she finally peeled her focus away from Mel.

"Harris!" the sergeant yelled. "What do you think you are doing?"

Lai looked back to Mel, the only kid still alive on the wall. Mel was breathing heavily, and her forehead was slick with sweat.

"Lailani Harris!"

Lai forced herself to look her sergeant squarely in the eye and tried to keep her voice from shaking.

"That's my cousin," she replied in a weak voice. The other students around her gasped. Jaime stepped up beside her but did nothing more.

"Why didn't you shoot her?" the sergeant demanded. Lai blinked several times, unsure she had heard correctly.

"She's my cousin," Lai said again. She realized she was holding her gun in a death grip and relaxed her fingers.

"That does not mean you are allowed to let this felon live."

Lai sucked in a sharp breath. She had never heard of this happening before. Even if a family member of a student were on death row, they would never be assigned to that student. No one could be that careless. Perhaps it was because she and Mel were only cousins through marriage and did not share the same last name.

"But—" Lai began, but was quickly cut off by the sergeant.

"I don't want excuses, Harris. I want that girl dead. You are going to face her and shoot her in the head. That is the exercise."

"I can't shoot my own cousin," Lai cries. Jaime finally spoke up.

"Sergeant, there must have been a mistake. Lai's cousin shouldn't have been at her station. She shouldn't have been assigned to this group at all. She's in shock. That's all."

"I don't want any excuses from you either, Martinez."

Jaime took a step back and said nothing more. Lai glanced back to where Mel was still chained to the wall. Her eyes were wild, pleading. She wanted to die about as much as Lai wanted to kill her.

"Harris, I don't care if she's your twin sister. If you don't put a bullet through her head this second, I will put you on kitchen duty for the next year and drop you to a Delta group!"

Lai knew she was serious. Sergeant Washington never put up with anything. Either you did what she instructed or you would find yourself dropped a year in training.

Lai's hands tightened around her gun again. She turned to face Mel, the girl she had been inseparable from since she moved to the Republic until she had left for training. With shaky hands she lifted her gun and trained it on Mel's forehead. Mel was crying openly now, and she fought weakly against her bonds. No officer moved to stop her. Lai took a deep breath and allowed herself to think for a short moment.

If she didn't shoot Mel, someone would. If she didn't shoot, Mel would die anyway and she would be dropped to a Delta training group for another year of basic training. There was nothing she could do. The logical part of her mind told her to do it. For Mel to be on death row, she had to have done something terrible.

What Oscar had told her floated back to Lai's mind. That wasn't necessarily true. She could have stolen a car. She could have hurt someone in a fight. She could have done any number of things that did not call for her life. In that moment, Lai made a decision she knew she could never return from.

In one fluid motion, Lai spun around to face Sergeant Washington and shot the woman in the leg.

Everyone was too shocked to move. The sergeant gave a pained cry and dropped to one knee, now bleeding from the wound in her thigh. Lai quickly set up her gun for another shot, but she had no idea what to do next. She heard someone come up behind her and place a hand on her shoulder.

"Take me hostage," Jaime whispered.

Lai frowned and kept her eyes on the officers in the room. They all had their guns pulled but were unsure if they were to advance.

"Take me hostage, now!" he whispered with more urgency.

In a rush Lai understood his intent. She spun and flung an arm around her friend's neck. She shoved her gun into the side of his head and faced the room. She allowed her fury to show on her face.

"I am taking my cousin and I am leaving!" she shouted. "If we are not allowed to leave, I am going to shoot Jaime in the head."

"Please, don't hurt me," Jaime pleaded.

Lai could have kissed him for his cleverness. "Shut up." She pushed the gun harder into his head and hoped he would forgive her for the bruise he would have the next day.

"You don't have any bullets left," Kieran called from the other side of the room. The other students nodded their agreement. This caused the four officers standing guard to all come forward. Lai took her gun from Jaime's head for the moment and aimed it at the ceiling. She fired once and quickly returned it to her friend's head. Everyone flinched at the shot.

"I have plenty of bullets left, and I will use them all to get out of here," Lai warned. She fixed her glare on the sergeant, who sat on the ground in a small pool of her own blood. She pressed her hands firmly against the wound as she met Lai's death stare.

"Tell an officer to unchain her," Lai ordered.

The sergeant did nothing.

"Do it now or I'll shoot both of you!" Lai screamed.

After a long moment, the sergeant nodded to an officer. "Give her what she wants."

The officer in question frowned in confusion. "Sergeant Washington, are you sure—"

She cut him off. "That's an order, officer."

The officer nodded once and found the keys on his belt. He stopped next to Mel and undid her ankle shackles, followed by her handcuffs. She pulled the gag out of her mouth and walked quickly over to Lai. She was shaking wildly, and she was still crying.

"The three of us are going to walk out that door," Lai said quietly. She nodded to the door in the corner of the room that led outside. "If anyone tries to stop us, I will shoot the sergeant again, and this time I will shoot to kill."

No one moved. The four officers had their guns lowered. The sergeant met Lai's eyes with a cold glare of her own.

"You don't want to do this, Lailani," she said coolly.

"It's too late for that now," Lai hissed through clenched teeth. Without saying anything further, she began carefully walking herself and Jaime toward the door. Mel followed them with a hand on Lai's shoulder. A distant part of Lai's mind told her to stop this, to lower the gun and apologize and accept her punishment. The adrenaline pushed those thoughts aside and left her with only her objective.

She had to keep her cousin alive.

Chapter Four

WHEN THE three of them were through the door and outside the building, Lai began to let Jaime out of the choke hold she had him in. The moment she loosened her hold, he grabbed her arm and forced it to remain around his neck.

"We're still too close," he hissed to her. "If you let me go now, they'll shoot you."

Lai realized he was right. She turned them around and walked backward.

"Mel, get behind me," she ordered. "Don't try to run. They could shoot you. And believe me, they'll shoot to kill."

Mel said nothing and followed the order. Lai realized her cousin had said nothing since being released. She reasoned the girl was in shock from nearly dying and then being rescued. Lai shook her head to clear it. She couldn't think about that. She had to focus on getting them to safety.

Behind them stretched a large expanse of the Yuma Desert. Lai cursed their location in the southwestern Republic. The nearest city was miles away. On foot it would take them at least two days to reach it.

Lai regarded the academy building as they retreated. Officers poured out of the doors and aimed their weapons.

"I have a loaded gun, and I will use every bullet in it to get us out of here!" she shouted, loud enough for every officer to hear. She saw Sergeant Washington limping out with the aid of Kieran and Vineet. The sergeant had a bandage wrapped around her leg and a hand pressed to the bandage.

"Think about what you're doing, Harris." Pain colored the sergeant's voice. "This will not end how you want it to end."

"I don't care what you have to say, sergeant," Lai shouted in reply. No one said anything further. When a few officers made to follow them, the sergeant gave a command Lai couldn't hear that caused them to halt. She almost smiled. It was working.

"I hope you have a plan, *asere*," Jaime whispered to her.

"My plan is to keep Mel alive," she replied simply. She could hear her cousin breathing heavily behind her. "You okay, Mel?"

"As okay as I can be," came the reply.

Lai nodded once. "We're going to keep walking until they can't see us," she said. "The moment we're out of sight, we turn around and run."

"And then?" Jaime asked. When Lai didn't reply, his grip on her arm squeezed tighter. "Tell me you know what we're doing."

"I don't want to lie to you."

Jaime muttered a curse in Spanish as they continued backing up. It was a slow journey. They were all scared, and Lai was kept going only by the high of the adrenaline rushing through her system. She knew that as soon as they stopped, she would most likely have an anxiety attack at what she had done. For the time being, however, she would stay in control of herself to keep them all safe.

Her dark brown hair clung to her forehead, and her clothes stuck to her back, courtesy of the sweat that covered her body. The heat of the desert didn't help. They needed to find cover as soon as possible. The full-body black training outfits she and Jaime wore couldn't be helping either. Lai briefly envied Mel in her thin short-sleeved orange jumpsuit. She was about ready to request a clothing swap and accept being more visible if it meant less sweat.

Another twenty meters, Lai decided, and then they could turn and run. Even if the officers pursued, they had a big enough head start to find cover before being caught. Besides, the guns could not shoot them from that distance.

"On my word, we run," she told her companions.

Mel said nothing, but Jaime nodded. She made a mental note of the distance in her head and waited for the right moment. The forbidding gray of the academy was blurring with the sun in the distance. She took a deep breath before giving the command.

"Run!"

She quickly pulled her arm back and let Jaime go. They both turned around and ran after Mel, who was already running. Lai said a silent prayer in hopes that they could find somewhere to hide and rest rather than be caught. If they didn't, Mel would be dead before nightfall and she and Jaime would have run for nothing. They wouldn't just be demoted to a Delta group. She would be criminally charged and executed for shooting Sergeant Washington. That was something she had no interest in facing.

As they ran, Lai realized her gun had not been put to safety. She swiftly clicked it on, though she kept the weapon out as they ran. No one had to know it wasn't ready to shoot. Seeing the weapon might give pause to anyone who tried to stop them. Not that anyone would if they got away from the guards. There was barely anyone within a day of the academy. While that made it easier for them to hide, it would be that much more difficult to find any help. That is, if anyone wanted to help three felons.

"Lai?" came Jaime's panting voice.

"Yeah?"

"Do you know what she's in for?"

Lai stared ahead to where Mel ran several feet ahead of them. "No idea."

"So we probably helped a murderer escape."

"It's possible."

"And you never stopped to think that maybe she deserves—"

"No, Jaime, I did not stop to think that my cousin might deserve to die."

Jaime quickened his pace. Lai had to double her strides to catch up to him and Mel.

"You okay, Mel?" she asked when she was running beside her. Mel's dirty blonde hair whipped out behind as she ran.

"Oh yeah, Lani, I'm great," she huffed.

Lai thought she saw a hint of a smile on her face, but she couldn't be sure. "How long can you run for?"

"As long as I need to stay alive."

Lai could have laughed at the answer if she weren't so damn angry with everything. She was angry with herself for not thinking. She was angry with Jaime for questioning her. She was angry with Mel for getting on freaking death row. Most of all, she was angry with the government that condemned Melanie to death at nineteen.

Lai spared a glance behind her. The academy building was out of their sight now. They ran down a small hill, dodging around cacti and kicking up clouds of dust. There was no sign of anyone pursuing them. After another thirty seconds, Lai slowed her pace until she was walking. Jaime and Mel noticed and slowed down to wait for her. All three were breathing heavily. Jaime kept checking his prosthetic. Mel ran her hands through her hair and pulled it together behind her as if she were going to make a ponytail. Lai pulled at the tight material that stuck to her chest to allow air to filter through.

"What the hell did you do, Lani?" Mel asked with a half smile. Lai could only shake her head. Jaime glanced between the two girls that walked beside him.

"You never let anyone call you Lani," he pointed out.

Lai shrugged. "She's my cousin. I don't mind."

"You two don't look alike. At all."

"We're not related by blood," Mel explained.

"My mother married her uncle," Lai added. "Which is why you and I look more alike than she and I do."

"You got that right, *asere*." He chuckled for a moment. He glanced over to Mel and gave her a once-over. "This is an interesting introduction. I'm Jaime Martinez."

Mel echoed his laugh. "I guess it is. Melanie Hayes. Thank you for helping save my life."

Jaime shrugged as if he hadn't just been an accomplice in a crime. "*Olvídalo*," he said. When Mel raised an eyebrow, he realized she must not speak Spanish. "It means forget it."

Mel nodded her understanding. She pulled her hair behind her ear and regarded Lai. "I've never seen something like that before."

Lai met her gaze. "I didn't know I had it in me."

"Thanks for not shooting me."

Lai did laugh this time. "*Halika na*, I could never shoot my cousin."

"I swear to God, why is everyone I know bilingual?"

"Maybe because we weren't born in the Republic," Jaime offered.

Mel waved a hand at him. "I just sucked at languages in school. Lani tried to teach me Tagalog for a few days, but even she realized I was hopeless."

Jaime laughed once and looked ahead. Lai smiled for a moment before getting serious again.

"We need to figure out what we're going to do," she said firmly. Her companions nodded their agreement. She kept her focus on the desolate land ahead of them as she spoke.

"First things first, we need to find somewhere with food and water."

"That won't be easy," Jaime said. "Yuma is at least two days northwest."

"It's sixty-five miles northwest," Lai confirmed. "And there isn't much between us and the city."

"My family lives in a compound north of here," he offered.

"Your family would help us?" Mel asked.

Jaime thought for a moment. "They've never been sympathetic to the Republic."

"Then why do they live here?"

"Cuba was being torn apart by a civil war. My parents thought it would be better for us here. They didn't want to raise me and my sisters in a war."

"That war ended five years ago," Mel pointed out.

Jaime shrugged. "It will start again," he said with certainty.

Mel raised an eyebrow again but did not argue.

"Let's go to your family," Lai decided.

Jaime nodded and glanced up to check the position of the sun. "We can make it there by midnight if we keep walking," he told the girls.

Mel groaned. "That's a lot of walking. I've barely had anything to eat all day. They don't feed death-row prisoners very well."

"We don't have much of a choice," Lai countered.

Mel mumbled to herself. Lai shook her head. Mel never took things very seriously. It seemed nearly dying did not change that.

"You know the way?" Lai asked Jaime.

Jaime nodded and turned slightly to the right. Lai and Mel followed and allowed themselves to be led deeper into the desert.

CHAPTER FIVE

"WHAT MAKES you think your family won't turn us in?"

Jaime turned to Mel when she asked her question. When he didn't answer straightaway, she continued.

"I mean, you wouldn't get in trouble. Everyone saw you get kidnapped. And no one would believe a convicted felon and a girl who shot her sergeant over that."

"My family won't turn us in," he replied.

Mel regarded him curiously. "You said they weren't sympathetic to the Republic."

"That's right."

"What does that mean, exactly?"

"It means what it sounds like," he said with a half smile.

Mel frowned. "Then pretend I'm a child. How would you explain it to me?"

Jaime looked ahead to where Lai was walking several feet ahead of them. She wasn't exactly leading the way, only following the directions Jaime had given her, but she insisted on being their "scout," as she was the only one with a loaded weapon.

"Two years after I was born, Cuba fell into a civil war," Jaime began. He kept his focus on Lai's back as he spoke. "My father was in politics, and it destroyed his career. The people didn't want a government controlling their lives. They wanted to have a say in their own decisions. Ever since the Munez government took power in 2104, they had little say in how the country was run. My father was one of the good guys. He advocated for people's rights, but no one cared. They wanted every current official taken out of power. When I was four, my family was forced to flee the capital city to a smaller town for our own safety. We couldn't be somewhere where people knew our faces.

"My oldest sister, Angella, was part of the most outspoken group that called for the heads of officials, so to speak."

The smile had completely disappeared from Jaime's face. Mel watched him carefully. He clenched his jaw for a moment before continuing.

"She didn't leave the city with us. She chose to stay with *Partido de la Libertad Popular*, the People's Freedom Party. She was only sixteen when we left her behind. It broke my mother's heart. My father never forgave her for it."

"What happened to her?" Mel asked in a quiet voice.

Jaime took a deep breath. "She's all right now, if that's what you're asking. But we weren't all right fourteen years ago. She was in Havana when it was bombed. When we got the news, my father went to find her and bring her to us so she could be safe. While he was gone, the town we were staying in was also bombed. I lost my leg in one of the explosions.

"My father did find Angella. He had to drag her, quite literally, out of a building before it could explode. She screamed that she was fighting for the freedom of the people. He told her she couldn't fight if she was dead. My father tells me that when she got back to us and saw what had happened to my leg, she could only scream that she was right. That was when she told us that it wasn't *Partido de la Libertad Popular* that was responsible for the bombings. It turns out the government had staged them to seem like terrorist attacks from the party to keep them from getting any more supporters.

"When I was healed, we came to the Republic. No Latin American country was accepting Cuban refugees. They all said we would only bring a war into their countries. The Republic let us in because my father convinced them we had nothing to do with the fighting. Angella says she nearly bit her tongue in half to keep herself from disagreeing with the lies he was telling to get us in.

"When we moved here, my family realized that this government was as corrupt as any Cuba could have had. They thought Cuba had been a dictatorship, but the Republic made it look like a tea party. At least it seemed that way to my father and sister, and my mother before she passed. I grew up here. I remember very little from my time in Cuba.

"That is why my family has no sympathy for the Republic. We call it being nonsympathetic. The Republic may have let us in, but the government is too similar to what nearly destroyed Cuba. People do not have the freedoms they deserve. My family has been sure to teach this to me. I only tell you this because I know that even if you spoke of these views, your words would hold little stock. You are, after all, a convicted felon."

Mel had no words. From her wide-eyed expression, whatever story she had been expecting from Jaime was clearly not that. At least his story made it clear that his family wouldn't turn them in. With the hell they had been through with their own government, they were unlikely to place their fates in the hands of the Republic.

"You must not tell that story a lot," Mel said after a long minute of silence.

"I've only told half a dozen or so people," he confirmed. "Your cousin is one of them. I trust her. You're lucky to have her on your side."

"I am." Mel stretched her arms above her head and took a quick glance around. All she could see in any direction was more desert. She sighed and let her arms fall back to her sides.

"How much longer until we get to your house?" she asked.

Jaime tilted his head up to the sky. "Five hours," he replied with a nod.

Mel groaned.

Jaime chuckled and gave her a sidelong glance. "What's your story, Melanie? How did you end up on death row?"

Mel squeezed her eyes shut. "I don't want to talk about it."

"You are serious, *niña*?" he scoffed. "I just told you my family history and you won't tell me how you landed in prison?"

"I said I don't want to talk about it!" she yelled. She opened her eyes and sighed. Lai glanced back over her shoulder but said nothing to them.

"All right, don't tell me," he conceded with a shrug. "But I will ask again."

"Of course you will," she grumbled. She returned the sidelong glance he had given her a moment earlier. "Maybe I'll tell you if you tell me why you're training to be a protection officer for a Republic you clearly hate."

Jaime did not respond.

Mel smirked and focused her attention on Lai's back. "What happens after your family? Obviously we can't hide out there forever."

"My family has certain… connections that could help us. My sister especially."

Mel stared at him as if expecting more. When Jaime didn't reply again, she looked ahead. She kept her attention on Lai as the two of them fell back into silence.

CHAPTER SIX

IT WAS nearly midnight when the group reached the decrepit compound of houses. All three of them were beyond famished, parched, and dead tired. Jaime led them through the maze of buildings from the light cast by the moon. There were only a few illuminated windows, and Jaime skirted those. The girls kept low to avoid their heads peeking over windowsills. Lai still had her gun out and held it ready in her hands.

Before Jaime pointed out his house, Lai correctly guessed which one it was. It was one of the half dozen lit from within, and she could hear two people shouting at each other in rapid-fire Spanish. When Jaime turned back to them, she tilted her head. He gave her a half smile and nodded them ahead. The three teens stole silently across the compound until they reached the house the noise was coming from. Jaime held an arm out to stop the girls before they could go in.

"You should put that gun away," Jaime said to Lai. "In these outfits, my sister will think it's a raid."

Lai nodded and holstered her weapon. Jaime walked in front of them and pushed lightly on the door; it opened without resistance. He waved them forward and held his arms up as if in surrender. He waited until they both did the same and pushed into the house.

They were greeted by a gun pointed at Jaime's head.

"Angella, *soy yo*!" Jaime shouted. The woman holding the gun lowered it and frowned in confusion.

"Jaime?" she said.

He nodded frantically. She looked behind him and raised her weapon slightly. Her shoulder-length brown hair fell in front of her face. A tall man stood next to her with his arms crossed. He seemed less angry but equally suspicious.

"¿Quién diablos es la chica de naranja?" she asked Jaime with a fierce glare.

"Es una amiga," he replied. "Está bien, hermana."

"Could we speak English, please?" Mel spoke up.

Jaime lowered his arms and waved a hand at her. "Shut up," he hissed.

The woman finally lowered her weapon all the way and fixed her stare on Mel. "I asked my brother who you are," she said in accented English. She placed a hand on her hip. "You can put your arms down now. I'm not going to shoot you."

Mel realized Lai had already lowered her arms. She did the same with a sheepish expression.

"Lai, Mel, this is my sister, Angella," he told them.

Angella gave them both a nod.

Jaime nodded to the man. "This is my father, Jorge."

"I apologize for my daughter," he said to them with a pointed glare at Angella.

She ignored it and tilted her head. "You want to explain to me what you're doing here in the middle of the night?" She looked Mel up and down. "And with a criminal?"

"Mira quién habla," Jaime snapped at her.

"Te apareces sin previo aviso a la mitad de la noche y crees que me puedes decir eso?" she replied.

Mel sighed and took a step forward. "I'm sorry, but I speak about two words of Spanish, and none of those are it."

Angella raised an eyebrow to her brother.

He shrugged and returned the expression. "Can we come in? We need some help."

"Of course," Jorge spoke up. "Please, girls, come into the living room."

He disappeared through a doorway behind him. Angella shoved her gun into her waistband and gestured for them to follow him. Lai made a quick appraisal of the house as she did. The entry room was small and filled to the brim with shoes, jackets, and, she noted anxiously, a fair amount of firearms, more than she knew to be legal.

She had to duck as she went through the doorway. They emerged into a living room about twice as large as the entryway. Green paint peeled from the walls and littered the floor. There were two faded brown couches facing each other and a coffee table between with papers messily spread out. Angella went for them immediately and pulled them into a pile that she then deposited under the table. She stood next to one of the couches and watched the two girls. Jorge reached into a cabinet and pulled out three bottles of water. He handed one to each grateful teen and sat down next to where Angella stood. Jaime sat on the other couch and patted the spot next to him. Lai sat next to him and Mel next to her.

"You're not going to ask your brother how he is?" Jaime asked his sister.

She crossed her arms and tapped her fingers against one. "Something tells me we have more important things to talk about."

"It is good to see you, *mi hijo*," Jorge added. "But you must understand, we're very confused. Shouldn't you be in training?"

"It's not safe for any of us at the academy anymore," Lai said. All eyes turned to her. "Jaime said we can trust you, and I trust him. Angella, I've never met you, but if Jaime says you can help, then I believe him." She paused a moment to gather her thoughts before she spoke again. "My cousin, Melanie, was on death row. We rescued her and escaped."

"Válgame dios!" Angella exclaimed. She put a hand to her forehead and shook her head. Jorge regarded them calmly but said nothing.

"I couldn't kill my cousin," Lai continued. "I didn't think. I just acted. I shot my sergeant, and Jaime helped me get her out. We've been walking here for hours."

"Jaime, how could you be so reckless!" Angella chastised him. "You think we need this right now?"

"What was I supposed to do, Angella? Leave my friend to deal with this herself?" he challenged. "They never would have gotten out if not for me."

"So now it's our problem too," she hissed. She shook her head and directed a steely glare at Mel.

Mel shrunk back into the couch.

"Please don't blame your brother," Lai cut in. "I'm the one who did this. He was only trying to help."

"And if you bring officers here? Did you ever think of that! That is the last thing we need right now."

"Angella," Jaime said urgently. He stood up and walked over to his sister. He put a hand on her arm and spoke quietly in Spanish.

Jorge sighed and held his hands out to Lai and Mel. "Do not think you are unwelcome. This is simply an inconvenient time for surprises. But any friend of Jaime's is welcome in our home."

"Thank you, sir," Lai said with a smile. "I'm glad to hear that."

"Thank you," echoed Mel softly.

Lai put a hand on Mel's shoulder. "This isn't your fault, Mel."

"Of course it is," Mel replied. "If I had been assigned to another training group, you wouldn't have to do this."

"And then you would be dead."

To that Mel had no reply. Mel looked back to Jaime and Angella. He seemed to have calmed his sister down, though she still stood with her arms crossed tight across her chest.

"You sure they won't come here searching for you?" Angella asked.

Lai shook her head. "They won't. When we left, I kind of took Jaime hostage."

Lai thought she saw Angella's lips fighting a smile.

"You've got some nerve, *niña*." Angella finally sat down next to her father on the couch.

Jaime moved to stand in between the couches. "Eventually they will come here. We need to be long gone when that happens. *Papá*, Angella, if it's all right with you, we'd like to stay here tonight."

"Padre, honestamente no creo que sea una buena idea," Angella whispered to her father urgently. "Tenemos planes a partir de mañana y—"

"That's enough, *mija*," Jorge cut her off.

Angella huffed and settled on glaring at Mel.

"We only need to stay until morning," Jaime told them. "We need some supplies and new clothes, and then we'll figure it out for ourselves."

Jorge considered his son's words for moment and then turned to his daughter. "You could take them with you."

Her head whipped around to him, and she fixed him with an incredulous expression. "You can't be serious." She nearly laughed.

Lai and Mel frowned to each other.

"It would keep them out of trouble," Jorge continued.

"It would get us in more trouble," Angella argued. She spared a quick glance to her brother. "It would put him in danger."

"They can at least stay the night."

Angella sat back into the couch and ran a hand through her hair. Her brown eyes flicked over each face that watched her before they settled on her brother. "One night," she said flatly. "And then they have to go. The sooner they leave, the better it is for everyone."

Jorge nodded his agreement and turned to his son.

Jaime thought for a moment and then nodded his assent as well. He moved to sit next to Lai again. His prosthetic beeped when he was on the couch. He glanced down at it and sighed.

"Need a charge?" Angella asked him.

Jaime frowned up at her, a silent question on his face.

She smiled for the first time since they had arrived. "I have a charge." She stood up and walked across the room to a cabinet that leaned precariously against the wall. She rummaged through it for a moment and grabbed a small black box with red wires sticking out. She walked back to the couches and tossed the box to Jaime.

He inspected it for a moment before breaking out into his own smile. "How did you get this?"

Angella shrugged. "The usual way." The cousins were once again baffled as to what the family was talking about, and annoyed that no one deigned to explain.

Jaime saw their confusion. "I'll explain it later."

Mel nodded, satisfied with the response. Lai peered curiously at Angella but said nothing. Angella seemed not to notice and sat back down just as her father was standing up.

"You must be hungry," he guessed. "Would you like some Moros y Cristianos?"

"It's black beans and rice," Jaime explained to Mel.

She nodded eagerly. "Yes please. I haven't had a decent meal since…." She trailed off and fingered her outfit.

Jorge softened his expression and stood up. "Please, follow me to the kitchen."

Jaime and Mel both stood and followed his father out of the room. They left Lai and Angella alone.

Angella met her gaze evenly. "You did a very brave thing. And a very reckless thing."

Lai took another sip of water and used her thumb to wipe a stray bead of moisture from the corner of her mouth. "I had to help my cousin."

"And give up your own life in the process?"

"I'm not dead."

"But your old life is finished. You think they would let you be a protection officer now?"

Rather than reply, Lai decided it was time to ask her own question. "You're a member of the *Libertas Publica*, yes?"

Angella raised an eyebrow and smirked. "What would give you that idea?"

Lai leaned forward and rested her arms on her knees. "You have far more guns than this family could need. More than is legal. You said you have plans for the morning. That we would interfere. That we would bring trouble. Your father suggested we would be in less trouble with you."

Angella watched her with growing interest as she spoke.

"And then there is your history in Cuba," Lai added shrewdly.

Angella leaned back into the couch and studied Lai's face. Lai thought she looked impressed. "That's an interesting idea you have. If it were true, why would I tell a future protection officer?"

"You said it yourself. They'll never let me become one now."

Angella narrowed her eyes slightly. "Are you sympathetic?"

Lai shrugged a shoulder. "Less and less since I started my training. Jaime told me you aren't. It makes sense, really. You leave your country's freedom party and join the one here."

Angella cracked a smile and laughed. "Jaime never told me you were so clever. I like that."

Lai returned the smile. "So where did you get the charge? I'm sure you didn't buy it."

"You're a clever girl. Figure it out."

Lai thought for a moment. She tapped a finger against her knee as she thought. "I'd say the government facility that was raided a month ago," she said after half a dozen seconds. "Fifteen charges were stolen, along with food and weapons for a dispatch of twelve." The tapping ceased. "Were you in that raid?"

"No fue nada," Angella replied with a shrug. "We got in and out without a single person injured or detected." She leaned forward to match Lai's position. "So tell me, *niña*, how does a nonsympathizer end up in a training academy?"

Lai's smile vanished, and she leaned back.

"Touchy subject?"

Lai nodded after a moment. "I wasn't born here, like you. Maybe if I had lived here all my life, I would have known how silly I was being. I thought I would be keeping people safe. It's in the name, right? Protection."

"My little brother is like you," Angella cut in. When Lai did not respond, Angella stood up and walked over to take a seat next to her. "He thought he could help people too. Siempre el optimista...."

"That's why we're friends. Some of the others in our group, they don't see the problems with the Republic. They want to be a part of keeping things how they are. Jaime isn't like that."

"I made sure of that."

At Angella's remark, Lai turned to face her. "He really looks up to you."

Angella shook her head. "If I did so well, how did he end up in training?"

"He isn't like most of the kids there. He cares. He wants to do good. He just doesn't know how." Lai let her words hang in the air for a long moment. "Neither do I."

"Maybe you can figure it out now that you're not in training."

"Maybe," Lai echoed. She leaned back into the couch and put her head in her hands. "*Diyos*, I did something big, didn't I?"

"*Sí*." Angella nodded. "You made a real mess of things."

CHAPTER SEVEN

JAIME'S FORMER room was packed to the brim with boxes. There was barely an inch of clear floor to step foot in. When confronted about it, Angella shrugged and said she needed the space for storage.

"Típico," Jaime said as he spread out a blanket where the coffee table used to be. He had insisted Lai and Mel take the couches. Lai had argued for a short while, but Mel hadn't put up a fight.

"It'll be the most comfortable sleep I've had in weeks," she replied as she collapsed on the couch. Her orange jumpsuit had been replaced with a pair of long gray sweats with the words "*besa mi*" spelled out on the rear, and a plain black tee, courtesy of Angella. Lai wore the same with a white tee. Jaime had squeezed through the boxes to his old closet and retrieved a pair of loose linen pants and a blue long-sleeve.

"You kids good for the night?" Angella asked. She threw two pillows down to her brother and smirked when they hit him in the head.

Lai nodded. "We'll be fine here. Thanks again for the clothes, and the bullets."

"If you're running around with my baby brother, you might as well have protection," she replied.

Lai flashed her a smile before letting herself fall back onto the couch. She glanced over to where her now fully loaded gun rested on the coffee table that had been moved over to the wall. Next to it was Jaime's gun, also fully loaded. When Mel had asked if she got a gun, Angella said she would give her one when she told her what she got arrested for. Mel hadn't asked again.

"If you need anything, don't knock on the door at the end of the hall," Angella said as she headed toward the hall.

"Why not?" Lai questioned.

"That's my door," she answered with a wink.

Lai watched until Angella was out of sight. She then turned to Jaime. "I like your sister."

Jaime shook his head and lay back onto the blankets. "You would."

When all three had settled into their beds for the night, there was a lengthy pause. Each refused to be the first to voice the question weighing their minds, as if speaking it aloud would somehow make it more of a reality. After a solid minute of silence, it was Mel who finally broke it.

"What are we going to do in the morning?"

Lai sighed heavily. "I have no idea. Jaime?"

"Don't look at me, *asere*." He pulled his blanket up to his chin.

"What does that mean, *asere*?" Mel asked.

"It means friend," he explained. "It's used in Cuba."

"Hey," Lai cut in. "We need to figure this out."

"We can't stay around here for very long," Jaime said.

"We could take her back south."

"To the border? No way Mexico lets her in, even if the Republic didn't notice her getting out."

"Does your family still have contacts in Cuba?"

"You don't want to go there."

"You don't need to talk about me like I'm not here," Mel complained. "If you're going to, at least do it in a language I don't understand."

"Sorry, Mel, we're just trying to talk through it," Lai apologized.

"I get it. I just wish we knew what we were doing tomorrow."

"Don't we all."

"Maybe we could find some other people to help us," Jaime suggested.

"Like the *Libertas Publica*?" Lai said. "You think they'd want a felon?"

"We're all felons now," Jaime reasoned. "I heard most of their members are ex-cons, or current cons."

"And what does that mean for us? Do we also keep running, keep hiding?"

"We don't have much of a choice anymore. We made that decision when we ran."

"No, I made that decision when I shot the sergeant," Lai groaned as she rolled over to lie on her stomach. She closed her eyes and shoved her face into her pillow. There was a pregnant pause as her companions considered her words.

"None of us would be here if I hadn't gotten myself a death sentence."

Jaime twisted his head around to peer at Mel in the darkness. "So how did you get a death sentence?"

"Back off, Jaime," Lai warned.

"I said I'd ask again. We have a right to know who we're traveling with."

"We're traveling with my cousin! Besides, did you forget what Oscar told us?"

"We don't know what this is until she tells us!"

"Stop it!" Mel nearly shouted.

Lai and Jaime both fell silent at her outburst.

Mel clutched at her blanket and took few deep breaths. "I killed someone."

"*Dios mío*, I knew it!" Jaime said.

"You got your answer. Now leave it alone," Lai told him.

"Leave it alone? We helped a murderer escape."

"And how is what we do any better?"

To that Jaime did not reply. He mumbled to himself and turned on his side. No one spoke for several minutes. Jaime was the first to fall asleep.

When he was snoring softly, she rolled over again and propped herself up on her elbow to face Mel. "Just promise me you're not a serial killer."

Mel let out a nervous, breathy laugh. "I'm not a serial killer. But that's all I'm saying for now."

"For now," Lai echoed. She fell back into the couch and stared up at the ceiling.

"How's Oscar doing?" Mel asked.

Lai wasn't surprised Mel had asked about Oscar. Lai had met him only a few days after she met her new cousin. Though the two of them were never as close as Lai was with either of them, they spent enough time together before he and Lai left for the academy together.

"He had a breakdown a week ago," Lai replied after a moment.

"Oh." Mel shuffled on the couch. "What happened?"

"He was pulled from training and taken to a hospital."

"Why did he have a breakdown?"

Lai declined to respond. Mel got the message and asked no further questions.

After a long pause, Lai let out a breath through her teeth. "We really need a plan."

"Any bright ideas?" Mel asked.

Lai shook her head. "Not in the past ten minutes."

"The Confederacy?"

"That's funny," Lai said flatly.

"What about Canada?"

"Come on, Mel, you know the borders are closed. They have been for forty years."

"Maybe they would give me refuge. Let me serve a prison sentence there instead."

"I doubt it. No one but smugglers cross that border."

Mel lifted her head. "What about smugglers?"

"You mean have them smuggle you across?" Lai asked in disbelief.

Mel hummed her agreement.

"That sounds dangerous. They could just as easily turn us over for a price."

"What else am I supposed to do?"

Lai frowned. It sounded like Mel was crying, but she couldn't see any tears in the darkness.

"I'm scared, Lani," she whispered.

"I know, Mel. So am I."

"You're not the one they want to execute."

"Who knows. After shooting my sergeant, maybe they'll execute me too."

"If they can get you." Mel wiped a tear off her cheek. "You were pretty badass today."

Lai laughed and looked back up at the roof. "I guess I was."

"Thank you."

Lai allowed herself to smile and closed her eyes. She listened to Mel's breathing until she fell into a dreamless sleep.

CHAPTER EIGHT

A GROUP of half a dozen officers in varying positions of authority stood in a semicircle around a large computer screen. The machine emitted the occasional *beep* as it processed information. In the middle of the screen was the insignia for Colonel Parks Academy, a handgun over a shield in a blue circle with a white rim. Occupying the room were another twenty or so people sitting at computers.

"Pull up a map of Yuma and surrounding settlements," a burly man instructed. A woman sitting several feet away tapped at her keyboard and the map came into view on the screen.

"They couldn't have gotten far," another woman in the semicircle spoke up. "Three kids with no supplies. They must be headed for the city."

"I wouldn't rule out other options, Lieutenant," the man replied. "After all, the city is the most obvious choice. They likely want to stay under the radar."

Lieutenant Kagome Yori looked to the man. "The only other settlements for miles are houses, Captain Chor. You think they would risk seeking help from strangers?"

"I think these are impulsive children. They could risk anything."

"These are more than children, Captain," came a voice from behind the group. They all turned their attention to the woman sitting on a stool near a group of computers.

"Please explain, Sergeant," Captain Chor said.

Sergeant Washington nodded, rubbed her injured leg, and held back a wince. "Harris is one of my top students. What she did was impulsive, yes, but she's not careless. She'll be taking every precaution to keep them out of our scope."

"What about the boy?"

"I can't say with certainty that Martinez was a victim. He and Harris are close. It's likely they were working together."

"So we have two high-level students with a loaded weapon attempting to hide a dangerous felon," Lieutenant Yori said. "Tell us again how you let them get away."

"That's enough, Lieutenant," the captain ordered.

"I made a judgment call," Sergeant Washington replied anyway. "One that resulted in no casualties."

"Which is one less than there should have been," another officer cut in.

"Would you have risked the lives of every student and officer in that room, Sergeant Jenkins?" Sergeant Washington challenged.

The captain raised his fist, and the other officers fell silent. "That's enough arguing. We have enough problems without my people going at each other's throats."

"Yes, sir," Sergeant Washington and the officer replied as one.

"Back to the matter at hand. What do we know about these settlements? Jenkins?"

"They're mostly low-income families," the man answered. "Quite a few immigrants. None would be likely to want trouble."

"Even if they were threatened?" Lieutenant Yori asked.

Jenkins shrugged. "I couldn't say, ma'am. I've never been to any in person."

"Washington, do you think your students would seek shelter by force?" the captain asked her.

She considered the question for a moment. "Harris is trying to keep her cousin alive. I think she is capable of more than usual. We shouldn't underestimate her."

"Captain!" a man called from across the room. The captain turned to see a lower-ranking officer, one he did not know by name, enter the command room in a hurry.

"Yes, officer?"

"Sir, I found something you should see." He went to the computer next to Sergeant Washington and tapped away at the keyboard. On the large screen, a file opened in front of the map and a picture of a woman appeared, along with a list of information next to it.

"Tell me what I'm seeing," the captain ordered.

The officer squeezed past him to stand beside the screen. "This is Angella Martinez." He pointed to the picture.

"Martinez… she is related to Jaime Martinez?"

"She's his older sister," the officer confirmed. "She's been flagged recently."

"For what?"

"She is a suspected member of the *Libertas Publica*."

Captain Chor bristled at the mention of the self-proclaimed "freedom fighters" that tormented those who kept order in the Republic.

"How was the Martinez boy allowed into our academy given his family?" he demanded.

"She was only flagged a month ago. Her name came up when a supplies facility was raided. There was never any solid evidence against her, so we couldn't make an arrest. I only found it when doing a system-wide search into the kids."

The captain turned to Sergeant Washington. "Are you certain they could have been working together?"

"I can't be certain, but with this information I'm more convinced."

"Officer, where does Angella Martinez live?" the captain asked.

The officer peered at the information on the screen. "She lives in a compound about thirty miles north of the academy."

The captain smiled a toothy grin. "Well done, officer."

The officer beamed with pride. "Thank you, sir. I'm always happy to be of assistance."

"Lieutenant, how soon can we have a team ready to mobilize?" the captain asked.

She hesitated for a long moment. "They can be ready to leave by sunrise," she replied with a frown.

The captain returned the expression. "What are you waiting for, Yori? Prepare a team."

"Sir," she began tentatively. "We have no legal grounds to search the house, much less raid it. According to these reports, she is not a confirmed member. Given that Jaime Martinez was taken hostage in a room with twenty witnesses, we can say with no certainty that the kids would have gone to his family."

"I don't want to hear why we can't do it," the captain growled through his teeth. "I want a 'yes, sir' and immediate action."

"But, sir—"

"You are dismissed, Lieutenant."

Lieutenant Yori leaned back in surprise. When she opened her mouth to speak, the captain beat her to it.

"Unless the next words out of your mouth are 'yes, sir,' I don't want to hear it," he warned.

The lieutenant shut her mouth and nodded once. She quickly walked across the room and out the door the officer had entered. All eyes watched her leave. When she had gone, the captain turned to Jenkins.

"Sergeant, tell me how to legally get into that house," he ordered.

Jenkins thought for a few seconds. "I just got an anonymous tip," he lied. "A neighbor reported seeing drugs being moved into the house. The concerned citizen called us and reported it."

"That's what I want to hear. How soon can you have a team ready to mobilize?"

"Two hours, sir," he said. "Well before sunrise."

"Tell them to be well stocked. They're going on a raid."

CHAPTER NINE

LAI WAS woken suddenly when a shoe slammed into her head.

"Letse!" she exclaimed as she shot into an upright position. She glanced around, dazed, to see Angella throwing various articles of clothing at her friends.

"Angella, *kung ano ang impiyerno?*" Lai continued. In her half-awake stupor, she began rambling in Tagalog. "Ang ibig mo sineseryoso magtapon ng isang palabas sa aking ulo? Hindi ka maaaring gisingin mo ako sa isang nicer paraan?"

"Inglés o español, niña," Angella replied. "English or Spanish."

"English, please," Mel groaned as she sat up.

"What the hell is going on?" Lai snapped.

Angella barely spared her a glance. "We need to get out here right now. There's a raid coming."

The fog of sleep quickly cleared from Lai's mind. "A raid? How do you know?"

"A few of our scouts saw them and sent word ahead. They'll be here in fifteen minutes, maybe less. We need to move, *rápido.*"

Lai's mind switched to autopilot. She stood up and quickly stripped off her sweatpants. She replaced them with a pair of light gray cargo pants that Angella had thrown at her after the shoe. She kept the T-shirt and pulled on a green jacket that Angella tossed to her. She was pulling her shoes on, with Jaime getting ready as well. Mel seemed confused and tired, but she still put on a jacket that Angella dropped on her head.

When Lai was dressed, she grabbed her gun from the coffee table and double-checked it was loaded.

"Hey," Angella called, and tossed her two additional clips, which Lai shoved into her pockets. She noted that Angella was already dressed and had two weapons of her own, or at least two that were visible.

"Are these scouts reliable?" Lai asked. She checked her pants for a place to safely holster her gun. Unlike Angella, she was not comfortable with putting it in her waistband.

"They're friends. I'd trust them with my life," Angella replied. She saw Lai searching for a place to put her gun. She went to the cabinet and riffled around in it. She pulled out two belts with holsters and tossed one each to Lai and Jaime.

"It's not just your life at stake here," Lai pointed out as she looped the belt through her pants. She received no reply.

"Why don't we just wear our academy uniforms?" Jaime asked. "They're more practical."

"They're also more conspicuous," his sister replied. She was still going through the cabinet. "We don't need to attract attention."

"I think those weapons will do that for you," Lai said.

Angella turned her head to glare at her. "You can be smart with me after I've saved your lives."

Lai didn't want to argue with her. She holstered her gun and turned to Mel, who was pulling on her own pair of cargo pants. She seemed terrified.

"You good, Mel?" Lai asked.

Mel gave her an unconvincing smile. "I'll be better once we're out of here."

"Maldita sea, ¿dónde está?" Angella exclaimed. She smacked her hand against the wall next to the cabinet.

Jaime walked over to his sister. "Did you lose something?"

She shook her head. "I don't know. I can't find a flash drive."

"Is it important?"

"I wouldn't waste time looking for it if it weren't," she snapped.

Jaime raised an eyebrow but did not comment on her tone. "Maybe it's in one of the boxes in my room."

Angella instantly spun on her heels and headed toward his bedroom. "Get some food and water," she called over her shoulder. "We leave in five minutes."

Jaime pulled three backpacks out of the open cabinet and handed one to Lai. "Mel and I will get food. Check the cabinet. If anything looks useful, take it."

Lai nodded and headed for the cabinet. Jaime grabbed Mel's arm and pulled her along to the kitchen. When Lai was alone, she took an appraisal of the cabinet. There was everything from charges to brightly colored folders with papers spilling out to boxes of instant coffee. Lai saw at least five laptops stacked on top of one another. She figured a laptop could be useful, but it would also be heavy. She ignored them and turned her attention to the rest of the cabinet.

She grabbed a charge and dropped it to the bottom of her pack. There was a box of handguns and clips in the bottom left corner. Angella was very unprepared for a raid, she noted. She grabbed another clip and added it to her bag. She also grabbed another handgun and holster. On the topmost shelf, there was a medium-sized black case. Lai pulled it out and placed it carefully on the coffee table. There was some writing in Spanish on the top that Lai couldn't read. She ignored it and opened the box.

Whatever she had been expecting to find inside, it wasn't explosives. Lai wasn't an expert on explosives, but she knew these were not homemade. They looked to be military grade weapons.

"What are you doing with that?"

Angella stood in the doorway, seeming as if she were about to implode from her worry.

"Jaime told me to go through the cabinet for anything useful," Lai explained.

Angella hurried over to her and shut the lid on the black box.

"I'll take that," she said. "You cannot touch my stuff, ¿de acuerdo?"

Lai nodded once and left to join Jaime and Mel in the kitchen. When she went in, she found Jorge was with them. He was helping them go through the cupboards and handing them various food items.

"Are you coming with us, Jorge?" Lai asked him.

He threw her a water bottle. "I'll be staying here to buy you time."

"What?" Jaime cried. He whipped around to face his father. "They'll arrest you and charge you with possession of every illegal item in this house. And there are a lot."

"Son, what's important is that you and your sister get out safely. You have to help her keep these two safe." He gestured to Mel and Lai. "I'll get them off your trail and get to safety. I'll be all right."

"You're in, too, aren't you?" Lai asked him.

Jorge stared at her for a long moment before nodding.

Jaime sighed.

Mel frowned up at them. "What are we talking about?"

"Nothing," Jaime lied. "Let's go, now."

Mel zipped up her backpack and followed Jaime back into the living room. When Jorge went to follow them, Lai stopped him with a hand on his arm. She waited until he met her gaze.

"Thank you," she said.

The man gave her a terse nod. "You are a very courageous young woman. I am sorry you had to grow up in this place."

He pulled his arm away and exited the room. Lai followed close behind. In the living room, Jaime, Mel, and Angella all stood ready to go. Each had a pack on. Angella's pack bulged as if a box pressed against the sides.

"We're going out the back," Angella pulled a gun from her belt. "Keep your guns out, but don't fire unless necessary. If we end up in a shooting match, we will lose."

Without another word, Angella nodded to her father and started for the back of the house. Jaime hurried over to give Jorge a quick hug and followed his sister. Lai tightened the straps on her bag and went after them. Mel fell into step behind her.

They went past the bedrooms to a doorway. Angella pushed through and led them into the dry morning air. The sun had just risen over the horizon and offered them enough light to see well. Lai wished it were earlier; they would be less easily spotted in the dark.

"We're heading northeast," Angella told them as they filed out the door. "We'll be traveling for five days until we reach a base."

"Is this base in Phoenix?" Lai asked.

"It's in Maricopa," Angella corrected. "We'll be safe once we get there."

"And until we get there?" Mel asked.

Angella did not reply.

Mel squeezed her eyes shut and took a few deep breaths. "What's this base we're going to?"

"It's a sort of safe haven," Angella explained. "The *Libertas Publica* use it as a way station."

"Wait, the State Freedom?" Mel gasped. "They're going to help us?"

Angella raised an eyebrow to her. "We already are."

Whatever Mel's response was, it was cut off by the sounds of vehicles charging in at high speeds. Angella waved for the group to follow her as she ducked behind a house for cover. All four squatted in the dust. Angella peeked around a corner and pulled her head back just as quickly.

"Mierda," she cursed. "They're here."

The vehicles screeched to a stop. Lai shuffled forward and peered around the corner herself. She saw groups of heavily armed officers, about a dozen total, jumping out of two black military vans. They headed straight for the Martinez house and busted right through the front door. People shouted and Lai pulled her head back.

"What do we do now?" she asked fearfully.

Angella pulled her backpack off and dug around inside. She opened the black box and pulled out a small white canister. "We do this," she said through clenched teeth. She held the canister to her chest and looked to her companions. "On my word we run left. Do not lag behind."

Angella stood up and removed a pin from the canister. She pulled her arm back and threw it as far as she could. It sailed through the air and landed behind another house in a patch of brush. She motioned them up with her, mouthing to herself.

"Three, two, one," she whispered. "Now!"

The four of them broke into a run. As if on cue, there was a loud bang from behind them. Lai spared a glance over her shoulder to see smoke spiraling into the air from where Angella had tossed what was evidently a smoke bomb. People ran in the direction of the smoke but Lai did not dare risk another look behind her. All four panted as they ran around houses, getting progressively farther from the raid taking place at the house. Angella led them along as the houses got closer together. Lai said a silent prayer of thanks in her head. This made it less likely for them to be seen.

"Angella, what do—" Mel began.

"Shut up!" Angella hissed.

Mel snapped her mouth shut and continued running. As they ran, the ground underneath them changed from dust to concrete. Lai finally understood all the seemingly random turns through the maze of houses. Angella was following a predetermined escape route. The concrete would prevent there from being any footprints to follow.

Angella suddenly turned to the right and changed their course. The three teens followed without a word. She led them on for another five minutes at a pace that made their hearts race. Just when Lai thought her lungs were going to burst, Angella slowed and waved them toward a generic-looking building with boarded-up windows. An unreadable sign hung unevenly above the door.

"Get inside," she ordered. Lai ran ahead to take the lead. She pushed open the door and led them all inside. Angella glanced back over her shoulder before following.

Inside the building it was cool, a welcome change from the hot desert air. Lai took in the building. It appeared to be a supplies store. There were shelves filled with cans and boxes, and farther back, clothing hung on racks against the back wall. In the opposite corner, there were outdoor supplies: rope and tarps and tents. It was not a large store, but it seemed to have a little bit of everything.

A short Hispanic woman with curly brown hair stood behind a reception desk. She glanced up when she heard the group enter the building. When she saw them, a concerned frown came to her face.

"*Dios mío,* Angella, *lo que está sucediendo?*" she asked.

Angella gave her a smile and took her backpack off one shoulder. "Mariana, we need to lay low for a little while," she panted. She waved a hand to the others. "These three are with me."

"Of course, *chica*, of course," Mariana nodded. "Into the back room."

"*Muchas gracias,* Mariana," Angella thanked her with another smile. She headed toward the back of the store to a low doorway. She pushed through it and held it open for Lai, Jaime, and Mel to go inside. They entered a small room piled high with boxes. Angella went in after them and closed the door. She took off her backpack and slid down the wall until she was seated. She held her gun in her lap and panted openly.

"Who was that?" Lai asked her.

"That was Mariana. She will hide us until it's safe to leave. We can trust her. She's helped me in the past."

Jaime and Mel sat down as well. Lai opted to remain standing and held her gun ready. She faced the door as if she expected officers to burst through at any moment.

"They must have figured out I wasn't taken hostage," Jaime reasoned.

Mel groaned and put her head in her lap. "How are we going to get out of this?" she whined.

"We are going to wait for one hour," Angella told her. "Then I will check outside. If it's clear we'll keep heading for the base."

Mel lifted her head and narrowed her eyes at the woman. "You're a member of *Libertas Publica*."

Angella rolled her eyes. "Como si pudiera ser más obvio," she muttered.

Mel frowned at her.

Jaime placed a hand on her shoulder. "My sister just wants to help us. Her group has no love for the Republic."

"You don't seem surprised to learn your sister is a freedom fighter."

Jaime met Lai's gaze before he replied. "It isn't new information to me."

Lai did not react to his comment. She looked back to the door and focused on standing guard.

CHAPTER TEN

"SO YOU'RE saying we shouldn't have a singular law enforcement group?" Mel asked.

Angella gestured enthusiastically with her hands as she spoke. "I'm saying the Republic doesn't need a militarized police force. Most countries have a police and a military. They have no connection. But then President Emilia started preaching about the need for a single force to protect the people, and now you have protection officers. Making the police and the military a single entity gives them more power to oppress the people. It was bad enough when the police were shooting innocent kids in the streets. Now they can raid houses on a whim. I bet they had to lie to get the approval for the raid on our house."

Lai watched Angella and Mel debating. They had been at it for nearly twenty minutes. Sitting in the storage room had made Mel antsy, and Angella had indulged her with a lively conversation.

"That is one of the objectives of the *Libertas Publica*," Angella continued. "We want a separate military. Personally, I believe the Protection Force should be dissolved completely, but some think that's too radical to happen right away. First we need to get back to a democracy. That's why we're called State Freedom. We believe the state system should return and be allowed to have their own laws."

"But you said you don't believe in government control," Mel said.

Angella raised an eyebrow and gave her a smile. "*Bueno*, you've been paying attention. I don't. But I know the best way to get there is to first get rid of the Republic, and the best way to do that—"

"Is to be a member of the *Libertas Publica*," Mel finished.

Angella leaned back against a box and spread her hands out in front of her. "Esta chica entiende," she said to her brother. "This girl understands."

There was a sudden knock at the door. Lai raised her weapon and trained it at head level.

Angella instantly stood up and put her hand on Lai's arm. She listened to the knocking pattern and breathed a sigh of relief. "It's

Mariana." She opened the door to reveal the woman standing on the other side.

"Prisa," she said. "You have to get moving."

"Is everything all right?" Angella asked. The kids filed out the door in front of her.

"An officer came in to ask me some questions," Mariana told her. "I said I have no love for the *Libertas Publica*. I told him I saw you circling back around to the south to confuse them."

"*Gracias*, Mariana," Angella thanked her. She took the other woman's hand for a moment, then followed the others back into the store. "We need to get moving."

She led them back outside. Her gun was held ready in front of her. She did a quick sweep of the area and then waved them along. "Jaime, take the back. Lai, you're up front with me."

Everyone fell into position with Mel in the middle. Without another word the group started off to the northeast.

As they walked, the buildings thinned out. After about half an hour of walking, they passed the last house in sight and entered the open desert once again. Lai scanned their surroundings. There didn't appear to be anything or anyone ahead of them.

"Why don't we get a car?" Mel asked to break the lengthy silence.

"I don't have a car," Angella told her. "We'd have to steal one. That would raise attention."

"Wouldn't it be faster?"

"It would. But there are no roads around here. Besides, we'd run out of gas before we made it there."

"How do you even know where we're going?"

Angella shoved her gun into her waistband and reached into her pocket. She pulled out a small gray device.

Lai recognized it with a start. "Where did you get a GeoScanner?" Lai asked with wide eyes.

Angella punched coordinates into the small machine. "Courtesy of Mariana. She's my supplier in this area."

"Your supplier for what?" Mel asked.

Angella raised an eyebrow and tapped a finger on her gun. "Everything."

The group fell into silence again as Angella worked on the machine. Lai spun around in a tight circle to take stock of the surrounding area.

The houses behind them were barely visible in the distance. She wiped her brow and cursed the heat. When her mother brought her and her little sister to the Republic, they'd lived in the north where her new stepfather stayed when not on an international posting. The temperature was much more to Lai's liking. Even in the three years since joining the academy Lai hadn't gotten used to the dry heat. She hadn't seen so much as a speck of snow in the past three years, and she missed it.

Lai glanced over when Angella pulled off her jacket. The woman tied it around her waist and stretched her arms above her head. When she lowered them, Lai noticed something for the first time.

"That's an interesting tattoo," Lai said.

Angella looked to her right shoulder. The tattoo was slightly faded, at least ten years old if Lai figured correctly. A thick black circle held the letters PLP in sharp red lettering. The pattern of a Cuban flag, blue and white horizontal stripes with a white star in a red triangle on the left, was inked behind the letters.

"It's the logo of the *Partido de la Libertad Popular*," Angella explained. "I got it when I was sixteen."

"I like it."

"It almost fits the *Libertas Publica* letters."

"Seems fitting you would end up in a similar group," Lai observed.

Angella gave a sly smile. "The politics are rather ironic."

"Does the tattoo ever give you trouble here?"

"Most people don't know what it means. I don't have trouble, even though *mi madre* nearly had an aneurysm when she saw it. It's high enough on my arm that I can usually cover it."

Lai smiled along with her. They both looked ahead of them as they continued walking.

"I've been meaning to ask," Lai began. "Your house, it was full of illegal items. They were just sitting out in the open. Isn't that a big risk?"

Angella glanced at Lai out of the corner of her eye. "You are a nonsympathizer," Angella said rather than answer the question. "You are now a wanted fugitive. That doesn't mean I trust you with group secrets."

"Angella, you can trust me," Lai said. She reached back into her pack and took out her water bottle. She took a quick swig and offered it to Angella. The woman grabbed it after a moment and took a drink herself before handing it back.

"We all have to take risks," Angella replied cryptically. "Sometimes they don't pay off."

Lai realized that was all she was going to get from her at the moment. Angella's gaze was hard. This was a member of the *Libertas Publica*, not just Jaime's older sister.

"¿Puedo preguntarte algo?" Lai asked.

Angella regarded her with obvious surprise. "You actually speak Spanish."

Lai thought she sounded impressed. "Jaime tries to teach me." She shrugged.

Angella gave her a tight-lipped smile. "Ask away."

"How did you become a *Libertas Publica* member?"

Angella took a deep breath. "That is a complicated question with a long answer."

"I think we have time."

Angella stared openly at Lai for a long moment. Before she spoke she turned forward again and looked off toward the horizon.

"My brother said he already told you about my affiliation in Cuba. When we came here, I didn't want to live under a second oppressive government, especially not a racist one. It started with a friend I had at school. I was taking classes in politics, but I did not speak very much English when I was seventeen. My classmate, Salomé, spoke English and Spanish. She translated in class for me and gave me English lessons after school. She warned me about my writing. She said it was too radical, that it would get me in trouble. But she also told me she agreed with me. She told me if I was serious about my opinions, then I could come with her to a meeting one night. She wouldn't tell me what the meeting was for.

"When we arrived I saw the flag on the wall. It was a *Libertas Publica* meeting. I told them my opinions on the Republic and about my affiliations in Cuba. Salomé translated for me. When I was finished explaining, they asked me if I wanted to join."

"Just like that, you were a member?" Lai asked.

"I was only doing little tasks in the first few years. I would put up fliers around the campus that spoke of the evil of the Republic. I carried messages. I didn't get a real assignment until I was twenty-three."

"What happened to Salomé?"

Angella took a long time to answer. "She was captured five years ago during a raid at one of our bases. She was tried for treason. They put her on death row and executed her."

Lai frowned. "*Lo siento*, Angella."

"You're sorry, yet you've killed dozens of people like her," Angella hissed.

"I never wanted to do that," Lai argued.

"But you did!"

Lai fell silent at her words. She knew Angella was right. She had no right to argue. She glanced behind them. Mel was kicking a rock around and did not appear to be paying attention. Jaime was keeping an eye on the desert around them. Lai caught his eye. He offered her a sympathetic smile. He had clearly been listening.

She faced forward again and cleared her throat. "Angella, I'm sorry about your friend. No one should be killed for their beliefs. I mean that." She looked hard at Angella and did not speak until their eyes met. "And I don't think it's right to kill people, period."

Angella let out a noisy breath that almost sounded like a laugh. "You were killing people just yesterday, *niña*."

Lai echoed the sound. "Maybe it took seeing my cousin about to die to make me realize how screwed up this system is."

Angella smiled in spite of herself. "You would make a good member."

Lai did not disagree.

CHAPTER ELEVEN

THE SUN was well across the sky behind them when they saw the truck. Lai was walking in the back with Mel and Jaime several meters ahead of her. Angella led them with the help of the GeoScanner. The truck appeared to be standard Republic issue with a faded green tent covering the back.

The moment it came into view ahead of them, Angella dropped to her one knee and aimed her weapon.

"Get behind me," she growled. Lai and Jaime fell in to flank her with their guns raised while Mel kneeled on the ground between them.

"Get the box out of my bag, *rápidamente*," Angella ordered. Jaime frowned. Lai knew what she was referring to and quickly unzipped the pack. She pulled out the black box and opened it next to her.

"Find a black canister and hand it to me."

Lai did as she was told and closed the box. Angella held her gun in one hand and brought the canister to her mouth in the other. She held the pin between her teeth and waited. Lai returned her focus to the truck.

"There's no way we can shoot our way out of here," Jaime warned.

Angella removed the pin from her mouth. "That's why I'm going to throw a stun grenade at them. We only shoot if we need to." She returned the pin to her mouth. As the truck approached them, it began to slow. Angella pulled her arm back. Just as she was about to throw the grenade, there was a shout from the truck.

"Vivat populus!" a man shouted.

Angella's arm stopped above her head. She lowered it and turned to her companions. Lai was shocked to see a smile on her face.

"They're *Libertas Publica*," she told them as she replaced the grenade pin. "That's our friend code. It means 'long live the people.'"

All four of them breathed a sigh of relief. Angella put the grenade back into the box and returned the box to her backpack. Lai and Jaime both holstered their weapons. They all stood as two men jumped out of the truck and jogged over to the group. Lai quickly appraised them.

The man running in front was about the same age as Angella. His short brown hair was sticking up from his head. He wore a loose black tee and cargo pants. The man a few steps behind him was at least forty. His white clothing contrasted with his dark skin and cropped black hair. Both men came to a halt when they reached the group. The man in front pulled Angella in for a tight hug the moment he reached her.

"I can't believe you're alive," he laughed. She returned the hug with equal force. "The scouts said you were raided."

"I was," she groaned. When they pulled away from each other, Angella was instantly grabbed by the other man for another hug. She laughed as he squeezed her tight.

"Okay, okay, Carlton, I need air," she gasped.

The man chuckled and let her go. "How did you get out of there?"

"The scouts got word to me," she explained. "We got out with seconds to spare."

Both men gazed at the teens in front of them.

"Who is this *we*?" Carlton asked.

"This is my brother, Jaime, his friend Lai, and her cousin, Mel," Angella said. She gestured to each of them in turn. "Melanie here is a death-row escapee."

Sydney whistled. "Death row. That's harsh. You don't look a day over twenty."

"I'm nineteen," Mel corrected.

"How is she an escapee?" Carlton asked.

Angella glanced at the girl in question. "Es complicado. And it's better told in a truck, and not in the open."

"We got you," Sydney said with a nod. He walked back to the truck. "You taking them to Maricopa?"

Angella nodded and followed after him. Everyone else fell into step behind them.

"We were going to walk before you so graciously showed up," she said.

"Lucky you," Sydney teased. Angella turned and gave him a friendly slap on the shoulder. When they reached the truck, Lai noticed that there was a woman sitting behind the wheel. She followed them with her eyes as they walked around the back of the truck. Sydney pulled the back open.

"All aboard," he said with a flourish of his hand.

He and Angella helped the teens up and then followed them inside. They had to duck when they stood to avoid the cover. Carlton sat on the left side of the truck with Angella next to him. Lai, Jaime, and Mel all sat on the right side. When everyone else was seated, Sydney signaled to the driver and hopped up next to Carlton. The engine revved to a start and the truck turned around.

"I assume the cargo was lost in the raid," Sydney said to Angella.

She grimaced and nodded. "*Sí*. Most of it, anyway. I got a few guns, the flash drive, and the box of explosives."

"Explosives? What'd you bring for us this time?" Sydney asked while rubbing his hands together.

Angella rolled her eyes and pulled the black box out of her pack again. She opened it on her lap and let the men take a peek inside.

"You got any salted bombs in there?" Carlton asked.

"Of course not, *bicho raro*," she replied. "It's mostly smoke bombs and stun grenades. There's also three fragmentation grenades and an ammonium nitrate bomb."

"Can I touch one?" Sydney asked as he reached for the box.

Angella slapped his hand away. "Not unless you want to lose that hand."

"Any Semtex?" Carlton asked. When she shook her head, he grumbled, "Those are my favorite…."

"Enough drooling over grenades," she said as she closed the box.

"You're right," Sydney sighed. "Besides, we've got questions. Starting with those three." He raised an eyebrow to the three teens across from him.

Lai met his eyes. "It's not that complicated." She ignored the pointed look Angella gave her. "Jaime and I were in training. Mel showed up at my station. I shot my sergeant and we rescued her."

"You're in training?" Carlton asked in alarm. His hand moved to rest on his hip. Lai could see the bulge of a handgun under his shirt.

"We used to be," she clarified. "I think we dropped out the moment I shot a superior officer."

There was a long pause that was broken when Sydney laughed.

"I like this one," he said with a smirk directed at Angella. "We should keep her."

"All we're doing is getting them to the base," she said firmly. "I only ended up being a babysitter because we were raided. I wasn't about to leave my own brother to the mercy of the Republic."

"Who said anything about babysitting?" Jaime complained. That got a laugh out of everyone in the truck. Carlton removed his hand from his gun, though he remained tense.

"We should be there in two hours, *sí*?" Angella inquired.

"Two hours," Carlton nodded.

"If we don't run into any officers," Sydney added.

"Isn't that what this truck is for?" she asked with a raised eyebrow. "How did you get a standard issue truck, anyway?"

"Now that is a very long and very complicated story," Sydney told her.

"I want to hear this," Angella said with a sly grin.

Carlton shook his head as Sydney began telling the story. Lai did her best to tune him out and tapped a finger on the legs of Jaime and Mel.

"What are we going to do when we get to the base?" she asked in a hushed voice once she had their attention.

"I think we should stay there for a while," Mel said. "We'll be safe."

"As safe as you can be with the most wanted group in the Republic," Jaime pointed out.

"It's still safer than we'd be on our own," Lai reasoned. Neither could disagree with her.

"That doesn't mean we're joining the group," Jaime continued. "We can stay for a few days while we make a better plan."

"What plan are we going to make?" Lai asked. "Once we get Mel somewhere safe, then what? We don't have anywhere to go back to. We're fugitives. If we don't stop somewhere, we'll be running for the rest of our lives."

"Then we leave the Republic."

"And go where? To Cuba? To the Philippines?"

"The Philippines isn't a bad idea."

"We would still need to get out, and it won't be as easy as getting out of the academy. These borders are the most heavily guarded in the world."

"Why don't we join them?" Mel spoke up.

Lai tilted her head.

"You can't be serious," Jaime said with wide eyes.

"Why not? We're practically members already."

"It's different for them. Most of them are members in secret. They can still have lives. We can't. We would be known. The *Libertas Publica* would be our lives."

"None of us have lives anymore," Lai cut in. When five pairs of eyes turned to her, she realized she had spoken louder than intended.

"You three all right?" Carlton asked.

"We're just talking about what to do next," Jaime explained.

"My cousin suggested we seek membership," Lai added.

Angella raised an eyebrow.

Sydney laughed once. "You might as well. The girl is right. Your lives are effectively over."

"¡Cállate!" Angella said. She gave Sydney a smack on his arm. "These kids have been through enough. They don't need you saying things like that."

"Has someone gone soft?" Sydney teased. When Angella raised her hand again, he flinched back. She smirked and ran the hand through her hair instead.

"You can talk about joining rebel groups when we get to Maricopa," Carlton said. "You three should try to get some sleep while you can. You may not get that much at the base."

"Why not?" Mel inquired.

Sydney gave her a wicked grin. "Haven't you heard? The Republic isn't the only group that knows how to go on a raid."

CHAPTER TWELVE

THE TWO teens slipped silently into the dorm room. Tamsin took one last glance around the halls outside before gently closing the door. They walked through the rows of beds to the farthest row where their friends sat waiting.

"Did you find anything?" Virginia asked hopefully.

"We couldn't get anything," Rylen said with a shake of his head. "Security is tight."

"We couldn't even get into a lab, much less hack into the server," Tamsin added.

Siobhan groaned and fell back onto the mattress. "I wish they would tell us something," she whined.

"Protocol says they're not our problem anymore," Deirdre sighed. "We don't have the clearance to ask questions about fugitives that aren't inside the academy."

"Good riddance," Kieran called from across the room. Five pairs of eyes turned to the girl lying with her back to them on her bunk. She had her sheet pulled tight around her shoulders.

"Come on, Kier. These are our friends," Deirdre said.

"They're fugitives," Kieran countered. She sat up and threw her sheet off. Her curly black hair stuck up at odd angles.

"You heard Lai. That was her cousin," Virginia said.

"Come here." Deirdre held her arms out and waved Kieran over. The girl rolled her eyes and stood up to walk across the room. She plopped down next to her girlfriend and crossed her arms.

"You all sound very nonsympathetic," Kieran scoffed. Deirdre idly smoothed down the girl's unruly curls.

"We're just worried," she said. "They could be anywhere."

"They could even be dead," Tamsin added.

"You think they'd kill Jaime?" Rylen asked. "He didn't seem like he wanted to leave."

"Do any of you honestly believe he wasn't helping her?" Kieran interjected. "If Lai were taking someone hostage, it wouldn't be her best friend."

Everyone considered her words for a moment. Rylen stood up and paced in a tight circle.

"I wonder what Lai's cousin did," Siobhan said.

"*I* wonder if Lai knew before she saved her," Deirdre added.

"I doubt it," Tamsin replied. "My station is next to hers. Lai seemed pretty surprised."

"Makes you wonder if her cousin deserved to be there," Virginia said.

"Oh, so now we're against capital punishment?" Kieran scoffed.

"I think we should question the morality of a system that sentences half of its prison population to death, especially considering what Oscar said."

"Oscar had a breakdown," Kieran said dismissively.

"He did," Deirdre agreed. "But you have to wonder why. If he really did see the things he said he did, shouldn't we all be skeptical?"

"Let's say Oscar had anything real to tell us." Kieran stood up and faced her four dorm mates on the beds. "What are we supposed to do about it? We're seven months away from finishing our training. The only thing we could do is quit. That still changes nothing."

"If we could find the truth, we could put a stop to it," Virginia suggested.

"And after your failed information-gathering trip, do you think you'll have much success?"

"So we're just supposed to sit by and execute people who may be innocent?"

Kieran bristled for a moment before her expression lost its fire.

"If Oscar was telling the truth, if he wasn't delusional, then we shouldn't be doing this," Virginia pressed on. "Even you couldn't argue with that."

Kieran sighed and rubbed her eyes with the heels of her hands. She took several deep breaths before she spoke again. "Then what are we supposed to do about it?" she repeated.

"We could ask the sergeant if what Oscar said is true," Tamsin suggested.

"You think the sergeant would tell us?" Deirdre asked. "If she knows, I doubt she would help."

"We could appeal to her humanity," Kieran said. She crossed her arms and gave a humorless laugh.

"If we could just get into the system, we could figure out the truth," Rylen said.

"Have you ever hacked into a system this protected?" Virginia asked him.

"There's a first time for everything."

"Even if we could get this information, we would still need to know what to do with it," Deirdre pointed out.

"We would have a hard time getting it to the media," Siobhan said.

"She's right," Tamsin agreed. "There's hardly a station out there that isn't controlled by the Republic."

"Underground radio?" Rylen suggested.

"Good luck getting enough people to listen," Kieran said.

"Do you have any suggestions, or are you just going to shoot down ours?"

"I still think this is absurd."

"I think you wouldn't be talking to us if you didn't agree with what we're saying."

Kieran gave him an even expression. She glanced over to the four girls sitting on the beds, and her gaze rested on Deirdre. She sighed heavily.

"Damn it," she mumbled. She shook her head quickly. "How did I end up in a training group with nonsympathizers?"

"So let's pretend we have the information we need," Rylen continued. "What do we do with it?"

"We obviously can't take it to the sergeant, or anyone with strong sympathies," Virginia said.

"We don't have the resources to spread it on our own," Kieran argued. "That's assuming we even want to let it out."

"Why wouldn't we?" Siobhan asked.

"This kind of information is dangerous. It needs to be contained. If we just release it, we could end up with riots in major cities."

"There's always the LP," Rylen suggested.

Kieran looked as if she could have slapped him. "That is one step too far," she hissed. The intensity of her glare caused Rylen to take a step back.

"Kieran, this isn't as simple as we thought it was," Deirdre said. Kieran looked over to her, and her glare broke. Deirdre gave her a pleading expression. "We need to figure out what we're fighting for before we decide to keep fighting."

"But the *Libertas Publica*?" Kieran said in a hushed tone. "They're a group of radicals and terrorists. They're on the opposite side of the political spectrum than we're on right now."

"I have to agree with Kieran on this one," Tamsin spoke up. "The LP takes things too far. We don't have to agree with them to disagree with this."

"Did Lai really throw this much of a wrench into our group?" Kieran asked. "She's got us talking about joining a resistance group that wants to dissolve the government."

"Maybe she gave us the reason we needed to question it," Virginia said. "Hasn't it ever bothered you that they make teenagers into executioners?"

"If we're going to be protection officers, we need to be able to kill someone," Kieran reasoned, though it was obvious from her expression that she was unsure of her own words.

"But why do we need to be so skilled at shooting people? Why is killing supposed to be our first response?"

"Especially if you consider we're training for a domestic position," Rylen added. "We won't be fighting in any wars. We're supposed to be protecting people."

"Do you remember reading about the police in history class?" Deirdre asked. Everyone nodded in acknowledgment. "Killing a person was only supposed to be their last resort."

"That never seemed to stop them from doing it anyway," Kieran pointed out.

"Maybe not, but before the Republic they weren't supposed to. Now it's our first option in almost every situation. Have you ever had a problem with that?"

"Damn it, we're not supposed to be talking like this!" Kieran exclaimed. She fell back onto the nearest bed and threw her arms up. "If anyone heard us, they could have us knocked down to a Delta group, or worse."

"Come on, Kier. I know you," Deirdre continued. "You believe in justice. How is a death penalty for so many things just?"

Kieran rolled her head around to meet the eyes of her girlfriend. She sighed heavily and sat up. "This shouldn't be making sense."

"Then ask yourself why it is."

No one spoke for nearly a minute. The air was thick with the realizations of what had been said.

It was Siobhan who finally broke the silence. "So what happens now?" she asked in a quiet voice.

Kieran gave a bitter laugh. "As if any of us know."

CHAPTER THIRTEEN

NO ONE got a wink of sleep on the way to the base in Maricopa. The desert terrain proved uneven, the roads at the outskirts of the city even more so. When the truck bed lurched over a bump in the road for the umpteenth time, Mel nearly fell across onto Angella.

"Who gave that lady a license?" she grumbled.

Sydney held back a smirk.

"Romana drives quickly, not carefully," Carlton told her. "Careful drivers get caught."

Mel sighed and held on tighter to the seat. Lai opened her eyes and glanced over to her. After attempting to get some rest on and off for the past two hours, Lai finally gave up ten minutes earlier. She had settled for closing her eyes and ignoring her companions.

"What happens at this base?" Lai asked.

"Apparently we prepare for a raid," Angella said with a pointed glare to Sydney.

He shrugged and ignored the expression. "We got word this morning that a supply truck was coming through the city. It was too good an opportunity to pass up."

"Despite the fact that the Maricopa base is not stocked for a raid. It is stocked to be a refuge, a way station. How many people are even going on this raid?"

"About six," Sydney admitted.

Lai thought Angella's eyes would pop out of her head and end up bouncing around on the floor.

"Six!" she exclaimed. "¿Lo dice en serio? That's not a raid. That's a suicide mission."

"You could come with us," Sydney suggested.

Angella scoffed. "I don't raid trucks. I raid bases, and I do it discreetly. I don't walk right up to a truck and demand their surrender."

"We would have a better chance with you," Carlton reasoned. "Protocol calls for a team of at least eight for a standard supply truck."

"Even with me you're a person short," Angella said. She crossed her arms and leaned back. "Esto es una mala idea."

"We can't miss a chance like this," Sydney pressed. "The base is understocked as it is. With these three we need all we can get."

Angella sighed and squeezed her eyes shut. She stayed silent for a long moment. When she opened her eyes again, she glared at her friend. "If I get shot out there, I'm blaming you."

Sydney smiled victoriously. "Now that that's settled, the raid will go off without a hitch."

"We're still a person short," Angella reminded him.

"I could go with you."

All eyes turned to Lai.

"What could possibly make you think that's a good idea?" Angella demanded.

"You're a person short," Lai said. "I have a gun. I've been through training."

"You're a child," Angella argued with a wave of her hand.

Lai could have laughed if she hadn't been serious. "You were only sixteen when you were nearly blown up in Havana," Lai countered coolly. She fixed Angella with an even stare. "None of us are children anymore."

Lai and Angella stared each other down. They both likely would have remained in their perpetual state of tension had their glaring match not been interrupted by Sydney laughing. Both shifted their glares to him, though he hardly seemed to care.

"I like this one," he snickered. "I vote to let her tag along."

"You can't be serious." Angella said. When Sydney nodded, she stared at him for a long moment before she shook her head. "*Bueno*, it's your funeral."

Lai fought a smile and turned to Jaime and Mel. Jaime seemed about as happy as his sister.

"Are you sure you want to do this, *asere*?" he asked.

"We'll be fine," she assured, giving him a half smile. "Everyone will be safer with my help."

"You won't be safer," Mel whispered.

Lai put her hand on Mel's arm. Her expression turned serious. "Hey." She waited until they both looked at her. "This is what happens now. We made our decisions. Now we have to live with them."

"You're a smart girl," Carlton interjected.

Lai's smile reappeared.

Angella was still wearing her frown. "Who authorized this raid? Who's in charge at the base now?"

Sydney ran a hand through his hair. "Technically, Jackie is."

Angella rolled her eyes, and when she spoke, Lai thought she could detect a tone of bitterness. "Who the hell put Jackie in charge?"

"She put herself in charge, as usual. When the four of us showed up at the base a week ago, there was no one running anything."

"The four of us being…."

"Me, Carlton, Romana, and Jackie," he replied. "We had no assignments until we were supposed to meet you and pick up the cargo. Jackie saw the absence of leadership and started calling the shots."

Sydney saw Angella's concerned expression. "A lot has changed since you went dark. Most of our people left this area. Once we picked you up, we were supposed to tell you to pack up and head north. There's too many officers around here for us to operate safely."

"Since when has safety been our main concern?" she questioned.

Sydney shrugged.

"There's no use in having us die needlessly," Carlton said.

Before the conversation could continue, the truck screeched to a halt. The group all lurched in their seats.

"Looks like we're here," Sydney said. He hopped up and opened the back of the truck, then jumped off and offered a hand to Angella. She took it and jumped off after him, and the others followed. When Lai's feet hit the ground, she lifted her head and assessed the area.

They had stopped outside what appeared to be a large warehouse. All around them were buildings of the same design and capacity. The one in front of them had no obvious signage, save for a metal plate nailed next to the doorway that read 1125 Maricopa Storage. The woman Carlton had named as Romana came around the side of the truck to where the group waited. She gave a cursory glance to the three teens but said nothing. She pulled a key out of her pocket and unlocked the door with a gesture for everyone to enter. Lai followed closely behind Mel as they entered the warehouse.

Inside it was anything but a nondescript storage facility. Two armed guards were posted by the door. They nodded to Sydney as he led them in. The building was at least six stories high. Off to the left, there were half a dozen shipping containers in a row against the wall. Past them Lai could see several tables where a group of armed people sat, eating. Against the far wall, there were doorways spaced evenly.

"I can see three white people in this entire building," Lai observed, "and one of them is Mel."

Angella gave her a pointed look. "Is it any wonder those who don't enlist end up with us? They offer safety, but we offer change."

Lai nodded her understanding and returned her attention to where they were going.

Along the right wall, where they were being led, were more tables with a few computers and numerous papers spread chaotically around.

A tall Native American woman stood with her arms crossed, staring down at said papers. She glanced up when the group approached. "You brought more kids." She sighed. "Why am I not surprised?"

"Nice to see you, too, Jackie," Sydney greeted her. "And these kids have quite an interesting story."

"Don't we all," she said.

"This is one you'll want to hear," Angella added.

Jackie turned to Angella and shook her head. "Angella Martinez, still alive and here to cause me trouble."

Angella regarded her with a strained grin. "Always a pleasure, Jackie," she replied flatly. "I hear we're going on a raid."

"I invited her along," Sydney added. He nodded to Lai. "This one too."

"You invited a kid on a raid?" Jackie asked incredulously.

"I'm a kid who can shoot a gun," Lai said.

"There's more to executing a raid than knowing how to shoot."

"All right, Carlton, why don't you and Romana take Jaime and Mel and get them settled in," Sydney suggested. "We need to plan."

Carlton nodded his assent. He put a hand on Romana's shoulder and nodded to the other side of the warehouse. Mel and Jaime both hesitated beside Lai.

"I'll catch up with you before I go," Lai promised them.

Mel grabbed her hand. "Stay safe, Lani." She gave Lai's hand a squeeze before following Carlton and Romana away.

Jaime lingered for a moment. "Are you sure you'll be all right?"

"No," Lai admitted. "But I'm sure Angella won't let anything happen to me."

At hearing her name, Angella turned back to them. She gave her brother a wink. He sighed and turned to follow Mel.

"So, Lai, you ever been on a raid before?" Sydney asked.

Lai turned to see him leaning onto his elbows on the table. "Of course not. Students don't have outside assignments."

"Students?" Jackie echoed. She gave Lai a once-over and frowned in concern. "Don't tell me she's an academy kid."

"We can trust her," Angella cut in.

Lai raised an eyebrow to her but said nothing.

Jackie continued frowning at Lai. After a long moment, she sighed. "We don't have enough people here to worry about where she came from. As long as she's on our side, she'll do fine."

"Excellent!" Sydney exclaimed. He stood up straight and clapped his hands together. "We're all on the same page. Now let's fill her in."

"The supply truck will be driving through the outskirts of Maricopa at 2200 hours," Jackie said. "That only gives us two and a half hours to be ready and in position."

"How are you going to raid the truck?" Lai asked.

"We're going to shoot out their tires first. Then we're going to force them all out at gunpoint. Anyone who doesn't surrender their weapon is collateral damage."

"We're going to kill them?"

"Is the academy kid uncomfortable with killing people?" Jackie scoffed.

"Leave it alone, Jackie," Angella defended her. "We don't necessarily need to kill anyone. I managed to grab the explosives before the house was raided."

Angella swung off her backpack and laid it on the table in front of them. She pulled out the black box and opened it for Jackie to see. She picked up a black canister and held it out.

"This is a stun grenade," she said. "If we throw it into the truck, the officers will be disoriented." She returned the canister and pulled out a fragmentation grenade. "Or we use this. We throw it under the truck and let it take out the engine for us."

Jackie crossed her arms and tapped her fingers against her arm.

"Come on, Jackie, you don't have to like me to like my ideas," Angella appealed.

Jackie rolled her eyes. "Sydney, what do you think?"

"I think Angella is right. If we throw a smoke bomb as well, we can use our gas masks and go in without them even seeing us."

"What about the two officers that ride in the back?" Lai asked. When the others eyed her curiously, she elaborated. "We learn about these things at the academy. It's standard protocol. Three officers in the cab, two in the back with the supplies."

"Then we shoot the two in the back," Jackie answered. "Can you live with that?"

Lai met Jackie's gaze evenly. "I'm not sure I have a choice."

CHAPTER FOURTEEN

LAI SNAPPED to attention as an assault rifle was thrown at her head. Her arms shot up and caught it before it could give her a bloody nose.

"You ever fired an M4 carbine?" Jackie asked.

Lai held back her glare.

"I have," Lai replied coolly. "Semiautomatic, optional three-round bursts, shoulder-fired with .223 caliber rounds?"

"Someone has done her homework."

"It's part of standard training for Beta groups. We did a three-month rotation with assault rifles."

"Good, because you're going to use this one in the raid."

Lai gave a quick laugh and turned the weapon over in her hands. "I am not using this."

"What's wrong with it?" Jackie questioned.

"Nothing is wrong with it," Lai replied. "I just prefer my P30."

"This is not a training exercise. This is a raid. We will be up against armed guards. You need an assault rifle."

"What I need is a weapon I can rely on," Lai countered. She tossed the rifle back to Jackie before continuing. "I know how to fire an M4, but I know how to use my P30."

Jackie sighed loudly and threw her arms in the air. "I give up. This is what I get for letting a kid on my team."

As Jackie walked away, someone laughed behind Lai, and she turned to see Angella riffling through her bag.

"Something funny?" Lai asked.

"*Es interesante*; you get on her nerves more than I do," Angella said with a smile. She zipped the pack shut and grabbed a black jacket from the table. She put it on and nodded at the pile of clothes. "You should put yours on. We leave in ten."

"Do you think I should carry an assault rifle?" Lai asked her. She did as Angella suggested and pulled on a jacket of her own.

"Jackie likes to hit hard. Understated really isn't her style."

"A good leader should know when less is more," Lai pointed out. She zipped up her jacket and tapped her fingers against the gun in her holster.

Angella shrugged and stretched her arms above her head. "As long as we all get through this raid alive, I really could not care less how we do it."

She moved to walk away but paused momentarily. "It's interesting that you noticed. About most of us being nonwhite, I mean. In a country as messed up as this one, when it comes to race, unless you want to become a protection officer, this is your best option. Not that it's a safe one."

Angella walked away before Lai had a chance to respond. She took a moment to look around the base. By the main doors were several of the people in the group for the raid. Lai found she could not recall their names. She attributed her forgetfulness to the load of information she had been given in the past two hours. She had stood around maps and computer screens with Jackie and Angella while the former spouted off formations and escape routes. She detailed every aspect of the plan.

Lai had been paired with Angella. Lai was to be Angella's backup while the latter got close enough to throw the stun grenade. If there was any retaliation, she was to protect her while Angella set up to throw a fragmentation grenade. Lai was ordered to shoot to kill if necessary. When she pointed out that she did not take orders from Jackie, the woman gave her a glare that could freeze a lake.

"I guess you're heading out now."

Lai turned. Jaime had walked up beside her while she was lost in thought. She gave her friend a quick smile. "*Na tama*, any minute now. I have been given the task of protecting your sister."

"Make sure you protect yourself too," he requested.

Lai took in the worry in his eyes and grabbed his hand. "This is the kind of assignment we train for. We've been through practice raids."

"This isn't practice."

"It works the same."

"You're also going against the Republic."

Lai sighed and let go of his hand. "*Halika na,* you know I can do this."

"I'm worried that if you do, you can't come back from it," he admitted. He shoved his hands into his pockets. "We could talk our way out of you shooting the sergeant. You were shocked when you saw your cousin. You weren't thinking clearly."

"It sounds like you're suggesting we go back," Lai said warily.

Jaime kicked the ground with his good leg. "I'm suggesting we don't do anything that gets rid of that option."

"Jaime, I am going on this raid. My best option is to make these people trust me." Lai waved a hand toward the group by the door. "It's also Mel's best chance."

Jaime offered no reply.

Lai eyed her best friend and made an effort to soften her expression. "Keep an eye on her for me?"

Jaime nodded after a moment. "She was sleeping when I left her. She'll be fine."

"Harris, time to go!" Jackie called from across the room. Lai noticed that the other seven raid members had all converged by the door.

"I'll see you later," Lai promised.

Jaime gave her a forced smile.

Lai fingered the zipper on her jacket as she turned and walked toward the group. Surrounded by adults who had clearly been on raids before, she felt like a child. During practice raids she had been with her training group. No one was more than six months older than her.

But I'm not practicing anymore, she thought. In thinking that to herself, it finally set in just how real her life was becoming. She swallowed back the lump in her throat and focused on keeping her expression from betraying her anxiety.

"You ready, kid?" Jackie asked when Lai had joined the group.

"Ready." Lai nodded. Jackie raised the M4 in her arms and started toward the door. The rest of the group fell into step behind her. Sydney took up the rear behind Lai and Angella.

Angella leaned toward Lai. "You look nervous," she whispered.

"I'm trying not to," Lai replied.

Angella gave a soft hum but said nothing. Lai was glad to have her company. It seemed that Angella had warmed to her since their unorthodox meeting, and Lai was willing to accept any friend she could get.

As Lai followed the group out into the dry night air, she considered what Jaime had said to her. Not even three full days had passed since she had rescued Mel. Her life had changed in an instant, and it had gone much further than she expected. She never planned on aiding a known rebel group. Maybe Jaime was right, and when faced with executing her cousin, she had stopped thinking clearly.

But she could not ignore the curious feeling of being in the right place. At the academy she had grown further away from their ideals the longer she trained. In teaching her to protect the Republic, they had accomplished the exact opposite of what they intended; they had turned her into a nonsympathizer. When the job became executioner, the belief of protecting people seemed superficial. Perhaps that was what drove her to be a part of the raid. She could not think of a better explanation.

AFTER LAI and his sister disappeared out into the night, Jaime spun around on his heels and headed toward the back of the base. His mind reeled at what was taking place, and at what his friend had gotten herself into.

When Jaime told Lai to take him hostage, he was only thinking about keeping her safe. He knew that if she didn't have someone to protect her, quite literally, from the officers and their fellow students, she would probably end up with a bullet in her head. He had said the only thing he could think of to keep his friend and her cousin safe. He was still having trouble comprehending how it had taken him so far past what he wanted.

Then again, Jaime rarely knew what he wanted. He had grown up in unconventional circumstances. Though he was born in Cuba, the Republic was the only home he knew. His sisters were old enough to miss their home country. Angella had nearly stayed behind. He had only the dimmest memories of bombs being dropped.

While he went through the standard schooling of any child in the Republic, his family made sure he was raised to question authority. Though he was much more sympathetic to the Republic than any of them, their lessons could never be discarded or forgotten entirely.

He did his best to push the thoughts from his head as he reached the second door from the left at the back of the base. He knocked twice. When he received no reply, he shouldered the door open and went inside.

He had left Mel sleeping. He found her sitting against the far wall with her legs splayed out in front of her. She had her hands clasped in her lap and was staring ahead at nothing. She did not look up or move when Jaime walked over and sat down on the floor next to her.

"You should be sleeping," he told her.

"Who could sleep right now?" She rolled her head around. "I keep dreaming about getting shot."

"That's not going to happen," he promised.

Mel gave him a humorless laugh. She looked tired, both physically and mentally. "I would be kidding myself if I thought I could ever be safe again."

"You don't think they'll protect you here? You don't think we'll protect you?"

"I think you don't trust me. I think my cousin got in over her head. I think these people have targets bigger than the one on my back could ever hope to be."

Mel rolled her head back around and stared at the wall. One half of her mouth quirked up into an unconvincing smile. "I also think she left without saying goodbye."

Jaime slid across the ground to sit next to her against the wall. His back pressed against the cool metal plating. "I would tell you she's going to come back, but I don't think you would appreciate empty promises."

"You're right, I wouldn't," Mel replied. There was a long pause before she spoke again. When she did her voice was little more than a whisper. "I don't know if I can keep doing this."

Jaime glanced over to her and frowned. He said nothing and waited for her to continue speaking.

"When I was in prison, I knew I was just waiting to be executed. It was only a matter of time before my name came up and they would take me. I mostly cried at first, or screamed. If anyone tried to talk to me, I would just start screaming. After two weeks I got tired of that and stayed quiet. No one tried to talk to me, except for guards telling me to go somewhere. I had a lot of time to think.

"I mostly thought about my friends. I thought about how the last time I saw my best friend was when we said goodbye after a day trip. We caught a bus and hiked to a lake north of the city. We spent the day there together. When she got off the bus, I was checking my phone. I never said goodbye to her properly. That was the last time I saw her.

"The last time I saw my mother was in a courtroom. She wouldn't even look at me. When they sentenced me to death, I saw her crying, but she still wouldn't look at me. It was like she couldn't bear it. I still don't know if she couldn't bear to see me about to die, or if she couldn't bear to see proof that her daughter was a murderer. I like to tell myself it's the first.

"My girlfriend didn't even come to the trial."

Mel stopped talking when her voice broke. She pulled her knees up to her chest and wrapped her arms around them.

"Why didn't she come to the trial?" Jaime asked in a hushed voice.

Mel ignored the question and continued talking. "There was something a woman said to me in prison. It was only three days before they took me. She said to smile. She said it helped her pretend things weren't so bad. Smile and pretend. I started doing that. I've been doing that. I don't think I can do that anymore."

Mel sniffed loudly and rested her forehead against her arms. "If she dies tonight, I am never going to forgive myself."

Jaime reflected on her words for a long moment. Mel was indeed quite the actor. But now he understood. She was scared. Making herself seem happy was her coping mechanism. He would never have guessed at her inner feelings had she not imparted the information willingly.

"What can I do?" he asked after several minutes of silence.

Mel peeked up at him from behind her arm. "What do you mean?"

"I mean what can I do to help you? What can I do to make you feel better? What's bothering you right now?"

Mel hid her eyes again as she considered his question. Jaime waited in silence. Just when he thought she wasn't going to answer, she sighed loudly and lifted her head.

"I can't protect myself," she finally said.

Jaime frowned. "You want to know how to protect yourself?"

"I want to be able to keep myself safe," she confirmed. "If we're in danger again, I want to be able to look out for myself so she can look out for herself."

Jaime considered her request. He idly flicked a finger against his prosthetic as he thought. It emitted a metallic clang each time his nail struck against it.

"Are you familiar with firearms?" he inquired. "Have you ever used one before?"

Mel clicked her tongue. "Those questions have different answers. I'm not familiar with firearms."

Jaime noted her words left unsaid. "Would you like me to teach you how to use one?"

Mel thought for a moment before she nodded. "I think I would."

THE FIRST thing Lai noticed was that the truck was going too slow.

Republic shipment trucks were required to maintain a speed of at least twenty-five miles per hour while traveling along a stable road. The regulation made it possible for a truck to achieve a higher speed in a short amount of time, were it to be attacked. The truck that ambled up the road that wound between the ridges they were perched on couldn't be doing more than fifteen.

"Something isn't right," Lai said quietly.

Angella glanced over to her from where she kneeled two feet away. "What are you talking about?" she asked in a whisper.

Lai lifted her head a few inches to get a better look. "That truck isn't going fast enough."

Angella placed a hand on her shoulder and forced her down. "What does the speed of the truck have to do with anything?" she hissed.

Lai kept one eye on the truck and one eye on Angella. "It isn't following regulation." Her brow furrowed as she attempted to come up with an explanation as to why the truck would be going that slow.

"Why wouldn't it be? They don't know we're here."

In an instant the answer popped into Lai's mind. Her fingers clenched over her gun and her eyes went wide.

"Yes, they do."

Lai turned around and leaned back against the concrete barrier they were hiding behind. That had to be it. Her mind drifted back to her lessons at the academy. She recalled one particular day where they had learned about antiterrorism tactics. She had been paired with Kieran, which must have been why she had pushed the day from her mind.

"You can't know that."

Angella's words brought Lai's mind back to the present.

"Antiterrorism protocol seventeen point five subsection A," Lai recited. "In the event of the suspected or confirmed raid of a shipment truck with goods deemed necessary and/or invaluable to the order and safety of the Republic, a squad of ten will replace the goods and continue on the designated supply route. The goods will be taken to a secure location until they can be safely transported without the risk of destruction or confiscation."

Lai flicked her eyes to Angella. "What is supposed to be on that truck?"

Angella sucked in a deep breath. From the expression on her face, Lai could tell that her theory was correct.

"If you don't throw the bomb, the others can't safely get to the truck," Lai reasoned.

Angella shook her head quickly. "Jackie will do it anyway. She wants what is on that truck, or at least what she thinks is on there."

"We have to stop her. She'll be leading them into an ambush."

"¡Maldita sea!" Angella cursed. She smacked a hand against the ground and thought for a moment. It did not take long. "We're going to stop them. Watch my back. If we're seen, they're going to kill us, no questions asked."

Lai nodded as Angella came to her feet and crouched low to the ground. She shoved the stun grenade into her belt and pulled out her gun. Lai followed as they moved quickly through the night. They ducked to keep their heads below the barriers that lined the ridge above the road. When they came to the edge, Angella dropped and slid down the incline. Lai followed suit after a few seconds. They rounded a bend in the road and came face-to-face with Jackie and Sydney.

"What the hell are you doing here?" Jackie hissed. She seemed as though she wanted to rip Angella's head off.

"It's an ambush," Angella told her breathlessly. "They know we're here."

"That's ridiculous, there's no way they could—"

Jackie was cut off when there was a sudden explosion on the other side of the barriers. All four rushed to cover their heads as rubble and shrapnel rained down around them. Lai fell flat to the ground and squinted to see through the narrow opening between two barriers.

Two of the men on their team were lying on the road in pieces. The truck had stopped a safe distance away. Boots trampled along the road; then twelve Republic officers jogged past where they hid. Two of them stopped to inspect the dead *Libertas Publica* members before falling into formation in front of the truck with the other officers.

Lai barely dared to breathe. One wrong move and the officers would be alerted to their presence. She spared a glance over to the others.

Angella was pressed up against the barrier with Sydney next to her. Angella looked as if she might throw up at any moment. Sydney wasn't doing any better. Both were covered in scratches and cuts, and Angella had a piece of shrapnel sticking out of the crook of her right arm. Lai attributed her own sound state to her proximity to the barriers and the ground.

Jackie was lying flat the same as Lai, only she was much less alert than the situation warranted. Lai dragged herself closer. When she was a foot away, Jackie rolled her head. Lai finally saw the blood that matted her hair on the left side of her head.

Lai pushed aside her concern for Jackie and took a moment to consider their options. It was unlikely they could make their way back up to the ridge without the officers being alerted to their presence. They were outnumbered, and there was no way of knowing where the other two members were, if they were even still alive. If there was no movement, the officers would dispatch half of their squad to search for them. They would be found in an instant.

There was another option Lai was loath to turn to. It was, however, the only option she could think of to get them out alive. None of the others were well enough to do what needed to be done. Lai took a long breath. She was going to have to do it herself.

She carefully pulled herself along the ground until she could reach Angella's belt. She pulled three of the canisters out and attached them to her own belt. Angella gave her a questioning look but appeared too dazed to do anything. Lai ignored her and came to her feet. She kept her head ducked as low as possible as she scurried along behind the barriers. She figured she had about twenty seconds before the officers dispatched and they were all killed.

Lai followed the road around another bend. She fell to her knees. It would have to do. She pulled the three canisters from her belt. Two of them were fragmentation grenades, and one was a smoke bomb Lai recognized from when Angella had used one that morning. A new idea formed in her head. When she heard a shout from an officer, she knew it was time.

Lai held the smoke bomb in one hand and her P30 in the other. She said a silent prayer and tossed the canister into the air. Without a second of hesitation, Lai raised her gun and took aim at the canister. She fired a single bullet. Time seemed to slow as it sailed through the air toward the bomb. When it made contact with the canister, she allowed herself a smile as the bomb exploded in a cloud of white smoke. She picked up a grenade and pulled the pin out with her teeth. Without looking she threw it over the barrier toward where she knew the officers would be standing with their attention to the smoke in the air. The moment the grenade left her hand, Lai flattened herself to the ground and pressed herself as hard as she could against the barrier.

The explosion came seconds later. Lai hoped that her aim had been good enough. At the academy she had always prided herself on her accuracy, though that pride was usually the result of a gun. She idly wondered what the other Beta Five members would think of her now.

Screams came from the officers as they were shredded by the shrapnel. Lai closed her eyes and unsuccessfully tried to block out the sounds. She thought instead of Mel. She told herself she was doing this to protect her cousin. She was doing it all for Mel.

When the only sound Lai could hear was the ringing in her ears from having two bombs go off next to her, she peeked her head over the barrier. What she saw was a bloodbath. The road was slick with the blood of twelve officers. The officers themselves were in various states. A few who had clearly been at the center of the blast had shrapnel embedded in every inch of their bodies. The others were lying unmoving on the ground. Lai thought they were all dead until one man drew his leg in toward himself. When Lai was sure they were all accounted for, she rose to her feet and kept her weapon trained on the officer.

Movement came from her right and she snapped her weapon around. Sydney and Angella stood with Jackie between them. They held the woman up and helped her over the barriers. Lai walked to meet them. Her muscles ached, and her head was pounding with a headache that was sure to keep her awake all night.

"Did you do that?" Jackie moaned. When Lai nodded, she continued. "That was the craziest thing I have ever seen."

The four of them stopped next to the one officer who was still breathing. He had his eyes clenched shut, and he was gasping for air. Lai saw the shrapnel that protruded from his stomach. When they approached, he opened his eyes and his expression became fearful.

"Please," he groaned. "Help me."

Jackie removed her arm from around Angella's neck and reached down to her waist. She pulled her gun from its holster and aimed it at the man's head. No one could get a word in before she fired. Lai figured she had no right to complain after what she had just done.

"Let's find the others and get back," Jackie said. She coughed for a long moment as she holstered her gun. When her coughing subsided, she glanced over to Lai and a smile ghosted over her lips.

"Kid, you are a damn good shot," she said breathlessly.

Lai found she could not reply.

CHAPTER FIFTEEN

IT WAS nearing midnight when the group returned to the base. Lai wanted nothing more than to collapse into a bed and sleep for a day, though she doubted the pounding behind her eyes would allow it.

After they had determined that the injuries could be dealt with when they were in a safer location, she, Jackie, Angella, and Sydney had located the other two living raid members. They had fortunately been far enough away to be unaffected by the bombs and were able to help Jackie along while Lai guarded the rear. The slow journey back gave her time to think, despite the fact that thinking about what had just taken place was the last thing she wanted to be doing. The image of the aftermath of her grenade was plastered at the forefront of her mind.

Though she had killed numerous times before, the result was never so bloody and chaotic. Even the simulations could not compare to the real thing. She kept seeing the officers' lifeless bodies littering the road, most with their eyes open as they stared at nothing, the shrapnel protruding from their bodies. The blood had seeped out of them to create a single pool that surrounded all twelve of them. Lai knew that if she was able to fall asleep, it was all she would dream about.

When she at last entered the base, she was immediately tackled by her frantic cousin.

"I was so worried about you!" Mel exclaimed.

Lai pushed the tangle of blonde hair out of her face and returned the hug. She allowed herself a short moment of contentment. "I wasn't going to leave you," Lai replied as she pulled out of the hug.

Mel smiled for a moment before she took in the state of the group. "What happened?" she asked in concern.

"Your cousin saved our lives," Jackie spoke up. They turned to see her being set down in a chair near the wall. She held a hand where the blood had dried in her hair and winced.

"They knew we were there," Angella added. She sat down in a chair next to Jackie and held her right arm out, unmoving. "Lai threw a grenade and took them all out. We would have been dead without her. Right, Jackie?"

Jackie attempted to nod, but when she did, she immediately doubled over and moaned. Footsteps echoed along the floor from behind them. Romana pushed past Mel and knelt in front of Jackie. She said nothing and purposefully gestured with her hands. Jackie responded with gestures of her own.

"Romana is deaf," Angella replied when she saw Lai's puzzled expression. "She's also the best medic at this base."

"Is she going to be all right?" Lai asked.

Angella studied Romana's signing for a moment. "From what I can tell, she thinks Jackie has a concussion. There shouldn't be anything life-threatening."

Lai breathed a sigh of relief and eyed the shrapnel sticking out of Angella's arm. "Are you planning on making that a new accessory?"

Angella's lips twitched into a smile. "I'll get it taken out when Romana is done with Jackie. You should wait to get checked out too."

"I think I got the least of it." Lai shuffled her feet. She was ready to be alone. "Do you think I can get checked out in the morning?"

Angella tapped Romana on the shoulder and did her best to translate for Lai. Though her injury impeded her signing, Romana understood and took a quick look at Lai. After a few seconds, she nodded and signed to Angella before going back to Jackie.

"She says you can go, but only if you come see her first thing in the morning," Angella translated. She nodded toward the tables where they had done their planning earlier. "You can leave your gear over there. Mel will show you where your room is."

Lai nodded and spun on her heels to head for the tables. She walked quickly, leaving Mel to hurry along behind her. Lai didn't speak as she deposited her remaining grenade and took off her jacket. She slipped off her boots and replaced them with a pair of sneakers that had been left under the table. She kept her gun at her side.

"Carlton said they usually have four people per room, but the base is less than half full," Mel told her. "He said we can have a room to ourselves."

Lai held back a sigh. She was looking forward to being alone that night, but she supposed bunking with Mel was better than with strangers.

"Jaime is in the room next to ours," she continued. When Lai had finished removing her gear, Mel headed toward the back of the base. With Lai at her heels, she kept talking. "He's sharing a room with his sister. Carlton offered to let him stay with him and Sydney, but that would mean Angella would be stuck with Jackie and Romana. She and Jackie don't get along very well, if you hadn't already guessed."

Lai listened to Mel blather on without interrupting. She was in no mood for chatting. Either Mel was oblivious to that or she was filling the silence with idle chitchat to avoid broaching the subject of what Lai had done on the raid.

When they reached their room, Mel held the door open for Lai. Lai walked in without a word and let herself fall onto the nearest bed. It was not the most comfortable bed she had ever lain in, but that night it felt like heaven. Though she was tired, she kept her eyes open and stared at the ceiling. Mel shut the door behind them and moved to her own bunk. She sat down and leaned her elbows on her knees. She clasped her hands together and looked down at them as she spoke.

"Jaime is teaching me how to use a gun," she said.

That made Lai curious enough to finally speak. "Why is he doing that?"

Mel shrugged. "I asked him to. Well, I didn't ask him exactly. I told him I wanted to be able to protect myself, and he offered."

"That was nice of him."

Mel nodded and said nothing for a long moment. Lai let the silence build; she had no intention of breaking it.

"Do you want to talk about it?" Mel asked her.

"I don't think so," Lai replied with a shake of her head.

"If you change your mind…." She left the offer unsaid. Lai kicked off her sneakers and rolled over to face the wall. The bed creaked as Mel lay down. Lai forced herself to close her eyes and scanned her brain for an image to plant in her mind. Anything would be better than what she was seeing. She eventually settled on the face of her little sister, Imee. She concentrated hard on holding it there until she could drift off to sleep.

NEITHER OF the girls knew what time it was. Their room had no windows; only the dim lamp in the corner allowed them any light to see by. The noise of the base had long since died down, with only the occasional footsteps of a guard walking by their door.

Lai had been drifting in and out of sleep for what felt like a week. Just when it seemed as if she were going to get some real rest, her dreams were invaded by the sight of the dead officers lying in a pool of their own blood. She had now been lying awake for about half an hour while refusing to so much as blink for too long. From the incessant creaking of Mel's bed, she guessed her cousin was awake as well.

"It felt different this time," Lai said in a whisper. The creaking ceased.

"What felt different?" Mel asked groggily.

Lai glanced over and met her eyes in the poorly lit room. "I've killed people before. I killed over twice as many people a month at the academy. What I've never done is kill eleven people at once."

Lai rolled over onto her side to face her. Mel propped herself up on her elbow as she listened.

"This time it felt so different," Lai continued. "I've always been able to rationalize the target practice. I told myself those people were criminals. The law had condemned them justly. I wasn't the one making the decision to end their lives. I was simply carrying out the task. Maybe it didn't feel as wrong as it should have.

"I chose to do this. No one told me to. No one gave me any indication that I should. I made my own call. I chose to end the lives of twelve people. If I hadn't chosen that, they might still be alive."

"But they would have killed you," Mel whispered.

Lai squeezed her eyes shut for a moment. "I know that." She opened her eyes and kept her expression neutral. "I do know that. They would have killed all of us without a second thought. But I still chose to do it. I've never made that decision before. It feels so different."

Mel cast her gaze down and said nothing. Lai flipped over onto her back again and stared at a crack in the low ceiling.

"You probably know the feeling. You killed someone, right? It's a strange feeling. It reminds me of the first time I killed someone. That time it was an instruction, but it was still the first time I ever ended a life. I remember what she looked like. She was about five nine. She had long black hair and bangs cut straight across her forehead. She was East Asian. I couldn't see the color of her eyes from where I was standing.

"I cried for hours that night. I snuck out of my dorm and hid in a closet so no one would see me crying. Jaime found me. He joined the academy at the same time as I had, but he was in a different Delta group. He had killed for the first time two weeks before. He sat with me all night and let me cry. When I was finished, we found Oscar and the three of us went to the mess hall. They made me laugh by dancing together on the tables.

"That was only after I killed one person. They only made first-year students kill one person on their first day of target practice. I never really got used to killing people, but I guess I absolved myself of the responsibility by telling myself that if I didn't kill them, they were still going to die. I wasn't choosing to end their lives. Tonight that is exactly what I did."

"I do know the feeling," Mel replied softly. "I only killed one person, but I know what you mean. For just one moment, you had the power over life and death. You decided to end a life, and then you did. It makes you feel powerful before you realize what you've done."

Lai stared openly. The question burned in her mind, but she held it back. She had decided to wait until Mel was ready to tell her.

"I never felt powerful," Lai said.

Mel raised her eyes to meet Lai's. "Maybe I did because of who it was."

"You don't have to tell me if you're not ready," Lai told her instantly.

Mel's smile was unconvincing. "He was old-fashioned. He didn't agree with the Republic's view on gay rights. Probably learned it from his parents. Imagine his joy when his daughter brought me home."

"You killed your girlfriend's father," Lai said before she could stop herself.

Mel's smile disappeared, and she looked at the ceiling. "He didn't even pretend to tolerate us. I knew he had a temper, but I never thought he would take it out on her. He was supposed to be at work when he caught us together at her house. He started yelling at us, and I started yelling at him. Violet stayed very quiet. That's her name, Violet.

"He pushed me out of the way and started to hit her. I tried to get him away from her, but he was stronger than me. He just wouldn't stop. She was crying, and I couldn't make him stop."

Mel's voice broke, and she took a moment to take several deep breaths. "Violet told me he kept a gun in the house. I had seen it before, so I knew where it was. I went and got it and I pointed it at him. I told him if he didn't get off her right that second, I would shoot him. I don't think he believed me because he didn't stop. I don't even know if I meant to shoot him."

She took in several more gulps of air. "They told me it wasn't self-defense. For it to be self-defense, he would have to have been hitting me. Violet refused to testify. It didn't matter. My fingerprints were all over the gun, and I never told them I didn't do it. I thought she would still love me. She never even went to the trial.

"In those few seconds after I shot him, even if I didn't really mean to, I felt powerful. I had stopped him from hurting her, from hurting the girl I loved. Then she started screaming. She wasn't saying anything; she was just screaming. I don't think I got to tell her I love her before the officers came."

Lai closed her eyes. So that was it. She felt an odd sense of relief hearing that Mel had killed someone to protect another. It was better than killing out of anger or revenge.

It also helped to hear that Mel understood a little of what she was feeling at the moment. Though their situations were entirely different, in that moment, Lai felt she knew Mel better than ever before.

"So yes, I know the feeling," Mel said after a long silence. "It is very strange."

Lai opened her eyes and glanced over. "I'm glad you told me."

"You don't hate me now?"

"I could never hate you. Especially after what I did."

"It's not much different from what I did. We both did it to protect people we care about."

Lai blew out a long breath and considered the words. She realized that Mel was right. They weren't as different as she thought. She was suddenly glad that she was not alone. Had Mel not given her something else to think about, she likely would have brooded over her own experience the whole night.

"Is it wrong to say I'm glad you can sympathize?" Lai asked. She was heartened when Mel let out a small laugh.

"Only if it's wrong for me to say the same."

Chapter Sixteen

LAI HAD a moment of déjà vu when she was awoken by clothing being thrown at her face.

She started awake, and in her hazy state, she accidentally whacked her arm against the wall of the room.

"Letse!" she exclaimed. She was promptly shushed by someone she could not yet identify. She rubbed her eyes hard before opening them and waited for the lines to stop dancing in her vision. It took her a moment to remember where she was. When she did, she was inevitably reminded of the previous night.

Angella stood over her bunk with her hands on her hips. She was dressed in a tight-fitting black tank top, light beige short-sleeved jacket, and dark green cargo pants. She had a red-and-white bandana around her head that held her hair back from her face. Lai also noted the bandage around her right arm where the shrapnel had been.

Lai sat up and frowned. "What time is it?"

"Almost seven."

"In the morning?" Lai groaned. Across the room, Mel slept soundly in her own bed, apparently having not been woken by Lai's cursing.

"Así es la vida." Angella laughed. "I've got a job for you."

Lai glanced down at her lap to see similar clothing to what Angella wore, down to the red-and-white bandana.

"Does this job involve nearly being blown up again?" Lai asked.

Angella shook her head. "No explosions, no gun."

"Then what are we doing?"

"I'll explain on the way. Get dressed."

Lai considered Angella for a long moment before she tossed her covers off and swung her legs over the side of the bed. Though she was incredibly tired, both mentally and physically, she had to admit she was more curious. Besides, it was hardly the earliest she had been dragged out of bed. Advanced Delta groups were often subjected to surprise drills at all hours of the night. In Lai's second year at the academy, only a couple months before she went into Beta training, she and her group had been awoken at three o'clock in the morning by a thundering alarm for a surprise test raid. She and nineteen other sixteen-year-olds had stumbled through the course until their sergeant had set off the sprinkler system to wake them up. Since then Lai had gotten used to being woken up and made to get ready at a moment's notice, though she hardly enjoyed it.

Moving carefully so as to not wake Mel, Lai stood up and stretched her arms above her head with a yawn. She then stripped off her shirt and replaced it with the black tank top she had been supplied. After three years of living in a dorm room, she was no longer shy about changing in front of others.

Angella played with the corner of her bandage as Lai changed. She kept her eyes lowered.

"Wasn't Romana supposed to check me over?" Lai asked. She pulled her pants off and appraised the new pair of cargo pants.

Angella shrugged. "You seem fine. Do you feel fine?"

"I'm tired, but I don't feel like I was injured," she replied as she buttoned the cargo pants at her waist. "That doesn't mean I'm fine."

Angella sighed. "You can wait around for her if you want, but I've got to go."

As Lai pulled on the jacket, she did a quick check of herself to see how she was feeling. She still had a slight headache, but the sleep had helped, however short and restless it had been. Other than feeling a little sore, which if she was being honest with herself was her constant state from training, she could detect nothing awry within herself.

"Fine, I'll go with you," she decided.

Angella gave a half smile and headed to the door. Lai quickly pulled on her sneakers and grabbed the bandana before following her through into the main room of the warehouse.

Lai squinted against the sunlight that poured in through the windows. Angella led them toward the storage containers as she looked around the base again. It was much the same as it had been the previous night, except there were fewer people roaming about. She saw one armed guard by the door, as well as Sydney sitting at one of the tables next to the containers. He had his feet propped up on the table as he ate a bagel. He smiled with his mouth full when they approached.

"Jackie won't be happy you left without her," he told them.

"Jackie has a concussion," Angella said. "She'll thank me when she's better."

"I highly doubt that," he said with a chuckle. Still, he only smiled as they passed. He nodded once to Lai, and she returned it promptly.

Angella stopped next to an open storage container. "Wait out here," she ordered. Lai leaned back against the container as Angella went inside. She crossed her arms and tapped her fingers idly against her arm as she waited. Inside, she heard what sounded like boxes being shifted around.

"Catch," Sydney said.

She turned just in time to see him toss a plastic bag toward her, and caught it a moment before it whacked her in the face. Inside were two cheese bagels and two apples.

"Thanks," she said.

"For the road," he replied with a nod before going back to eating his own bagel.

Angella emerged from the container a moment later carrying a large duffel bag in her left hand. "Let's get out of here before everyone wakes up and tries to come with us. O convencerme de lo contrario...."

She headed for the door at a brisk pace, which left Lai to hurry to follow. She held up the bag Sydney had given her.

"Hungry?" Lai asked.

Angella glanced over and shook her head. "Maybe later."

Lai shrugged and pulled a bagel from the bag. She then tied the bag handles through a belt loop to let it hang from her waist.

Angella hefted the duffel bag onto her shoulder. "You're gonna want to put the bandana on."

Lai held the bagel in her mouth and unwrapped the bandana where she had been holding it around her wrist. She went to tie her hair back.

"Not like that." Angella reached up to remove her own bandana and tie it around her face instead so it covered the lower half. Lai frowned in confusion.

"Trust me, where we're going you'll want your face covered," Angella told her.

Though Lai was even less sure of what they were doing, she did as she was told and secured the fabric around the back of her head. She removed the bagel from her mouth and tore off smaller pieces to sneak in behind the bandana.

The woman guarding the door nodded to Angella and pulled it open for them. Lai followed Angella through and squinted hard against the harsh glare of the direct sunlight that reflected off the numerous other warehouses. In the light it seemed no different from the dusty desert she had grown used to, except she could better see the particles floating around in the air in the rays of the sun. She was suddenly grateful for the bandana to cover her nose and mouth.

Angella turned to the right and started down the dirt road that cut a straight line through the buildings. Lai glanced up to the sky and judged that they were heading north. She fell into step beside Angella and continued to eat her bagel.

"I never properly thanked you for saving my life last night," Angella said. "*Gracias.* You really know what you're doing."

"It's the kind of situation I trained for," Lai replied. "But you're welcome. I'm glad you're still alive."

From the way Angella's eyes crinkled at the corners, Lai assumed she was smiling behind the bandana.

"Are you going to tell me where we're going now?" Lai asked. She finished her bagel and wiped her hands on her pants.

Angella stared ahead of them as she spoke. "When President Emilia created the Republic forty-two years ago, she claimed to care for all people. She revolutionized gay rights and disability rights like never before. She solidified a foundation that allowed women equal opportunity to men. She stopped the political discord and created one law for every citizen of the country.

"She also made it hell for immigrants. One thing she could never get the people to agree on was closing the borders, so instead she made it nearly impossible for a noncitizen to get a job or decent health care. My family got lucky getting citizenship. The Republic sympathized with my father's situation of being an ousted official, even if he lied his way through the paperwork. Then you have the political posturing. The Republic likes the rest of the world to think they're welcoming to refugees during times of crisis. Helps their image, whatever the hell that's supposed to be.

"Even once you become a citizen, this entire system is weighted against people of color and lower-class citizens. I'm both. It's not only hard for me because I'm an immigrant. This government has been racist since before it was formed. Even in the United States, innocent black kids were being shot in the streets because a white officer thought they looked intimidating. They don't teach you this in school because they don't want you to know that these things happened and still happen every day.

"I learned everything I could when I came here. Once I joined the *Libertas Publica,* I learned even more. I already knew what it was to have my civil liberties violated, and I didn't need that here. I guess you could say I'm one of the lucky ones. Not everyone is. That is what we're doing today."

"We're helping the ones who weren't so lucky," Lai cut in.

Angella turned to her and nodded. "It's something we've always done. We go into communities with people in need, people who were screwed by the system, and we help them. Sometimes when we raid warehouses and bases, we get more supplies than we need. Rather than get rid of some of the food we get, or let it go to waste, we give it away.

"Maricopa has a large lower-class Hispanic population. A lot of them are immigrants who thought the Republic would offer them a better life than their home country. Since they're here, we try to make them more comfortable."

"Is this a way to recruit them?" Lai inquired.

"We do explain the benefits of joining if they ask," Angella replied, "but that isn't our main focus. We were founded, first and foremost, to make this a better country for everyone, something the former president was never able to do. She made a police state. We want a country where no person has to live on the streets and go hungry. Jackie would usually lead these types of trips, but she's in no shape to leave the base."

"I'm sure you don't mind her staying behind."

Angella raised an eyebrow to Lai. "*Sí?*"

"You don't like her very much," Lai continued. "Anyone could see it."

She hefted the duffel bag higher on her shoulder. "Es cierto," she said with a nod. "I don't mind going without her."

"What happened between you two?"

There was a long pause before Angella spoke. "I don't talk about it. Está en el pasado."

Lai said nothing. She decided it would be best to drop the subject. It was clearly something Angella did not enjoy discussing.

"Why did you invite me?" she asked instead.

At this Angella did turn to her again. "I thought you could use the distraction after last night. Do something useful instead of sitting around that warehouse for a week."

Lai smiled and raised her hands to adjust the bandana. "Does this mean you trust me now?"

"You did something to earn my trust. That's not an easy task, and I don't take it lightly." Angella held out a hand to Lai. "I'll take an apple now."

Lai reached into the plastic bag at her waist and pulled out one of the pale red apples. She handed it off to Angella, who promptly took a huge, juicy bite.

"Trust isn't something you should just give away," she continued after swallowing her bite. "A person needs to show they deserve it before I give it."

Lai nodded and reached her hands up again to shade her eyes.

Angella noticed and laughed once. "I don't think you're used to this climate."

Lai shook her head. "I grew up in the Gasan municipality in the province of Marinduque. It's on the coast of an island in the Philippines. It may have gotten hot, but it was never this dry. After we moved to the Republic, I lived in Baltimore for six years. This dry air is killing me."

"I've gotten used to it," Angella told her. "Then again, I've been here for fourteen years."

"Three years isn't enough time for me to get used to the southwest of the Republic."

Angella took another bite of her apple and shrugged. "You don't need to stay here now. You have some options."

"I don't plan on staying here if I don't have to," Lai agreed. "Besides, it's hardly safe to stick around for much longer."

Angella held the apple in her mouth and reached into her left pocket. She pulled out a small water canister and offered it to Lai. Lai took it gratefully and lifted the bandana to let the liquid pour into her mouth.

"Have you ever wanted to go back to the Philippines?" Angella asked.

Lai finished her drink and lowered the canister. She took a moment to wipe her mouth. "Sometimes," she admitted. She handed the water back to Angella and continued as the woman took a drink. "But then I think about how it's been nine years since we left. With my father gone, I don't know if I'd recognize it as home. I didn't keep in touch with my friends, and we didn't have much family. My grandmother, my father's mother, she died two years after we came here. I would be going back as a stranger.

"Still, it's better than staying in this country when the government most likely wants me dead."

Angella tucked the water back into her pocket and brushed a stray hair out of her eyes. "If I didn't know any better. I'd think you could read my mind."

LAI AND Angella arrived at their destination a half hour later, with only a short stop to apply sunscreen when their skin started to burn. The actual place they were going turned out to be a makeshift homeless shelter on a corner of two desolate streets. It looked much the same as the desert they had been walking through, except there were dozens of old brick buildings lining either side of the street headed north, and a fence cutting off a dry, patchy field on the far side of the east street. The building on the corner was run-down, with bricks falling out of the wall and wooden beams strategically placed to support areas where the original wall couldn't support itself. The entrance was an open doorway with a tarp hanging down to cover about a third of the space.

At least fifty people sat, stood, or lay around in the shaded room. Lai glanced up when they walked inside. The roof was in no better condition than the walls. The original brick had been entirely replaced by wooden sheets that were unevenly spaced to let through random beams of the beating sun. Tarps covered some of these openings, though most were left open.

At the back of the room were two doors on the right side that were held closed with heavy padlocks. Broken windows on the doors were covered by nailed-in boards. On the left side was a window where a man stood sorting through papers on the counter.

While most of the people in the shelter seemed fairly relaxed, or else were actually sleeping, one woman flitted around the room wildly, her slender frame darting from person to person, occasionally going to the man at the window to grab something from him and hand it off to someone else in the room.

Angella stopped just inside the entrance to the building and carefully dropped the duffel bag from her shoulder onto the ground. Lai stopped next to her and continued to look around.

"*Hola,* Genevieve!" Angella called.

The woman who had been rushing around waved to Angella and hurried over to meet them. Angella returned the wave.

"I didn't know if you'd be coming this week," Genevieve said as she skipped up to them. She smiled at Angella and then turned a curious eye to Lai. "And who might this be?"

"We're not sanctioned today," Angella replied. "I'd prefer to keep her name out of it."

Genevieve narrowed her eyes and smiled again. "Of course. Did you have any trouble getting here?"

"None. We took the longer route around the east to avoid major roads. The bandanas also helped."

"I'm glad to hear." Genevieve held out a hand to Lai. "I'm Genevieve. Pleased to meet you."

Lai grasped her hand and gave it a firm shake. "Nice to meet you."

"There's plenty to do around here." Genevieve gestured with wide sweeps of her arms as she spoke. "We're above capacity today, and undersupplied. Water is in very short supply, and the food we have is about to go bad. The tarps are in need of repair or replacement, and we need another section of wall repaired.

"There were also a few officers in here the other day harassing some of our guests. They hauled off Luis for God knows what."

Angella frowned and knelt down to the duffel bag. "I'm sorry to hear that. We can't help with fixing the wall, but I brought some water, water purifiers, and some canned food."

She emptied the bag as she spoke. "I got a first aid kit, a large tarp and a smaller one, a sewing set in case clothing needs repairs, and about seventeen clean needles."

"Needles?" Lai repeated with a frown.

Angella glanced up at her and pulled out one of said needles.

"Para los adictos," she said.

"You supply addicts with needles?" Lai asked incredulously.

Angella shrugged. "If we don't, they'll only use dirty ones. Until they decide to get help, we try to keep them safe."

Lai let out a little hum as she considered the idea.

When Angella had finished emptying the bag, she and Genevieve began sorting the contents.

"Hey, *niña*, can you take some water to anyone who looks like they need it?" Angella asked.

Lai nodded and grabbed as many water canisters as she could fit in the now empty bag at her waist. As Angella and Genevieve sorted the food, Lai started around the side of the room. She knelt down next to a man who was leaning back against the wall with his head on his knees.

"Would you like some water, sir?" she asked.

He raised his head when she spoke and gave her a wide, toothless grin.

"Thank you, young lady," he said.

She pulled out a canister and handed it to the man. He took it with a nod and opened it to pour the liquid into his mouth. Lai smiled and moved to the next person along the wall.

For the next hour, Lai and Angella helped Genevieve distribute the supplies Angella had brought from the base. Once she finished handing out water, Genevieve called her into one of the locked rooms, where they stored their supplies for safekeeping.

"We've had some trouble with theft in the past," she explained. "It's best to keep everything locked up."

"Trouble with any of them stealing?" Lai asked with a gesture of her head back to the main room.

Genevieve shook her head. "No, mostly people in the area who don't like having a shelter in their neighborhood. It's a shame. These are wonderful people who weren't dealt the best hand in life, and privileged folk still want to come in and take what little we can offer them."

After shelving half of the food, Lai and Angella handed the rest out to guests, along with whatever was left of their old supply. Genevieve explained that they often tried to stick with canned food, as it did not require any bowls or plates, which would only create more work and less time to help with other tasks.

Once they finished with whatever Genevieve could think to throw at them, she dragged Angella away to one of the back rooms to repair some ripped clothing with the sewing kit she brought. Lai was given permission to do as she pleased until they were done, though Angella insisted she remain in the building to be safe.

After wandering around for a few minutes, Lai found herself sitting against a wall next to an aging Filipina woman named Riza that Lai gave water to earlier. She pulled Lai over to join her and offered to share the blanket she was sitting on.

"Were you born in the Republic?" Riza asked in Tagalog.

Lai shook her head. "I'm Gaseños," she replied in the same tongue.

Riza smiled wide at that. "My mother was Gaseños. I was born in the United States, but before the Republic was formed, I went to her hometown for the Moriones Festival. Do you remember it?"

Lai smiled at the memory. "Vaguely. I left when I was nine." She latched on to something Riza said. "You were born before the forming of the Republic?"

Riza nodded. "Indeed I was. I was born in 2097, twenty years before the Republic was formed."

"Most people don't talk about the United States," Lai said with a sigh. "School doesn't teach much further back than 2110 unless you really ask about it. Even then, I think they don't tell us everything."

Lai played with a zipper on her pants. "Maaari mong sabihin sa akin ang tungkol dito?"

"Tell you about the United States," Riza echoed in English. "My my, very few people ask me. No one wants to hear the rambling of an old homeless woman."

Riza pursed her lips and seemed to think it over for a moment. "Let me see. When I was old enough to know what was going on around me, the country was already in political ruin. I didn't understand it at the time. My father used to come home every day and complain about the government being in a standstill. He explained it to me when I was a teenager.

"There were three leading political parties when I was born. The Democrats, the Republicans, and the Libertarians. There were other smaller parties, but those three made up the bulk of the representatives in the country. The problem was, they all disagreed about everything there was to disagree on. There was something called the Congress, which was divided into the Senate and the House of Representatives. The majority of politicians in the Senate and the House didn't always match up with the party of the President.

"You can imagine how difficult it was to get anything done."

Lai had stopped playing with her zipper and gave Riza her full attention.

"If the president was a Democrat," Riza continued, "and the House a majority of Republicans, the House would do everything in its power to go against whatever the president wanted. It may seem childish and spiteful, but it's the truth. Add to this the fact that the individual states all but ran themselves. In the years before the turn of the century, states were given more and more power to decide their own laws and legislations. The president couldn't pass a federal bill without going through every state leader. If one disagreed, the bill couldn't be passed without going through miles of red tape and vetoes."

Lai frowned and turned her gaze to the ground. "That sounds like a difficult way to run a country."

Riza nodded. "It was. President Emilia had quite an idea to abolish the states. Her problem was execution.

"In the years leading up to the forming of the Republic, she amassed quite a following on the idea that if the country were to survive, it was crucial to stop the conflict between states and think of the good of the nation. She spread these ideas throughout the country, allowing it to seep into the minds of everyone she could ensnare. This caused the country to break out in a revolution against the governing system."

"I never heard anything about violence," Lai cut in.

"Violence was limited and uncoordinated," Riza explained. "The real revolution came in the form of voting. Entire counties refused to vote for a representative. If they did, it was for one who only argued for the ideals Emilia Theodore was putting forward. The Senate fell to ruins when nothing could get through its doors. The House was barely filled, and those who did fill it fought tooth and nail against individual state welfare.

"In the year 2117, the president at the time resigned. Before a real election could take place, Emilia stepped forward and announced that she intended to bring harmony to the country through the abolishment of the states. The people who already followed her were thrilled. Those who didn't, found mostly in the south of the country... well, I'm sure you know what happened there."

Lai nodded as she picked at a thread on her jacket. "The Confederate States."

"Indeed. Her ideas of full unification were the last straw for the states that so dearly wanted their freedom. What they did not accomplish three hundred years ago in the civil war, they did forty-two years ago. I suppose President Emilia knew she would fight a losing battle in trying to make them stay, so she allowed them to leave without a fuss. After the eleven southern states seceded, she successfully took power with very little opposition from the rest of the country. It was the most sudden and elegant power shift I had ever lived to see.

"It was only after she became President of the Republic that the problems came. With her tightly knit group of politicians, she changed laws everywhere. The police and military were the first to be compacted into a singular entity, the Protection Force."

"Which is why even domestic officers have some military training," Lai mused. When Riza seemed confused, Lai waved a hand at her. "Never mind. Continue."

"The prison system was the next to be altered. Prisons were overcrowded from the United States. Her solution was to simply execute most of them. To get more prisoners for execution, she upped the penalty on crimes. Anyone already in the system was out of luck."

Lai didn't bother to hold back the alarm on her face. She never knew that the laws had been changed so drastically. It was likely something the government didn't want her to know.

"Immigration wasn't far behind," Riza continued. Her fists clenched as she spoke. "My mother was deported after living here for half of her life. I stayed with my father because this was the only life I had known. I haven't seen my mother in forty-two years."

"Ikinalulungkot ko," Lai said in a soft voice. All of a sudden, she was thinking about her own family, and how easy it had seemed for her stepfather to get them into the country as legal citizens. The perks of being a rich white man, she supposed.

Lai licked her dry lips before she pulled out her own water and took a long drink. She offered it to Riza, who took it gratefully and drank a few sips.

Lai wiped the drops from her mouth. "Not that I agree with President Emilia's tactics, but if the country was in such chaos, wasn't unification a good strategy? I mean, it should have been gone about differently, but it seemed to me that she had the right idea at heart."

Riza shrugged a shoulder. "There are many who agree with you, but few had more concrete ideas than that woman. I only wish her son wasn't her identical in so many ways."

Lai thought about their current leader, President Jonas Theodore, and had to agree. Though Emilia was before her time, Lai heard President Jonas was the spitting image of his mother, in looks and in mind.

"To rub salt in the wound, she went and named the country the American Republic. It was as if she wanted to make a mockery of democracy itself in every way possible."

Before Lai could think of another question to ask, she was interrupted when Angella strolled over to them.

"Time to get going, *niña*," she announced. She had the duffel bag on her shoulder again, though it appeared to be mostly empty.

"Tama," Lai said with a nod. "I'll just be a second."

Angella returned the nod and headed for the front of the building.

Lai turned her attention back to Riza. "Thank you for telling me this." She took the old woman's hands in hers. "Umaasa ako na mahanap ka ng mas magandang kapalaran sa iyong hinaharap."

Riza smiled and squeezed Lai's hand. "And I hope you find what you're looking for with them," she said with a slight nod in Angella's direction.

Lai dearly hoped she would.

"MAKE A new friend today?" Angella asked. Lai fell into step beside her as she walked back in the direction they came.

Lai twirled her water canister around by its string. "Riza's mother was *Gaseños*."

"Did you talk about home?"

"We actually talked about the formation of the Republic. Riza was twenty when it happened."

Angella raised an eyebrow to her. "A continued topic of interest to you?"

Lai snatched the canister out of the air with her other hand and put it back into her bag. "It makes me think about things."

"What kind of things?"

Lai glanced quickly to Angella before her gaze returned to the road. "Everything. The LP wants the states back."

"In a general sense, yes."

"But the states were chaotic. Riza lived through the changes."

Angella clicked her tongue and stretched her arms above her head. "Change comes one step at a time. Better return us to the framework of the old country rather than attempt to create a new one. People like what they're familiar with. They'll accept the states."

"But how does the *Libertas Publica* plan on making things better? What's to stop the country from going back into divided chaos?"

"It's very complicated," Angella told her. "There were good times and bad in the past. No one here wants the country we had in, say, 2016. But the New Deal? Higher taxation of the upper class? There's some good to be found in history too. I don't want to be in charge of deciding how the new system should work in full. I have my ideas, so I'll want my say, but in the end how things were before the Republic are better than what we have now. Do you disagree?"

After a moment, Lai shook her head. "I think anything would be better than this. If I had known what I do now when I was fifteen, I never would have joined an academy."

Angella gave her a gentle shove with her shoulder. "It's never too late to learn."

CHAPTER SEVENTEEN

THE BULLETS tore through the paper target and embedded themselves in the thick block of wood a few feet behind. Mel lowered the gun and studied the paper for a moment.

"I suck at this," she said.

From where Lai was sitting at a table behind Mel, she knew she was right. Lai chuckled quietly and took a bite of her apple. Mel let out a groan and handed the gun to Jaime.

"You don't suck," he told her. He holstered the weapon and walked to collect the paper. "This is only your fourth lesson. You should've seen your cousin when she started training."

"I will have you know that I was always an amazing shot," Lai contended. "You must be getting us mixed up."

Mel giggled and walked over to sit on the table in front of Lai. She dangled her feet over the edge as she snatched the apple out of Lai's hands and took a bite.

"I think you should teach me next time," Mel said with her mouth full. "All Jaime talks about is breathing and focusing your mind."

"I'm not going to teach you anything if you don't stop stealing my food," Lai replied.

She went to take her apple back, but Mel swiftly pulled it out of her reach. Lai conceded and leaned back in her chair. Mel grinned victoriously and took another bite.

"You're getting better."

Lai and Mel turned to see Sydney and Jackie walking toward them. Sydney, who had spoken, was twirling a gun around on his finger. Jackie followed along more slowly.

Romana had been correct in her diagnosis of a concussion and had ordered Jackie to take it easy for the next few days while she kept an eye on her. Jackie had grumbled for a while before agreeing. She hadn't left the base since the night of the raid and spent most of her time with Romana away from any excessive noise. Lai didn't mind her absence.

Jackie was irritable and had thrown up twice that Lai had seen. At least she hardly commented on Angella and Lai's trip.

"Yes, now I can actually hit the paper." Mel nodded back toward the wall, where three bullets were embedded in the metal panels.

"Lucky for you this is only a temporary base," Sydney said with a wave of his hand. "A few bullets in the wall gives it character for now."

Mel smiled and went back to her apple. Lai shuffled her chair back to give Jackie space to sit down next to her.

"Are you feeling any better?" Lai asked her.

"Romana thinks it's worse than it is," she said with a shrug. She brushed a finger over the bandage at the side of her head. "I haven't thrown up all day, so I think that's a good sign."

"If you do throw up again, make sure it isn't on my shirt," Sydney said.

Jackie ignored him and addressed Lai. "There's something I've been meaning to talk to you about." She paused for a moment and looked at her hands on the table. "The scouts say it's all clear in the surrounding area. We've been waiting for this so we can finally get out of Maricopa and join up with another group at a safer location."

Lai knew what she was referring to. Angella had told her they were originally planning on vacating the base as soon as she joined up with them. After the botched raid, no one was willing to make another move so quickly. Scouts had been keeping an eye on Maricopa and the desert for the past three days to determine if it was safe for them to leave. Lai, Jaime, and Mel had been allowed to stay for their own protection.

"Are we leaving today?" Lai asked.

When Jackie shook her head, she winced. "We're going to wait two more days to be sure. After that we head north. That's why I'm talking to you. What are you three planning on doing after we leave?"

Lai glanced to Mel sitting on the table. Mel was facing away from them and seemed to be paying more attention to where Jaime and Sydney stood near the wooden blocks on the wall.

"We've been talking about that. We think getting Mel out of the country is the safest thing for her."

"Would you consider sticking around instead?"

Lai whipped her head around to frown at Jackie. The woman was staring at her with a placid expression.

"Are you asking us to join the *Libertas Publica*?" Lai asked incredulously.

"I am," Jackie confirmed. "Well, I'm asking you to join."

Lai could hardly believe what she was hearing. When they had sought the help of the insurgent group, she had thought help was all they were going to get. She could believe Angella asking her to join them, but Jackie?

"Why would you be asking me to join? I thought you couldn't trust an academy kid."

"You saved my life," Jackie replied. "You thought on your feet and saved the lives of five members. And Angella trusts you. While I am admittedly not that woman's biggest admirer, I know it isn't easy to earn her trust. I think we could use someone like you."

Lai thought it looked as if Jackie was trying to hide physical pain at having to say nice things about another person. Nevertheless, she took a moment to consider the offer.

Joining the *Libertas Publica* did have its advantages. Rather than be on their own, they would have the protection of an entire organization. Of course, said organization was defined as a terrorist group. Still, Lai could not shake the feeling that it was the safest course for them to take to help keep Mel safe, not to mention her and Jaime.

Her mind drifted back to the events from three days prior. After killing those eleven officers, Lai wasn't sure she could handle something like it anytime soon. She was bound to get assignments if she joined, and those assignments would likely involve her proficiency with a gun.

Her gaze flicked over to where Mel sat on the table. Lai breathed out a sigh and turned back to Jackie.

"I'm interested," Lai said.

"You are?"

"Are you sure it's not just your concussion talking?" Lai asked wryly.

Jackie cracked a small smile. "I'm sure."

"Then so am I."

Jackie's smile widened, and she leaned back in her chair. "Good."

"I do have some questions first."

"Of course you do."

"What about Mel and Jaime?"

Jackie glanced to the two in question. "Neither of them have shown themselves to be of any value to our group."

"My agreement to join requires them being allowed to join too," Lai told her. She kept her expression neutral as she watched Jackie.

"That's quite a request." Jackie met Lai's eyes evenly. "I would have to think about that."

Lai let one corner of her mouth rise. "I'm not sure you have the authority to make recruitment decisions. You're not offering membership. You're offering to put in a word on my behalf to whomever can recruit me."

Jackie rolled her tongue around in her mouth and tapped a finger against the table. "I can see why Angella likes you."

"My request is the same," Lai continued. "I will consider joining if you put in the same effort to get Mel and Jaime recruited as you do for me."

Jackie stared at Lai for a long moment as she considered. Lai held her steady gaze and let her think.

After a dozen or so seconds, Jackie let herself smile again. "You've got a deal." She held out her hand, and Lai smiled and shook it.

"I still have a few questions," Lai said when her hand was released. "Where we're going is the first one."

Before Jackie could reply, the door of the base slammed against the wall as it opened. All eyes turned to see a scout hurrying in the direction of Lai and Jackie. Both sat up straighter when he stopped in front of them, his breathing heavy.

"We found four kids hiding down the road," he panted. "They all had guns. One of them threatened Carlton."

"Was he hurt?" Jackie demanded.

The man shook his head. "She was the only one who pulled a weapon on us. We disarmed them and got them in handcuffs." His attention turned to Lai. "They were all wearing academy uniforms. They said they were looking for you."

Lai whipped her head around in time to see the four kids being dragged into the base by Carlton and two other scouts. She jumped to her feet and offered Jackie a hand. Jackie stared at it for a moment before she accepted the help up. Lai didn't wait for her as she marched over to the group. She stopped in front of them just as the four kids were pushed to their knees. One girl saw Lai through her tangle of curly black hair and scowled.

"Oh wonderful, Lani is here to save us," Kieran sneered.

Lai put her hands on her hips and scanned the other three kneeling next to her. Rylen was to Kieran's right, with Deirdre and Virginia on her other side. All four were disheveled and worn out, as if they had been trekking through the desert for days, which, to be fair, they probably had been.

Lai wouldn't have believed they were there if she hadn't seen them with her own eyes. Her mind raced with a million questions. How could they have gotten out of the academy? Why would they be in Maricopa? Were they given a field assignment? Most of all, if they had run away, why the hell was Kieran with them?

"What the hell are you doing here?" Lai demanded. The other three broke out in relieved grins.

"Lai!" Virginia exclaimed. "Thank God we found you. Do you know how many warehouses there are around here?"

Lai frowned and eyed the scrapes and bruises on Virginia's arms. Upon further inspection, the others seemed to have similar injuries.

"Are you okay?" she asked in concern. She allowed her apprehension to fade momentarily as she kneeled down in front of Virginia. "Did these guys hurt you?"

"We're fine," Rylen replied. He coughed loudly for a moment. "Can't blame them for being cautious."

Lai glared up at Carlton, who stood with his gun ready behind her friends. "Did you do this?"

"They were already like this when we found them," Carlton told her with a shake of his head.

"Except for the bruise I'll have on my side where this guy kept ramming his gun," Kieran complained.

Lai turned her glare to the girl. "What is this?" Lai questioned. She rose to her feet as Jackie, Angella, Mel, Jaime, and Sydney joined her. Jackie and Angella maintained steady glares. Sydney seemed more curious than angry, as did Jaime. Mel apparently recognized the group from when she was on the firing line and stayed close to Lai's side.

"It's a long story," Deirdre said.

"Why don't you start with how you found us?" Lai suggested.

"Rylen hacked into the system at the academy. We found the locations of seven suspected bases in the area. A woman named Mariana told us this was the most likely one."

"Mariana told you about this base?" Angella said incredulously.

"It took a long time to convince her we were on your side," Virginia assured her.

"Speak for yourself," Kieran mumbled. She grunted when Rylen elbowed her in the ribs but did not say anything further.

"If this is a suspected base, why haven't we been raided yet?" Jackie asked.

"I fried the system," Rylen boasted. "After we got what we needed, I sent a bug to wipe everything. It wasn't as hard as I thought it would be. I just used a code with—"

"He took care of it," Deirdre interrupted. "They lost everything without a hard copy."

"Is that when you guys left?" Jaime inquired.

Deidre, Rylen, and Virginia all nodded.

"I let the bug trip some alarms," Rylen explained. "They were too busy trying to save their files to notice us sneaking out."

"I'm confused," Lai cut in. She put two fingers to each temple. "You four hacked into the server at the academy, stole some files, and then wiped the entire system so you could escape and find us?"

"That pretty much sums it up," Rylen agreed with a nod.

Virginia and Deirdre nodded their agreement as well.

"And Kieran suddenly decided she's a nonsympathizer?" Lai asked in disbelief.

"I'm only here because my suicidal girlfriend dragged me out with her," Kieran shot back.

Deirdre frowned at her but said nothing.

"What makes you think we'd believe this?" Jackie challenged. She took a step forward to stand beside Lai. "For all we know, you could have been sent to infiltrate us."

"Check my back pocket," Deirdre said.

Jackie paused a moment and then nodded to Angella. The woman walked around behind Deirdre and reached into her pocket. She pulled out a small black device that Lai recognized as a standard issue data tablet from the academy.

"That's everything we stole," Deirdre explained. "Lai, you remember what Oscar told us? We have proof, and it's on that tablet."

"Is she talking about innocent people ending up on death row?" Jackie whispered to Lai.

Lai kept her eyes on Deirdre and nodded once. She had told them all a few days prior about what Oscar had discovered.

"Angella, check the tablet on one of the computers," Jackie ordered. "Disconnect it from the server first in case it's bugged. If it checks out, transfer the information immediately and destroy the tablet."

"What's wrong with the tablet?" Jaime asked.

"A tablet can be hacked remotely. We don't operate with equipment manufactured recently enough to be affected by wireless security."

Angella clasped the tablet in her hand and headed to the computers on the far wall. After a moment Jaime fell into step behind his sister.

"What made you change your minds?" Lai asked. "I knew some of us had doubts, but I didn't think you would do something as impulsive as this."

"More impulsive than rescuing someone from death row?" Rylen teased. He eyed Mel where she still stood at Lai's side.

"It's still a pretty bold move," Lai said. "Bolder than I thought you were willing to do."

"We thought about what you said," Virginia told her, "and what you did. After seeing what those files said, we didn't want to support that system anymore. We knew the information needed to get out somehow, and we thought the *Libertas Publica* was the best way to do it."

"Kieran?" Lai prompted. She crossed her arms and turned her attention to the girl scowling at the ground.

Kieran lifted her head and let out a bitter laugh. "Like I said, I'm here for Deirdre. You're all crazy."

"She's scared to admit that she agrees with us," Rylen contradicted. This time it was his turn to be elbowed in the ribs.

All eyes turned when footsteps announced Angella and Jaime rejoining them. Angella stopped next to Jackie and eyed the teens kneeling on the ground with something resembling admiration.

"Voy a ser maldita," she said with a shake of her head. "They're telling the truth. They got files on at least two hundred people who were executed unwarrantedly. We've got everything. Names, ages, convicted crimes, the location they were taken to be executed. We even have the student they were assigned to."

"Now can we get these handcuffs off?" Kieran asked.

Jackie put a hand each on Lai and Angella's arms and pulled them back a few steps. She waved Sydney over to join them and pulled them into a tight circle.

"You know these four?" Jackie asked Lai.

She nodded. "They were in my training group." She glanced over Jackie's shoulder at them. "I knew some of them had doubts about the Republic, but I never thought they'd do anything like this."

"Can we trust them?" Angella inquired.

Lai took a long moment to study her former group members. While Virginia and Rylen seemed to be getting a bit worried, Deirdre looked as confident as ever. Kieran was still glaring at anything and everything in her sight.

"I believe they're telling the truth," she finally told them. "If this was trick, they wouldn't have given us real information."

"Are you sure it's real?" Sydney urged. "If this isn't the real thing and we release it, we're in big trouble."

"I should check it first, but I do believe them," Lai repeated. "Virginia, Rylen, and Deirdre aren't going to betray us."

"And Kieran?" Jackie asked.

Lai stared at the girl in question for a long moment. As if sensing eyes on her, Kieran met Lai's gaze evenly.

"I've never trusted Kieran," Lai admitted. "The fact that she's here at all, even if it's for Deirdre, is more than I ever expected from her."

"So what do we do with her?" Sydney wondered. He looked to Jackie.

"We can't let her go, and it isn't safe to keep her here," Angella reasoned.

"So we kill her," Jackie said.

"Hold on. I never said she was that dangerous," Lai argued urgently. "She may not be trustworthy, but I'm not going to let you kill her."

"What do you propose we do with her, then?"

Lai sighed heavily and thought for a moment. She wished Kieran hadn't come at all. It was clear she didn't want to be where she was.

"We should keep her in one of the back rooms until we leave," Lai suggested. "Keep her in handcuffs. If she decides she wants us to trust her, then she can prove she deserves that trust. Until then, she stays locked up."

The other three considered Lai's words.

"I can live with that," Sydney agreed.

"If she's locked up, she can't do any harm," Angella added.

Jackie groaned and shook her head. "Do not make me regret this," she said firmly. She turned around and walked back to the others. Lai, Angella, and Sydney followed close behind.

"Uncuff those three," Jackie ordered with a wave of her hand. She pointed to Kieran. "She stays as she is."

"What?" Kieran cried. When she went to stand up, Carlton put a firm hand on her shoulder and forced her back to her knees.

"She isn't going to do anything," Deirdre argued. When her cuffs were off, she rubbed her wrists and stayed kneeling beside her girlfriend. "I'll make sure of that."

"We can't take any risks," Jackie said simply. "Until she proves we can trust her, the handcuffs stay on."

"Don't worry, Deirdre, I'm not going to let anything happen to her," Lai assured her.

"No, you're only going to let them keep me locked up after I risked my life to get this tablet here," Kieran seethed.

With a nod from Jackie, Carlton brought Kieran to her feet.

"Keep a guard outside her door at all times," Jackie ordered.

Carlton nodded and began pulling Kieran along to the back of the base.

"Wait!" Deirdre pleaded.

Carlton halted.

Deirdre hurried over to give Kieran a quick kiss and placed a hand on her cheek. "It'll be fine," Deirdre promised. "We won't let them do anything to you."

Kieran stopped glaring for the first time since she arrived at the base. She allowed Deirdre to place another kiss on her forehead before Carlton pulled her away again.

Virginia came up behind Deirdre and placed a hand on her shoulder. "She'll be better once she's cooled down."

Deirdre sighed. "I hope so. I just wish she would stop doing this. Her stubbornness is going to get her into more trouble."

"You don't need to worry about Kieran," Lai cut in. Deirdre and Virginia turned to her. "I have some influence here. She's safe."

Deirdre gave her a grateful smile. "Thank you."

Virginia suddenly launched forward and wrapped her arms around Lai. Lai staggered back a step before she laughed and returned the hug.

"You had me worried sick," Virginia scolded. She pulled back but kept her hands on Lai's shoulders. "You need to tell us everything."

"Only if you tell me how you really got out of the academy," Lai said. "That's got to be an interesting story."

"It is," Rylen agreed as he came to stand beside Deirdre. "I had no idea Virginia could drive like that."

"Was it just the four of you?" Lai asked. "Not even Siobhan?"

"We tried to convince Siobhan and Tamsin to come with us," Deirdre told her. "Tamsin thought the LP was too extreme, and Siobhan was too scared of what would happen if she left."

Lai sighed and closed her eyes. Those girls were her friends. It comforted her a little to know that they were at least out of harm's way.

"Seriously, you have to tell us how you got this so called 'influence' with the biggest opposition group in the Republic," Rylen pleaded.

Lai opened her eyes and allowed her a small smile. "Let's just say I am a very good shot."

Chapter Eighteen

MEL CLASPED her hands behind her back and strode purposefully toward the back of the base. She headed for the door on the far right. It had to be the right one, as it was the only door being guarded.

The guard stood up and placed himself in front of the door when he saw her approaching. Mel stopped a few feet in front of him and rocked back and forth on her heels.

"Hello, Benjamin," she greeted him cheerfully.

"No one is allowed in here."

"If no one is allowed in, how does she get any food?"

"No one is allowed in without Jackie's permission," he revised.

Mel stuck out her bottom lip and ceased her rocking motion. "I just want to talk to her. She must be lonely."

"Her girlfriend has already visited her three times today."

Mel sighed. "Jackie!" she called back over her shoulder. She glanced behind her to see Jackie sitting at a table on the opposite side of the base with Romana.

Jackie looked up when her name was called. "What?" she shouted back.

Benjamin rolled his eyes.

"Can I talk to Kieran?" Mel asked.

Jackie waved a hand and went back to signing to her friend.

Mel beamed at the guard. He huffed loudly and stepped aside.

"Thank you," Mel sang as she walked forward and pushed the door open.

The room was exactly the same as the one she and Lai had been assigned, except the room she was now standing in had a window. Light filtered in through thick iron bars set in front of the glass. Against the far wall were two beds lined up side by side, and a small table sat against the wall under the window. A tin cup of water and a plate with bread and some fruit sat on the table.

Kieran sat on one of the beds, leaning against the wall as she stared at the window. Her expression betrayed no emotion. Her gaze flicked briefly to Mel before returning to the window.

Mel noted the handcuffs that held Kieran's wrists together.

"Well isn't this something?" Kieran said.

Mel frowned and leaned back against the wall next to the door. "What do you mean?"

Kieran laughed once without humor. "The irony of this situation. Here I am, the trainee who has killed hundreds of prisoners, being locked up by a radical group. And here you are, the escaped death-row prisoner, visiting me to gloat."

"I'm not here to gloat. I thought you might be lonely."

"Yes, I'm sure you are genuinely concerned about my mental state."

Mel sighed and looked to the window. "You have this idea about what kind of person I am, do you?"

Kieran shrugged but did not reply.

"You don't know anything about me." Mel pointed to the second bed. "Can I sit?" When Kieran nodded, Mel sat cross-legged on the bed facing the other girl. "When you saw me on that line, you saw me as a criminal."

"Are you not a criminal?" Kieran challenged. She finally brought her gaze to focus on Mel.

"I committed a crime," Mel corrected. "That doesn't make me a criminal."

"It does in the eyes of the law."

"Okay, I didn't come here to argue about the law with you." Mel scooted herself forward a few inches and clasped her hands in her lap.

"Well, you certainly didn't come here because you were worried about me."

"No, I didn't," Mel admitted. "But I do want to talk."

"Why don't we talk about you first?" Kieran suggested. She leaned forward and narrowed her eyes at Mel. "I saw a few things when we hacked the academy. I saw your file."

"Did you see anything interesting?"

"I did, as a matter of fact. I saw that you killed a man. The report said you shot him in the back twice. Terrence Anderson was his name, I think. He had a daughter, you know. The report said she was there when you shot him.

"You shot a man in front of his daughter, and you have the nerve to come in here and silently judge me for killing people? Don't pretend you're not."

Mel squeezed her hands tightly together and took a deep breath. She kept her gaze even as she stared at the girl in front of her.

"I know he had a daughter," Mel said evenly. "She was the reason I killed him. He was beating her because he didn't like us being together."

Kieran's expression softened and she raised her eyebrows. She leaned back against the wall, and her eyes lost any trace of malice.

"I guess the file didn't tell you that."

"It didn't," Kieran said softly. She tilted her head but said nothing.

Mel let out a long breath and fell back on the bed, grateful that her head didn't slam into the wall when she did so.

"I wasn't judging you," she mumbled. "I'm curious about you."

Kieran brought a knee up to her chest and frowned. "Curious? Why?"

"The other three kids you were with all wanted to be here. You seem like you want to stab everybody."

"I only came because of Deirdre."

"You said that. Twice, actually."

"Your point?"

Mel pulled herself back up and turned so she was leaning against the wall. She glanced sideways at Kieran. "My point is that you must love that girl more than anything to follow her here."

A smile ghosted over Kieran's lips. "I do."

"I guess we'll both do crazy things for the girls we love."

Kieran caught the meaning and the smile reappeared. "I didn't know you were clever."

Mel shrugged and played with the hem of her shirt.

"Is that all you were curious about?" Kieran asked her.

"No," Mel admitted. "I wanted to ask you something specific."

Kieran waited while Mel glanced down at her lap and picked at threads in her shirt.

After a long silence, she finally looked up and spoke. "Why did you join an academy?"

Kieran lost her smile and leaned back again, clearly on the defensive. "That's not really any of your business."

"I told you about how I killed someone."

"Only because I already knew half of it," Kieran pointed out. "Why do you want to know?"

"I want to know what makes a person want to be a protection officer."

"Why don't you ask your cousin? You're obviously much closer with her."

"I know why she joined," Mel said dismissively. "She's not you. You called us crazy. You clearly sympathize with the Republic. I want to know why you joined."

"So you came in here to have a political debate with me."

Mel let out a frustrated growl and rolled her eyes. "Everyone here thinks the same thing. No one is even the slightest bit sympathetic. I'm curious what someone like you thinks."

"Someone like me? You mean someone who isn't trying to destroy the system that protects us?"

"It didn't protect me!" Mel shot back. "I may have killed someone, but I did it to protect someone I care about. That should have meant something. You don't need to kill a nineteen-year-old for trying to keep someone safe!"

Mel realized she was nearly shouting and worked to slow her breathing.

Kieran fixed her with a frown that was equal parts concerned and confused. "The laws are harsh for a reason," Kieran said with little conviction. "Prisons used to be overcrowded. It cost the country more than it could afford."

"So instead we turned prison into population control," Mel muttered.

If Kieran had a response, she kept it to herself.

"Yes, I am curious about why someone would willingly sign up to uphold these laws and come out of it still believing they're right."

Kieran's frown suddenly morphed into a glare. "Maybe when you said someone like me you meant a black girl," Kieran hissed. "Why would a black girl want to protect a racist system that has never bothered to protect her? It's simple. I don't know where you grew up, but I grew up right next to the Confederate border. People aren't so accepting there. Did you ever read about innocent black kids being shot in the streets back in the United States? Now, if the officers don't shoot us, they arrest us for anything that gets us a death sentence. In the south the government lets the officers take the lead. They get fewer orders. That lets them target us.

"In my neighborhood, kids were getting arrested left and right. I only managed to stay out of prison because my father taught me how to act. He taught me never to question the system, never to question an officer. It was how he stayed alive, and he taught me to do the same thing. Do you have any idea what that was like? When I was nine years old, I watched my best friend get shot because she asked an officer why he was following her. I didn't say a thing. If I had, I would've been dead too.

"When my father died, I was passed off to my mother. She didn't give a damn about me. I got myself emancipated when I was fourteen. I needed to figure something out. All I knew was that my father always taught me to respect the system, that it was the way to stay alive. I headed west and signed up for the academy. They don't target you when you're one of them.

"You want to know how I could fight for a system like this one? You're looking at a girl who was taught from the day she could process words that she should always respect it. She should never question it. I guess somewhere along the way that became all I had."

Kieran's tirade ended abruptly. She seemed to notice for the first time that tears were streaming down her face, and she brought her hands up to wipe them away. She held a hard glare as she breathed heavily and kept her eyes fixed firmly on the wall.

"Fighting against the system would only get me killed," she rasped. She heaved in a shaky breath and fell silent.

Mel was completely stunned. She didn't know where she was supposed to look, so she fixed her attention back to the threads that hung from her shirt.

She suddenly understood. Here was this girl who had spent her life in fear, in total submission just to keep herself alive. Why wouldn't she gravitate to an academy? It was a surefire way to ensure her own safety. It was something she could hardly be faulted for.

Mel couldn't help asking her next question. "How could you run away after all that?"

Kieran sighed and let her head fall back against the wall with a quiet thud. She sniffed back her tears and stared at the ceiling. "I met Deirdre. She didn't care about any fucked-up past I had. She just cared about me. She never told me I was wrong for joining the academy. She never told me I was wrong for any of it. Eventually I started loving her more than I feared for myself." She finally met Mel's eyes again. "I'm sure you can understand that."

Mel nodded as her mind drifted back to memories of Violet. "I'm sorry I asked."

Kieran stared for a long moment before she started laughing. It was only for a moment, and it was more a sob than a laugh, but Mel knew it was more than Kieran was used to doing in front of people.

"I don't tell people that story," Kieran admitted when she got herself back under control, "ever. Deirdre is the only person I've told, before today."

"Why did you decide to trust me?" Mel asked.

Kieran laughed again. "Trust? That wasn't trust. You just pissed me off enough to make me stop thinking about what I was saying."

Mel let out her own laugh. "Of course."

All at once Kieran stopped laughing and her expression got serious. "You're not going to repeat this to anyone," she ordered. "Not even your cousin."

"It might help you get those handcuffs off if they knew why you're so against them," Mel pointed out. She bit her tongue at Kieran's glower.

"I'm serious."

"All right," Mel agreed. "Not a word."

Kieran seemed to settle down at Mel's assurance. She let her shoulders sag and rested herself more comfortably against the wall.

"I think people misjudge you," Mel said. "Lai told me about you. You surprised me."

"Good surprise?" Kieran questioned.

Mel felt herself smile. "Yeah." She peered at Kieran for a moment. "Can I ask you another question?"

"Only if you promise not to make me shout at you again."

Mel's smile widened, and she shook her head slightly. "I wanted to know about the tablet, or the information on it."

"It's real, if that's what you're wondering," Kieran told her.

"You know what will happen when it gets out?"

"I do. People will end up rioting in the streets."

"And that's what you want?"

Kieran considered the question for a moment. "I've been in denial ever since I joined the academy. I only realized that in the past few days.

I didn't want to believe they were executing people unjustly, but it's the truth. How am I supposed to fight for a system that can't protect me even if I follow all the rules?"

"You still called us crazy," Mel pointed out.

"The LP *are* crazy. But they're also the best way for this to happen. The four of us didn't stand a chance on our own."

"You don't agree with how the *Libertas Publica* handle things."

"And you do?" Kieran challenged. "I heard about the bombing three days ago. This is what they do. They're radicals."

"Don't you want things to change?"

"Yes, but not how these people define it."

"How do you think change should look?"

"I didn't say I had a solution." Kieran brought her hands up to her forehead and rested them there. "I just said this isn't the right one."

Mel had to concede the point. "Fine, it isn't the right one. Maybe we should be thinking about the right one."

Kieran gave Mel a teasing smile. "You did just come in here to debate politics with me."

CHAPTER NINETEEN

SORTING BULLETS had to be the most tedious task Lai could possibly imagine. It was also the task Jackie had saddled her with.

Evidently it was a bad idea to complain that you were bored within earshot of Jackie. The words had hardly left Lai's mouth before Jackie had dragged her over to a bin of loose bullets alongside a small bin of empty clips and a notebook and pen. She sat Lai down on the ground and instructed her to sort and catalog the entire supply and report back to her at the end. She had then walked off without another word and left Lai to wonder how she had ended up sitting on the ground with a job to do.

Despite the menial nature of the work, it did serve to occupy her time. The fact that the LP stole rather than bought their supplies meant they rarely had a full set of anything. Bullets were no exception. While they did have a good supply of 9×19mm bullets, an hour into sorting, Lai found that nearly a third of them were for models of guns they didn't have. After she consulted Jackie about the issue, she was ordered to file them down to fit into their guns.

Her friends seemed greatly amused by Lai's work, though none of them got too close lest she try to pull them in to help her. At one point, Lai paused in her work when Mel headed in the direction of the room Kieran was being held in. After asking permission from Jackie, Mel went in. Why she would want to talk to Kieran was beyond Lai, but she wasn't concerned enough to do anything. Kieran might be vexatious, but she wasn't truly dangerous, especially not handcuffed in a back room.

It took Lai about two hours to get all the bullets sorted, cataloged, and attached into clips for easier use. She had just begun the even more tedious process of filing down the outliers when Deirdre suddenly appeared next to her. Lai jumped slightly, not having seen her walk up. Deirdre only smiled and lowered herself until she was sitting cross-legged next to Lai.

"This looks boring," Deirdre commented.

"You think?"

Deirdre shrugged and glanced around the warehouse. "I suppose someone has to do it."

"Well I don't suppose you would like to help me?"

"Not particularly. I have a better idea."

Lai inspected the bullet she had been working on and, finding it to her standards, added it to the finished pile before picking up another. "What's that?"

"I need a shooting partner."

Lai frowned and halted in her work. "You want to practice shooting? Now?"

"Why not?" Deirdre shrugged her shoulders again and gave Lai a borderline pleading grin. "I like to keep my skills sharp. You never know what's going to happen to you, especially when we're housed with a terrorist group."

"Terrorist?"

"That *is* the official designation," Deirdre pointed out.

Lai rolled her eyes. "Fine. Why me?"

"You've always been a good shooting partner."

"I thought you liked pairing with Kieran."

Deirdre smirked and stood up. She offered Lai a hand. "I never said you were my favorite."

At that, Lai found herself smiling. She really could use a break from her task. Since Lai had finished the main part of the job, Jackie would likely be more amenable to letting her finish later. Or not at all. Someone else finishing would not bother Lai in the slightest.

Lai grabbed Deirdre's hand and let herself be pulled to her feet. She groaned as the muscles in her legs were stretched properly for the first time in hours.

"I don't think Jackie wants us to waste bullets," she commented.

Deirdre reached around behind her back and unclipped a clear plastic bag from her belt. She held it out for Lai to see.

"I made wooden bullets last night."

Lai's eyes widened. "You *made* wooden bullets?"

"About four and a half dozen."

"You made fifty-four wooden bullets."

"Fifty-two, I think, but yes, bullets with a little gun powder and an old cartridge. Come on, I made them for my Ruger, so they'll fit your gun too."

Lai shook her head and gestured for Deirdre to get walking. "And I thought my job was boring."

The two of them walked across the base to where Jackie sat, signing with Romana.

Jackie glanced up as they approached and quirked an eyebrow.

"We're going out for shooting practice," Deirdre told her. "I made bullets."

Jackie turned her gaze to Lai. "You're finished?"

"Sorting and cataloging, yes," Lai confirmed.

Jackie tilted her head ever so slightly. "And filing?"

"I'll help her finish tonight," Deirdre cut in with a wave of her hand. Lai glanced to her and smiled.

Her fingers tapping away on the table, Jackie sighed and waved her hand dismissively. "Fine, go shoot things. Just don't do it outside. Use the warehouse next door, the one with the single blue door. It's empty."

"Thank you," Deirdre said with a nod. In a flash, she hooked her arm through Lai's and had the two of them headed toward the storage bins near the door. Deirdre left Lai outside and went in to rummage around in the contents. She emerged a few moments later with a paper bag, two pairs of safety glasses, and, to Lai's surprise and amusement, an old torn mattress. She handed the bag and glasses off to Lai to focus on carrying the mattress.

"We need something to shoot at," Deirdre explained.

Lai chuckled and followed her toward the door.

Virginia and Jaime stood near the door, apparently joking about something, as they were laughing when Lai and Deirdre approached. The two waved as they passed and gave them a few strange looks, before going back to their conversation.

Outside, the air was as dry as Lai had ever felt it. Deirdre apparently felt it, too, as she coughed a few paces from the door. The midday sun beat down on them from straight above, not a cloud in sight to offer shade. Lai was all at once grateful they were going to be shooting inside. Even a warehouse without air-conditioning was better than outside.

The warehouse in question was only just smaller than the base. It was empty save for a group of metal storage containers at the far end, all of which were open and boasted nothing inside.

"Help me with this," Deirdre panted. The added burden of carrying the mattress already had her sweating. Deirdre had grown up in the north, though on the other side of the country, so she had to be about as used to the dry air was Lai was.

Lai took one end of the mattress, and the two of them lugged it across to the storage containers. When they reached the one closest to the center of the back wall, they tipped it up on its end and rested it against the metal box.

"Right!" Deirdre exclaimed with a clap of her hands. "Let's get started."

LAI HAD shot at many strange targets in her training, not the least of which were living human beings, but a busted-up old mattress was certainly unique. While not as sophisticated as the variety of targets they utilized at the academy, it did serve its purpose well enough.

The wooden bullets fit perfectly in Lai's P30, as Deirdre had said they would. Had she not joined the academy, that girl could have had quite the future in carving. She only scoffed when Lai told her so.

The two of them took full advantage of the empty space and ran through a handful of their training techniques, from running back and forth across the room to firing after spinning around to jumping from the top of the storage containers. The last might not have been a technique they had ever practiced before, but it made things interesting.

After an hour of practice, when their supply of bullets had been nearly exhausted and they were both panting, they climbed to the top of one of the containers and sat for a lunch break. The paper bag Deirdre had swiped earlier contained half a dozen juicy red apples. Though it had become half of her diet since arriving at the base, Lai never got tired of them.

"Here's to successfully staying vegetarian on the run," Deirdre toasted with a wink.

Lai smiled and tapped her apple against Deirdre's before taking a huge bite. Juice ran down her chin, and she caught it with the back of her hand just before it could dirty her clothing.

"I needed this," Deirdre said after she swallowed her first bite.

"What, the apple or the practice?" Lai asked.

Deirdre shrugged a shoulder and took another bite. "Both. Mostly the practice, though. This was fun. It was a nice respite from all of this... mess."

"Even if we created another mess of our own," Lai joked.

The mattress lay in tatters on the ground before them. The bullets had torn into the fabric like it was nothing and left it shredded beyond use before they were halfway through. Loose springs either stuck out of what was left of the frame or littered the ground among the rest. Luckily for them, no one would care if they left the warehouse as it was.

Deirdre let out a quick chuckle and swallowed her bite. "I mean it. Thank you for doing this with me. We all went from zero to sixty in what seems like no time. I'm still on day two, so you three have got that on me."

"It hasn't exactly settled in for me either," Lai admitted. "But it has to eventually. I just don't see it happening until we're out of this base."

"Jaime told me you went on that raid. It sounded rough."

Rough didn't begin to cover it. "We nearly died." Lai shrugged a shoulder in a thinly veiled attempt at nonchalance. "I shot a smoke bomb out of midair. All in a day's work."

Before Lai could take another bite of her half-finished apple, Deirdre snatched it from her hand and tossed it into the air. She took less than a second to aim her gun before she fired. The apple exploded and splattered against the nearest wall.

Lai smacked her friend in the arm and frowned. "Now you're just showing off. And I wasn't finished with that!"

Deirdre gave a cheeky smile and took the last few bites of her own apple. "Come on," she said as she jumped down from the container. She pulled off her jacket and discarded it and her gun on the ground.

Lai's annoyance fell away to make room for her curiosity. "Come on what?"

"Target practice is still your thing." Deirdre jogged out to the middle of the warehouse and beckoned Lai closer. "I want to brush up on my hand-to-hand skills."

Now that was something Lai could get behind. She matched Deirdre's smile and jumped down to discard her own things.

"How much contact?" Lai asked as she stopped a few feet away from Deirdre and took up her fighting stance.

"Let's stay away from faces," Deidre decided. "Light hits only. We don't need anything breaking."

"I can agree to tha—"

Lai hardly had time to dodge when Deirdre came at her from the side. Lai pivoted on her feet and swung back in a wide arc. She caught Deirdre's forearm on her own and smiled wide.

The two of them traded punches and blocks for a while, their hits firm but gentle compared to what they could do in full protective gear. No one wanted to end up on the floor with Deirdre when they had no restrictions.

Lai ducked to her left and dropped to the ground as Deirdre's leg swung inches over her head. She shot out her own leg, hoping to catch Deirdre off balance and send her tumbling to the ground. Instead, Deirdre danced out of the way and came in low with a strong forearm. Lai dove to the side and rolled back to her feet. She spun around immediately and held both arms in front, one just below her jawline and one at her midsection, as Deirdre came at her with another kick. She caught Deirdre's foot on her lower arm and gave a mighty shove.

That was exactly what Deirdre had been waiting for. She used the extra momentum Lai gave her to spin around at a wicked speed and bring her other leg to Lai's now unguarded left side. The kick landed, and Lai felt the breath go from her lungs. Deirdre swept back around just as quickly and took Lai's feet out from under her. Lai went sprawling to the ground with a gasp. Just before her back hit, Deirdre came in at her side and used a shoulder to keep Lai from hitting at full force. Once she had halted the worst of it, she let Lai drop the rest of the way and placed a hand gently on her midsection.

"I win," Deirdre sang through her own gasps for air.

Lai groaned and used her elbows to lift herself partway off the ground.

When it came to shooting, Lai was easily the best in her group. Hand-to-hand combat, however, was Deirdre's domain, and they both knew it.

They also knew that Lai could have been injured for real, rather than just winded, had Deirdre not held back as she did.

"Letse," she gasped. Despite herself, she smiled. "I'll be feeling that tomorrow."

Deirdre seemed quite worried all of a sudden. "Did I hit you too hard?"

Lai lifted one wrist and let it fall back. "I remember why no one ever wants to fight you."

A pleased laugh burst from Deidre's lips. She stood up and stretched her arms above her head before offering a hand to Lai. Lai took it and allowed herself to be pulled to her feet. She winced slightly and took several deep breaths before she attempted to speak.

"Romana won't be happy we did this," Lai told her. "But I should be fine. You caught me just in time."

Deirdre's smile betrayed exuberance after the type of fight she enjoyed. "You're very fun to fight with, Lailani. More than Kieran, I'd say."

"That's because you refuse to hit her," Lai countered.

Deirdre scrunched her nose up and smiled some more.

"How is Kieran?" Lai asked as they made their way back to the storage containers. Rather than try to climb back on top, they sat down near their gear and leaned back against it.

Deirdre took a long moment to reply. "She's handling it. She isn't happy, of course, but I wouldn't be either if I was locked up."

A wave of guilt fell over Lai. She had gotten the others out free, but Kieran was kept under lock and key because Lai had told them she couldn't be trusted. She couldn't lie and say she had changed her mind about that, but that didn't make her feel any better when faced with Kieran's girlfriend.

"I really did make her come with us," Deirdre continued. Her previous joyfulness at their fight had evaporated, and a cool demeanor replaced it. "She never would have done this if I hadn't begged her to. Literally begged. I was almost on my knees. I couldn't leave her behind. I doubt I would have left if she had refused. I never would have forgiven myself for that.

"Even if she isn't entirely happy here, at least she's with me. I feel like I can do something for her when we're together. If she was back there and I was here, I think we'd both be hopeless."

Deirdre smiled a second later, an impulsive half smile that betrayed something of her feelings for her girlfriend. "She is such a patriot," Deirdre said.

Lai suddenly had the feeling that they weren't having a conversation anymore.

"She fights so hard all the time. She never stops fighting. Never has since she was a kid. She doesn't know what else she's supposed to do. It's always a fight to survive with her. Always trying to survive...."

She didn't speak for a full minute. Lai sat there, breathing as silently as she could, afraid to break whatever had come over Deirdre all of a sudden.

It was then that Lai saw something she couldn't remember ever seeing before. She had seen Deirdre and Kieran together hundreds of times. They all bunked together. Those two were like magnets, always keeping their eyes on one another, even in the middle of training. They got antsy when apart for what they deemed too long. It sometimes seemed five minutes was too long. Over the years, Lai had seen them look at each other in any number of ways, some sickeningly romantic enough to make Lai want to gag.

The expression Deirdre now had on her face was as clear as if she had the words painted on her face. She would go into hell if needed to keep Kieran safe. Given that Kieran had followed her to the base, it was clear Kieran already had.

Lai couldn't pretend to know the feeling. She had never, and most likely would never, feel the type of love those two felt for one another. She loved her sister, her mother, her cousin, even Jaime, each in their own special way, but what she could see from Deirdre at that moment was altogether different. There was a passion there that Lai couldn't match.

She didn't miss it, but it was as mystifying a feeling as she could ever imagine.

Deirdre seemed to come out of a trance and noticed Lai staring at her. She blushed and turned her face away, something else Lai had never seen her do before.

"Sorry," she breathed. "I was thinking. This whole mess has put Kieran in a difficult position. If I wasn't so glad she's here, I might feel sorry for dragging her along."

Deirdre took a deep breath and at once fell into a coughing fit. Lai unhooked her water canister from where it hung from her jacket and handed it over to her friend. Deirdre took it gratefully and emptied half of it before handing it back. She coughed a few final times and laughed as she wiped away a few stray drops from her mouth.

"Ahhhh. I will never get used to this air," Deirdre said.

"I understand. I grew up on the coast of an island and then in Baltimore, remember?"

"I do. I think everyone but Jaime grew up somewhere humid."

"Havana is pretty damn humid," Lai pointed out.

Deirdre shrugged and waved a hand. "Yes, but he's been here since he was, what, four? Fourteen years gives more time to adapt than three for us."

Lai thought for a moment. "You lived near Olympia, right?"

"About thirty-five miles west, but yes, I'm from the Northwest."

"Can I ask something?" When Deirdre nodded, she continued. "I'm not old enough to remember it, and I guess neither are you, but I know that's where most Irish refugees went when the war broke out."

"Posturing for the rest of the world," Deirdre said bitterly. "The Republic likes to appear nice to immigrants and refugees in times of crisis. But you know what happens once we get here."

She picked up her gun and idly twirled it in her hands. She glanced over to Lai and gave her a slight frown. "You want to ask me what it was like."

Lai nodded once. She knew less about many of her group members than she cared to admit. All of a sudden, Deirdre seemed all the more intriguing to her. She needn't worry about prying. If Deirdre didn't want to answer, she would make that clear enough.

Apparently Lai's lack of worry was correct. Deirdre took a moment to gather her thoughts before she replied.

"Yes, most Irish refugees went there when war broke out in Ireland. Siobhan grew up in the same town as me, you know."

"She mentioned that," Lai said with a nod.

"Mmmm, it was a strange time and place to grow up. I was born here. Siobhan too. Our community was ninety percent Irish, hence the accents. Most, like my grandfather, were so unbelievably grateful to have been allowed in and given fast-track visas that they became the most loyal citizens you could ask for. Without my mother to tell me otherwise, I believed every word everyone in my town said."

Deirdre paused for a long moment, apparently mulling over her next words. She flipped her gun over in her hands as she stared ahead to the mess of their target mattress.

"You know my mother was a law professor, yes?" Deirdre waited until Lai nodded to continue. "She didn't only teach. She was also an active defense attorney. Ever since leaving Ireland, it was all she wanted to do. She believed in the law more than anything else. She trusted it, let it guide her life. It *was* her life.

"That is, until she actually began practicing here. It didn't take more than a year for her to realize that the system is stacked against people. It doesn't want people to be innocent. It wants them to be controlled. Prison is a very efficient way to control people. To scare them into compliance. Add onto that death sentence after death sentence attached to the most ridiculous crimes. Even without the illegal executions, this country doesn't care about its citizens. It cares about government. It cares about keeping everything this way. Why do you think we don't have elections anymore? Why the unofficial yet advocated for motto of the country is *Democracy is Chaos*?

"My mother couldn't handle it. She spent seven years working with accused criminals who nearly all ended up incarcerated or dead. It drained everything from her. I was only a child, but even I could see it. She was never quite there. I didn't know it at the time, but her job was killing her. Eventually, it actually did."

Lai's mouth drew into a tight line. This was further than she had expected Deirdre's story to go. She wanted to speak, to say anything at all, but nothing she could say would help. She knew Deirdre's mother was long dead, but until now she never knew why or how.

"She just couldn't take it anymore. She shot herself in open court. She walked up to a bailiff, took the gun from their belt, and shot a bullet through the roof of her mouth."

Deirdre's hand tightened around her own gun. "I was four. We were already living with my grandfather. After his husband died, we moved in with him. After my mother... he raised me. Never once did he tell me why she killed herself. I asked, maybe more than I should have, but he always told me he didn't know.

"Ever since he came to the Republic, he couldn't say a bad thing about the country. But he knew. I didn't know he was lying for the longest time. When he died last year, he had most of his things donated or auctioned off, but he left me a box of old journals belonging to him and my mother. That's where I read the truth.

"I don't think I'll ever know if he really meant for me to find out this way, or if he simply wasn't thinking when he had them sent to the academy. Either way, I read the last entry my mother made, the morning she went to court and left in a body bag. In an entry in my grandfather's journal a day later, he wrote about it. He wrote that I would never know the truth, that I didn't need to know the truth. It would only confuse me.

"Maybe he thought at seventeen I would be ready, or I deserved to know why I grew up without a mother. I suppose it hardly matters now. They're both gone, and I'm at a *Libertas Publica* base with you people."

A nostalgic smile crept in at the tail end of her story. "What my mother would think of me now."

"I'm sure we've all done enough to give any family member an aneurysm."

Lai's comment made Deirdre laugh for a moment. Lai joined her, glad to see her friend smile genuinely after her frankly depressing story. She had never known all of those things about Deirdre. She knew that her family were Irish immigrants and that her mother had passed but precious little else. In a way, Deirdre was like Kieran in that regard. She spoke little of her past, instead focusing on her future as an officer.

The laughter didn't last for long. Almost as soon as it had begun, Deirdre's funereal demeanor was back.

"For a while I couldn't accept it. I believed wholeheartedly in the Republic, in what it stands for. In what I thought it stands for, anyway. I knew enough of the truth that I could have turned unsympathetic, but it took more than that.

"In all honesty, it took you."

Lai's brow shot up at Deirdre's words. Sure, she knew she had sparked something, but to actually hear it said so plainly was a different matter.

"You did something a lot of us wish we could have done," Deirdre said.

"What, shoot a sergeant and rescue my cousin?"

Deirdre's smile returned. "Not exactly. You said no. You were faced with a situation you couldn't reconcile your beliefs with. Instead of continuing to deny what was in front of you, the very clear truth of what this country does, you acted with what you know is right. It may have been instinct, but it was the right instinct. In that moment, you told the rest of us that we're allowed to think another way too.

"You really did start something when you saved your cousin, Lailani. I could see it that very night. It forced all of us to think. It forced every single member of Beta Five to ask ourselves why we were working to uphold the ways of the Republic if we had doubts. You made us wish we had done it instead. Not save your cousin, that is, but say no. You said no in such a loud way that everyone else had to hear it."

"I don't know about all of that," Lai cut in. She could feel her cheeks heating up at the praise Deirdre was heaping on. "I just set you off. Everyone already thought what they did."

Deirdre only shrugged. "Beta Five is a strange group of teenagers," she continued, as if Lai hadn't spoken. "It was as if they found the doubters and threw us all into a training group. Though it wasn't just us, you know. Word got around about what you did. Word travels fast in the academy, but you knew that. At dinner, I heard some whispers. No one would have believed things were this bad, especially since they weren't there when Oscar gave his little speech, but I noticed it.

"Things aren't the same at Colonel Parks. I don't think they ever will be."

"But that's not a bad thing, right?"

"Are you kidding? It's the best thing any of us could have asked for."

The air in the building suddenly seemed quite a bit colder. "Let's just hope it doesn't end up killing us."

Deirdre turned to Lai, her eyes alight. "Even if it does, at least we can say it was worth it."

CHAPTER TWENTY

LAI CURSED under her breath as she fumbled with the zipper on her backpack. The teeth had caught in the lining, and no amount of pulling was making it budge.

"Jaime!" she called over her shoulder. Footsteps sounded behind her, announcing his approach.

"I've seen you empty a clip into the center of a target at seventy-five yards, and you can't get a zipper to cooperate?" Jaime teased. He snatched the bag from her hands and worked the zipper in his fingers for half a dozen seconds until it could slide smoothly.

"Shut up." She laughed. She gave him a friendly shove and grabbed her bag.

Lai double-checked that her gun was loaded and holstered it. She took a moment to check over her supplies laid out on the table in front of her, not wanting to miss anything.

"You look ready," Jaime observed.

"It's at least three days to St. Louis," Lai said absently. "Maybe more if we have to cut to the north. We all need to be ready."

Earlier that morning, Jackie had gathered all fourteen of them, minus Kieran, to explain in full what their plan was. They were to pack all of the supplies that could fit into the two trucks without slowing them down, as well as their own personal supplies. She told them to take everything they needed because once they left, they were driving to St. Louis.

When Lai asked what was in St. Louis, Jackie revealed it was the location of a permanent base. Unlike the one they currently inhabited, it was completely secure and used for main operations. With its encrypted network, it would be the optimal location for spreading the information they had acquired, aside from their main headquarters. Jackie refused to give up that location.

In the three days since the four students had arrived from the academy, Jackie had spent most of her time on the computers. Lai had been with her for half of it as they pored over files and determined they were legitimate. She then shooed Lai away with the claim that she needed to go over confidential information. That was when she would call over Sydney or Romana to assist her. When Lai talked to Angella, the woman simply shrugged and joked that it was above her pay grade.

Lai was glad that they finally had a plan. She was getting tired of the week spent in the warehouse and would be more than happy to never see it again. Jackie instructed them to leave at noon and threatened that anyone who kept them waiting would be walking to St. Louis.

Lai tapped her fingers against her holstered weapon and went through her mental checklist. She scanned the items on the table. She had her backpack with food and water for herself, an extra set of clothes, two extra handguns (courtesy of Angella), and half a dozen clips. Next to her bag was her jacket and belt. The belt had been given to her, along with two grenades and a smoke bomb. Though Lai had been less than pleased about the explosives, Jackie had insisted she keep a few on her for safety.

She brought her hand around to tap her right pocket. Inside was a flash drive entrusted to her by Jackie. She was told it contained a portion of the files recovered from the academy. Jackie explained that in the event they were captured, a few of them could still manage to get away with their files and find a way to release them to the public.

"How many charges do you have?" Lai asked when she was satisfied she had everything she needed.

"I've got two in my bag," Jaime told her. "My sister has another."

"Did you hear that Jackie is bringing two of the computers?"

"Es ridículo. Don't they have enough hard drives to store everything?"

"Apparently she has an attachment to the monitors themselves."

The two friends shared a laugh. Lai pulled on her jacket and looped the belt around her waist. She winced slightly as the muscles at her side pulled where Deirdre had hit her the day before. While nowhere near a serious injury, it still ached and likely would for the rest of the day at least.

"I'm just glad we have trucks this time," Jaime said. "I've done enough all-day walking."

"Agreed." Lai nodded.

"Usted niños están listos?" came a question from behind them. They both turned to see Angella making her way over.

"We're ready," Jaime confirmed.

"Have you ever been to this base?" Lai asked as Angella stopped next to them.

"*Sí*," Angella replied. "Twice. I haven't been in four years, though."

"What's it like?"

"It's a lot nicer than this one. For one thing, it's secure." Angella looked around them. "This was never supposed to be an active base. It used to be a refuge. Desperate times."

"I'm excited for the air-conditioning we have in St. Louis," Jackie told them as she strolled up to join them. "No more abandoned warehouses in the southwest."

"Damn it, Jackie, that's my gun," Angella said. She snatched the weapon out of Jackie's holster and shoved it into her own. "Lo robé en la redada, y yo soy el único que puede usarlo, ¿de acuerdo?"

"She always does this," Jackie complained. "Angella, you know Spanish was never one of my stronger languages."

"She basically told you not to touch her gun," Jaime explained.

"I didn't come over here to argue about weapons. I'm here to talk to the two of you." Jackie eyed Angella and Jaime. "We got a transmission from Jorge."

Angella instantly perked up. "Our father contacted you? When was this?"

"About two minutes ago. I only caught it because I was on the computer. I was about to wipe it. He's lucky he caught us in time. He sent the message through a back channel I didn't even know was still open."

"What did he say?" Angella demanded.

"He said that he managed to get away from the officers and get to a safe house in Wellton. He says it isn't safe for him to leave yet. I told him where we were going when he wanted to catch up."

"Can we talk to him?" Jaime asked.

"I wiped the computer after I sent the message," Jackie told them with a shake of her head.

"You couldn't have waited a minute to let us talk to him?" Angella groaned.

"We're leaving in five minutes. There wasn't time."

Angella let out a sigh but nonetheless seemed cheered by the news that her father was safe. Jaime seemed just as relieved.

Jackie turned to Lai. "You and Mel are riding with me," she said. "Grab her and meet me when you have your things."

"Got it." Lai nodded.

Jackie returned the nod and walked off without another word.

When Jackie had gone, Angella broke into a smile. "Nuestro padre está vivo," she said to her brother. Jaime returned the grin.

As the siblings spoke to each other in Spanish, Lai grabbed her things and excused herself. She let her backpack hang from one shoulder as she scanned the base for Mel. Her focus locked on to her as she came out of the room Kieran had been held in for the past three days. Deirdre came out after her, followed by Kieran and Benjamin, who held on to her arm. When Mel caught sight of Lai, she said something Lai couldn't catch and jogged over to meet her.

"That has to be the fourth time you've visited Kieran," Lai pointed out as Mel stopped beside her.

"It's still about twenty times less than her girlfriend visited her." Mel shrugged. "She's nice."

"She's sympathetic."

"Have you ever taken the time to get to know her?"

Lai couldn't say she had.

"Try talking to her without accusing her of anything," Mel suggested.

Lai clicked her tongue and gave her cousin a once-over. "You got everything you need? We're riding with Jackie."

"I'm going to say goodbye to Kieran for now. She's in the other truck, and I won't get to talk to her until tonight. I'll be a minute."

"Hurry!" Lai called after Mel as she jogged back to Kieran and Deirdre. Lai hiked her bag farther up on her shoulder and walked over to join Jackie.

Jackie stood by the computers with Romana and Sydney. She was speaking and signing to them as Lai approached. Angella and Jaime joined them a moment later.

"All right, people!" Jackie shouted, her hands moving as well to translate for Romana. All eyes turned to her. "We're ready to go. Make sure you take everything you need, because this is the last time you'll ever see this warehouse."

She lowered her voice and looked to Romana, signing as she spoke. "Can you grab Harrison and get the trucks ready? He should be just outside."

Romana nodded and headed for the door. Lai tuned out of the conversation and took a last look around the base. Mel was speaking with Kieran, and she waved to catch her eye. Mel gave her a thumbs-up. Lai's gaze fell to Romana as she reached the door.

Romana swung the door open and was greeted by a bullet through her skull.

The warehouse exploded with movement. Everything happened so fast that only thanks to her extensive training could Lai process it all.

Before Romana even hit the ground, Republic officers began swarming into the base. They were armed with handguns, a few with assault rifles, and all carried ballistic shields. They stormed through the door without pause and opened fire.

Lai's training kicked in. She dropped to the ground and rolled under the nearest table. She immediately kicked it over in front of her to form her own shield against the bullets raining down on them. It was nowhere near perfect, but a table was better than being out in the open.

Lai did her best to ignore the persistent ache in her side. She pulled her gun out and clicked off the safety as Jackie, Angella, and Jaime dove behind the table next to her. She spared a glance across the base to where she had seen Mel before the chaos. It seemed that Deirdre had a similar idea and had pulled down two tables to shield herself, Kieran, and Mel. Benjamin had gone behind the storage containers against the wall and was returning fire. Lai briefly searched for Sydney but saw no sign of him.

Jaime suddenly cried out and clutched at his prosthetic. Lai immediately noticed the bullet that had penetrated it. Wiring was sticking out of the hole and emitting sparks.

"We need better protection," Lai told the others urgently. As Angella was helping Jaime move farther behind cover, Lai directed her instruction to Jackie. The woman was staring ahead at nothing, her back pressed against the table. Lai figured she was in shock at seeing her friend murdered in front of her.

"Jackie!" Lai shouted. She gave Jackie's arm a shake until she looked over. "Romana is gone. Let's make the sure the rest of us stay alive."

The words seemed to snap Jackie out of her shock. "We can get some of the panels off the walls. Angella, help me."

Angella had gotten Jaime's prosthetic off and crawled over to join Jackie. The two of them dove for cover under another table and quickly flipped it to extend their barrier. They did the same with a third table and created a path to the wall. They began prying off the metal paneling.

Lai turned to Jaime. He seemed shaken by the malfunction of his prosthetic but otherwise unharmed. He had his own gun out in his lap.

"I'm going to return fire," Lai told him. She went to rise but came crashing back to the floor when Jaime grabbed her arm.

"Don't you dare, *asere*," he ordered. "You won't stand a chance."

"If I do nothing, we'll all end up dead," Lai said through clenched teeth. She yanked her arm away and spun around on her knees. Before Jaime could voice another plea, Lai had her head clear of the table and was firing back at the officers.

In the few seconds she was firing, Lai was able to quickly take stock of the situation. She counted at least fifteen officers, all firing at the various groups that hid behind tables or storage units. She could see at least three of the officers carried assault rifles, though none were firing with them yet. They had fallen into a standard formation that allowed half the squad to kneel in the front with their shields on the ground and half to stand behind them and fire over their heads.

An officer went down with a cry. Not wanting to push her luck any further, she ducked back behind the table.

Angella and Jackie were crawling back over with two metal panels each. They leaned all four of them up against the table.

"Does this base have a plan for a raid?" Lai asked.

"It doesn't," Jackie groaned. "It has never had a reason to be on their radar until now."

"*Letse*," Lai cursed under her breath. She reached for her backpack, for the first time noticing that it was no longer hanging from her shoulder. She instead reached into her pocket and pulled out one of the two extra clips she had decided to carry on her person. She loaded one into her gun.

"I counted fifteen," Lai told Jackie and Angella. "Three assault rifles, not in use for the time being. They've created a wall."

"Can we get through it?" Angella asked.

"We can, but it won't be easy. They're not messing around. They have real shields, not wall panels."

Lai looked back over to her cousin. Mel was crouched behind the table Deidre had flipped. Kieran kneeled next to her. Deirdre was rising above the table to return fire before quickly ducking back down.

"Why don't you throw a grenade?" Jackie suggested.

"We're too close," Lai argued. "We risk blowing every one of us up too."

Jackie replied by rising to barrage the officers with her own bullets.

Lai squeezed her eyes shut for a moment. To anyone speaking with her, she appeared to be collected and sure of herself. On the inside, she was scared to death.

This was entirely different from the raid on the truck. Five days earlier when she had bombed the officers, none of them had been shooting at her or her friends. She had been able to sneak right up to them and throw the grenade.

This time she was facing a squad that knew exactly where she was and that she and everyone else had very little protection. The thought alone terrified her.

She sucked in a deep breath and forced herself to focus. There would be time enough to have a breakdown when they got out alive.

As Jackie dropped behind the barrier, Lai rose to replace her. She focused her efforts on the officers standing. There were more openings for her bullets to sneak through. One of the officers in the back row convulsed where she stood and fell to the ground. Lai was sure it had been her bullet that hit its mark.

When she dropped down again, she spared another glance across the warehouse. Lai counted the clips that littered the ground. Deirdre appeared to have already gone through four of them, and likely had only another one or two left. If she ran out, they would be practically helpless.

Jaime grabbed Lai's arm again. "My prosthetic is ruined. I can't help you."

"We've got it," Lai assured him, hardly convinced she was telling the truth. She fingered one of the canisters on her belt. With a glance down, she picked out the smoke bomb.

"I can still throw this," Lai said. She held the bomb out for Jackie and Angella to see. Both women nodded their approval.

"Not just yet," Jackie decided. "We don't know where everyone else is. Sydney just disappeared."

As if on cue, Lai rose just in time to see Sydney and Carlton burst out of a storage unit with assault rifles on their shoulders. They shouted wordlessly and opened fire on the officers. Taken by surprise, they had little time to reposition their shields as bullets rained down on them. Lai saw four more fall to the ground.

Carlton suddenly crumpled to his knees as a bullet made contact with his stomach. Sydney moved to protect him. Before the officers could get their footing back, Angella and Jackie joined Lai and Sydney as they sent bullet after bullet flying through the air. The officers turned their attention to them as Sydney dragged Carlton back into a storage container. Lai saw two of the officers reach for their assault rifles.

The three of them ducked back down before they could sustain any injuries. Lai had to ditch another empty clip and replace it with her final one. A hand grasped her arm, and she turned to find Jaime holding out his gun to her.

"It's only got one clip, but it's better than nothing," he said.

Lai took it and nodded to her friend.

As she rested, Lai sought out her cousin once again. From what she could see, Mel was absolutely terrified. Kieran kneeled next to her and struggled with her handcuffs, to no avail. Deirdre loaded another clip into her gun. She placed a hand on Kieran's shoulder for a moment before she came up to fire another round.

A bullet embedded itself between Deirdre's eyes. She didn't make a sound as she fell to the ground.

Kieran let out the most heart-wrenching scream Lai had ever heard.

Lai froze. Her attention fixed on Deirdre's dead form and she refused to move.

Everything they had talked about the previous day flashed through her mind in a second.

"Let's just hope it doesn't end up killing us."

"Even if it does, at least we can say it was worth it."

She had seen dead bodies before. She had seen hundreds of dead bodies before.

She had never once seen the dead body of a friend.

Kieran struggled to pull Deirdre's head into her lap. Though the handcuffs impeded her abilities, Kieran finally managed. She leaned over as if to shield Deirdre's body.

A wave of emotions tumbled through Lai's head.

Sadness. A friend of hers had just died.

Fear. They were severely outmatched.

Anger. A friend of hers had just died.

Doubt. Deirdre was nearly as good a shot as Lai, and ten times as careful, and she was still dead.

Lai struggled to push her feelings aside and focus. She brought a hand to her head and grabbed a fistful of hair. She gave it a hard tug and felt tears spring to her eyes. She forced herself to take several deep breaths to get her racing thoughts under control.

"This isn't working," Angella mumbled beside her. Lai took comfort in Angella's steady tone and hooked on to it to bring herself back to the task at hand. She realized she was still fixed on the scene across the warehouse.

Kieran no longer had Deirdre's head in her lap. Instead she was kneeling over and beating her wrists violently against the ground. Lai assumed it was to get the handcuffs off.

When Lai rose to fire again, half of the remaining officers were advancing toward the table where Kieran and Mel still hid. She quickly fell back to her knees and turned to Jackie.

"Give me the handcuff key," she demanded. The tone of her voice allowed no room for disobedience. Jackie fished around in her pocket and pulled out the key. She placed it in Lai's hand.

"What are you doing?" Jackie questioned.

Lai shove the key in her pocket. She didn't spare the time it took to reply.

She grabbed one of the metal panels from the table and held it firmly. She didn't hesitate for a second before she launched to her feet and ran in a dead sprint toward the other tables. She heard Jaime calling after her, but she ignored him. His voice was quickly drowned out by the bullets that slammed into the panel.

When she reached the overturned table, Lai whipped the panel in the direction of the officers and slid the final few feet until she was safely behind it. She deliberately avoided seeing Deirdre's body.

Kieran looked up with tears streaming down her cheeks.

Lai held out one hand to Kieran and grabbed the key with the other. She held it up for her to see. "Hands."

Kieran wordlessly placed her bloodied wrists in Lai's hand and let her fit the key into place and undo the handcuffs. The second they were off, Kieran threw them forcefully across the warehouse. She then picked up Deirdre's gun and clutched it tightly in her hands.

"We need to keep going," Lai told her. "Right now, we need to keep going."

Kieran nodded and sniffed back her tears. Her face set in a hard glare, and her eyes burned with hatred.

"Let's kill these bastards," she hissed.

She and Lai rose above the table as one and fired at the advancing officers. Realizing they would indeed find a fight, they began to retreat, but not before Kieran had buried a bullet in an officer's neck. The gun clicked to tell her she was out of bullets. She ducked back down and tossed the gun aside with a growl. Lai handed her Jaime's gun. Kieran immediately got to shooting again.

Lai took a moment to check on her cousin. Mel appeared entirely unharmed, if frozen in utter terror. When Lai placed a hand on her shoulder, Mel started and slapped it away. When she realized it was only Lai, some of the tension released from her body. Lai forced a comforting smile.

"We've got this," she assured her, once again aware that she was lying.

Kieran fell to her knees with a pained cry. Lai snapped her head around to find two bullet holes in her right shoulder. Lai took her place above the table and emptied the rest of her clip. She cursed as she crouched down again.

"Hey!" Lai shouted across to the others. She got Angella's attention and waved her gun. Angella seemed to get the meaning and pulled a clip out of her pocket. She tossed it through the air. Lai held up her hands to catch it but found it was unnecessary. The clip hit the ground a few feet away and skidded to a stop just short of the edge of the table.

Angella shouted a curse in Spanish. Lai held back a groan and quickly reached out to grab the clip.

A bullet tore through Lai's hand.

She let out a wail and snatched her hand back. She cradled it to her chest and forced herself to look elsewhere. She knew if she saw the wound, she was likely to start openly crying. That was the last thing she needed.

Still, it burned. Lai bit her lip so hard she tasted blood. The pain flared out from her palm and made her fingers numb. She held back a cry by biting down harder on her lower lip.

In that moment, Lai truly believed she was going to die.

At least we can say it was worth it.

She looked to her cousin. Mel hadn't moved, though she was staring at Lai in shock. Kieran pressed her left hand against her bullet wounds and gritted her teeth. Lai turned to look across to the others.

She met Angella's eyes. Angella clearly knew how badly she had messed up. If she had thrown the clip the slightest bit farther, Lai would have two good hands and another round of bullets. As it was, she had left them with nothing.

She wouldn't reach for the clip again. Even if she had the nerve, if she got her other hand injured. then she was definitely dead. Not just her, Kieran and Mel as well. Even with the extra bullets, she didn't like their odds.

All at once, there was determination in Angella's features. The woman reached over and grabbed one of the metal panels. She shoved her gun into her waistband and held the panel tightly with both hands. Makeshift shield in hand, she rose to her feet and sprinted across the base.

Bullets rained down on her shield, but Angella did not slow. She stayed focused on her destination. When she reached the table where Lai hid, she kicked the clip the extra foot it needed for Lai to safely reach it.

The first bullet tore through her calf. Angella buckled, and her hold on the panel slipped. The second bullet hit her knuckles, and she dropped it altogether. The third hit her squarely in the throat, and blood spurted out onto the ground. The fourth, as if for good measure, went in through her right eye and out the back of her head.

Someone screamed. It took her a long moment to realize that the scream was coming from her own throat. She didn't want to believe what she had just seen. She couldn't believe it.

And yet Angella was lying on her back in a pool of her own blood.

Lai felt the emotions coming once again. This time only one stuck.

Rage. They were going to pay for this.

Lai sprang into action. She held her gun between her thighs and used her right hand to insert the clip. The one Angella had just died for.

With her left hand hanging limply at her side, Lai rose to her knees and fired. She was not wasteful. She took the extra millisecond she needed to ascertain her aim and fired only one bullet at a time. The majority of them found their marks. Out of the corner of her eye, she could see Jackie was firing with her.

When she had only two bullets left, Lai crouched down and shoved her gun into her holster. Her gaze fell on Angella as she grabbed the smoke bomb and yanked the pin out with her teeth. She threw it over the table and waited for the explosion.

When it came, she didn't waste a second. She pulled her gun back out and this time stood. She walked out from behind the table, stepping over Angella's body. Jackie met her in the middle with a panel in one hand as a shield. They heard the cries from the few officers that were still alive. They fell out of the cloud of smoke and to the mercy of Lai and Jackie.

Jackie put a bullet in the heads of the first two who emerged from the cloud. When the third man staggered out, Lai fired twice. The first, a few seconds before the kill shot, she aimed at his crotch.

Just for good measure.

All of a sudden, it was over.

The smoke began to dissipate. Jackie kept her weapon raised in case there were any officers left alive. Lai didn't bother, as she knew she had used her last bullet. When they could see clearly, they knew there wasn't an officer still breathing.

"All clear," Lai called out, her voice hoarse. A few pairs of footsteps sounded as some of those left alive came out from where they had been hiding.

Lai turned around and took a few shaky steps forward. She only got half as far as she wanted to go before she fell to her knees. She heard a high-pitched whining, and once again realized that she was the source. She clamped her mouth shut and forced the sound to die in her throat.

Lai felt herself going numb. She went to clench her fists and remembered too late that her left hand was gravely injured. She hissed through her teeth and held the hand against her chest with the other atop it to stem the bleeding.

Jaime dragged himself out from behind the table. He pulled himself along to where his sister lay in a pool of red. When he reached her, he didn't make a sound. He simply knelt next to her, the blood soaking into his pants, and stared at her face. His expression was neutral except for his slightly widened eyes.

A cry came from behind her and she turned to see Jackie kneeling over Romana's body. She sobbed quietly to herself and let her head fall to rest on her friend's chest.

Footsteps alerted Lai to Virginia and Rylen approaching her. They appeared to have taken cover in the storage containers with Sydney and Carlton. Virginia's arms and the front of her shirt were covered in blood, though Lai could see no obvious injury. Rylen appeared unharmed.

Lai snapped her head back around when she heard a loud crash. Kieran had kicked the table over. She stood panting for a moment, the blood dripping from her shoulder, before she dropped to her knees and screamed.

Lai forced herself to her feet and walked calmly in the direction of her friends. Angella and Deirdre's bodies lay only a few feet apart. Lai stopped halfway between the two of them and stared at the floor, her breathing heavy. She felt dizzy from the blood loss.

Mel had snapped out of her stupor and was kneeling next to Kieran. As the girl screamed, Mel put pressure on her shoulder. Mel looked up and fixed her focus on her Lai, the tears pouring down her face.

"We're leaving in ten minutes!" Jackie yelled suddenly. Lai glanced behind her at the woman still kneeling over Romana. "If they send more officers, we're all dead. And somebody get handcuffs back on that kid!"

Benjamin limped toward Kieran. He pulled a pair of handcuffs from his belt. The sight, mixed with Kieran's screams, brought Lai back to herself.

"Don't you touch her!" Lai shouted. She planted herself firmly in front of Kieran. Benjamin faltered for a second before continuing on. When he reached Lai, she gave him a mighty shove with her good hand that nearly caused him to topple over.

"Don't you dare touch her!" Lai screeched. "No one is going to touch her!"

She fixed him with a look so intense that Benjamin didn't dare take another step forward.

Lai clenched her teeth and glared at everyone in front of her. When her gaze fell to Angella, and to Jaime still kneeling unmoving over her, she had to fight with everything she had to keep her composure.

With Kieran screaming over her dead girlfriend, Jaime staring numbly at his dead sister, the woman Lai had grown to admire lying on the ground with four bullets in her, one thought made its way to the forefront of Lai's mind.

This is my life now.

Chapter Twenty-One

OSCAR SPOONED a mouthful of cereal into his mouth and counted the number of times the entry door opened and closed. So far it had been used twenty-seven times that day. Most of the people going through were guards. Four had been prisoner transfers. Two were the cook.

It had become a habit of his to count things. It helped him keep a hold on the reality of his situation. He counted sounds, people, how many spoonfuls of cereal it took to finish his bowl. He counted the ceiling tiles, bars on the windows, chairs around the tables. He counted them all, and then counted them again. It was a constant task. It left him little time to consider his circumstances. Even on this day, the day he should be dreading, he counted as if nothing had changed.

As if it wasn't his execution day.

He brought the plastic bowl to his lips and drank the rest of the milk from the bottom. When he was finished, he wiped a hand over his mouth and placed the bowl gently on the table. He then counted the number of people in the holding room.

Fifty-six. Including himself, there were forty-five prisoners and eleven guards. Oscar knew that, as the prisoners outnumbered the guards four to one, it would be easy to overpower them. That is, if they weren't all shackled by their ankles to their tables. The farthest they could get was two feet from where they sat. In the past hour, four of the prisoners had tried to pull away. They had all been rewarded for their efforts with the sting of a Taser.

Oscar didn't bother with escape. Over the past two weeks, he hadn't tried to escape even once. The same could be said for only a handful of his fellow walking dead. It seemed that most of his group wanted to go out fighting. They had always been the easiest to kill.

The hardest were the ones who didn't try at all. They were the ones who shuffled into the training room, their feet dragging on the ground as the officers shoved them forward. They usually looked down and made very little noise, as if they had simply given up. It was hardly unexpected. When faced with certain death, it was a perfectly logical reaction for a person to shut down mentally, to make themselves numb rather than face the reality of where they were and what was about to happen to them.

Oscar was one such prisoner. He occupied himself with trivial tasks and kept his mind from his fate.

There was a girl, Nicola, who had taken to sitting next to him when they were gathered in the eating area. Oscar had spoken to her one week earlier when he first arrived at the academy as a live target. She told him she had been there for nearly a month. She didn't understand why they made prisoners wait for so long. She would have preferred to get it over with.

After that, Oscar hadn't spoken to her, though he let her speak to him. She didn't seem to mind his silence. She spoke of her family, of her friends, of her life before her crimes. She told him she was from Minneapolis, born and raised. This was the first time she had been away from home.

He didn't ask her what she had done, but she told him anyway. She had been on a walk with her younger brother, Thom. He was twelve, only five years younger than she. They walked through the back alleys of the city, as they had done countless times before.

She told him how a man had appeared out of nowhere and tried to grab Thom. A crowbar leaned against a garbage bin and she grabbed it. She swung it mightily and cleaved his head open.

Pleading self-defense did no good. She was sentenced to death by the courts.

Oscar took comfort in having her near, much as it pained him to know she would be dead soon. Still, it was better than being alone. Even his meaningless counting could not dispel the loneliness.

Nicola was also the only other person under twenty currently residing in the academy. If he wanted a friend, she was better than a grown man who had murdered someone out of spite rather than in defense of a loved one.

Oscar felt her hand rest on top of his where it lay on the table. He did not look over as she squeezed it and whispered a comfort to him. As if it would help. As if they weren't both about to be executed.

In a strange way, Oscar was glad he had been taken to an academy up north. There was no chance of seeing someone he knew. He knew everyone at Colonel Parks and couldn't imagine having one of his friends execute him. During one of the brief moments he allowed himself to truly think, he considered whether it was worse to be killed by a friend, or to be the one doing the killing.

He knew they were at the Duluth Academy, named after the city it resided in. It was one of the smaller training academies, and one without a standing Protection Force. Unlike Colonel Parks, which was remote enough to need a full operations center, Duluth Academy was like most northern academies. The only officers were guards and the ones who trained students.

It was a smart move to take him north. He knew the official story was that he was mentally unstable. After his breakdown, he had been pulled out of training and taken to the med bay. He was handcuffed to a bed and given a sedative that kept him out for the rest of the day. That night, when he finally awoke, it was to two guards pulling him upright and informing him that he had been sentenced to death for treason. In his highly medicated state, he wasn't coherent enough to argue as he was named a member of the *Libertas Publica*.

He was kept in a holding cell with other prisoners awaiting execution. When the sedative had fully worn off, he shouted that he was innocent, that he had been set up. The other prisoners mockingly claimed the same. For four days he reverted to much the same way he had been after learning of the wrongfully executed citizens, ranting and screaming of the injustices committed by the state. It infuriated him to learn of such a practice, even more so when he saw most of the victims were not white, though the latter part was hardly surprising.

By the time he was transferred to Duluth, it had set in that he was such a victim, and yet he found an odd peace with his circumstances. He knew he was innocent. He knew his only crime was finding those records, which was hardly something you could be executed for. His real crime, his crime in the eyes of the Republic, was being a threat to order. His knowledge made him dangerous, even if he was in a hospital.

Oscar had one small victory. He had told Lai and Jaime. He'd told them everything. He also got part of it out to the rest of his training unit before the guards dragged him away. Even if he couldn't live to get the information out, he trusted his friends to do it. That was what allowed him to be at peace.

When he heard the buzzing of the alarm, he knew it was time. Nicola removed her hand from his and placed hers flat on the table, the same as he did. Some of the other prisoners did the same, while some crossed their arms indignantly and scowled at the guards as they were forced into handcuffs.

Oscar didn't fight. He let a guard remove his ankle shackles, cuff his hands, and pull him up. Nicola was pulled up beside him, and she stifled a cry. All around, the forty-four inmates protested, some halfhearted, some more forcible. He did not bother to make a sound. He knew the end was near. He was going to retain a small shred of his dignity and keep his feelings to himself.

He counted the number of times a prisoner begged for their life.

It took about five minutes for the guards to get every prisoner under control. Though some still protested verbally, everyone was cooperating with the commands. The guards had everyone fall into a line along the side wall and around to the back. Oscar shuffled along with his feet still shackled together and took his place under one of the windows. Nicola fell in behind him and put her hands on his arm. He twitched his arm back in acknowledgment of the comfort but said nothing.

The guards separated them into groups of fifteen. Oscar's group cut off two behind Nicola. Their handcuffs were then connected with lengths of chain that prevented them from moving apart. The first group was taken out of the room. A few minutes passed, and a guard walked by and yanked on the chains between each prisoner before his group was led out as well.

They were stopped moments later and made to wait in the long hall outside of the eating area. The paneled blue walls were windowless, and the only light came from the flickering fluorescent bulbs in the ceiling. Oscar hated fluorescent lights. They had always given him a headache.

"Oscar?"

He twisted his head around to Nicola. Her tangle of dark brown hair hung in front of her face so her bangs hid her eyes. It did not fully hide the tears that slid down her cheeks.

"Thanks for letting me talk to you," she said quietly.

Oscar nodded once and went to turn back around.

"Oscar?"

He faced her once again after a quick glance at the guards. None seemed to be paying attention.

"You never told me what you're here for."

Oscar stared at her for a long moment. He liked Nicola. She talked a bit too much, but she was nice. She gave him something else to focus on. She didn't pressure him to talk. He knew if he were not to answer, she wouldn't ask again. But despite his decision to remain silent until the end, with the end being so close, he felt his resolve weakening.

"I was falsely accused of treason and sentenced to death because I discovered incriminating evidence against the Republic," he replied simply.

Nicola's mouth fell open.

Oscar turned his head back when a guard walked past them. He was carrying a black duffel bag, and he stopped before the first prisoner in line. He pulled smaller brown cloth bags out and placed them over the heads of the prisoners. When he was halfway through, Oscar turned back one last time to Nicola.

"Thank you for talking to me," he said.

It seemed that she could not manage a smile.

A bag was shoved over Oscar's head. He took several deep breaths and closed his eyes. Within seconds, he was being pulled along behind the prisoner in front of him. He counted the steps it took to reach the training area.

Eight hundred forty-two. A door opened in front of them, though they only slowed rather than came to a stop. Once through, the air was filled with the chatter of the fifteen students who were either distracting themselves with idle conversation or watching their targets being marched to their stations.

Someone put their hand on Oscar's shoulder to stop him. He was roughly turned around, and his handcuffs were yanked as the chain was released from them. His hands were then lifted over his head and connected to the bolts he knew were on the wall. He had seen this happen to countless prisoners since beginning his own training.

A moment later the bag was pulled from his head. He blinked against the sudden brightness of the lights in the training room. When his vision returned to him, he immediately looked to his left. Nicola already had her bag removed and was looking around the room in obvious fright. She met Oscar's eyes momentarily. The expression on her face could have made him cry.

Instead, he faced the students waiting to end his life. When their sergeant called for them to approach their stations, Oscar kept his focus on the girl who made her way over to the station he was at. She was about sixteen, with wide eyes and curly red hair. He idly wondered at her story, what had made her think to join an academy.

Perhaps she was a foster kid with no viable options but enlisting. Maybe it was the opposite, and she came from a rich family and felt the need to prove herself. Or maybe, like Oscar, she honestly thought she would be doing good, that her purpose was to help people.

For one odd moment, Oscar felt sorry for her. She had no idea what she was doing, no way of knowing that she was executing a falsely convicted teenager who only two weeks earlier had been in the same position as she.

The girl kept her eyes on Oscar as her sergeant gave the command to ready their weapons. She clicked off the safety without breaking her gaze.

It was then that Oscar did something even he could not explain. He smiled at her.

The girl frowned, and her grip on her gun faltered for a moment. He had expected as much of a reaction. He himself had never had a prisoner smile at him before they were to be executed. He had been yelled at, cursed, listened as they begged for their life, but never once had he seen his target smile.

He knew it wouldn't change anything. One smile wasn't going to save his life. What it would do was make her think, even for just a moment. That was something any other prisoner would never give her the opportunity to do.

On command, she raised her weapon and trained it between his eyes. Oscar spared a quick glance over to Nicola. She had ceased crying and now stared ahead with the most heartbroken expression he had ever seen. He wished he could say something to comfort her, but his words would be empty. When you were about to die, nothing could truly bring you solace. He returned his gaze forward and held the smile firmly on his face. He was determined to go out with it.

With only seconds left to live, Oscar closed his eyes and waited for death to find him.

Chapter Twenty-Two

THE TRUCK lurched underneath them, and Lai instinctively shot out her hand to steady herself. She remembered her injury too late and hissed at the pain of disturbing her gunshot wound.

"You're going to make it bleed again," Mel chided.

Lai rested her hand on her head and took several deep breaths. She forced herself not to glare at Mel. It was hardly her fault that Lai couldn't remember to be conscious of her injury.

Across the truck, Kieran sat, leaning against the fabric that covered the window to separate the cab from the bed. She pressed on her own wounds and directed a glare ahead of her. She had been sitting that way for the past two hours and had only moved to switch the recipient of her dirty look.

Lai couldn't blame her for her reaction. Everyone dealt with grief differently. It appeared that Kieran handled it by attempting to set fire to people and objects with her gaze.

Several feet down the bench sat Jaime. He had the same blank expression on his face, which he fixed on the floor of the truck bed. One of his hands rested on his ruined prosthetic. The nerve connections had been interrupted when he was shot, so now it hung limply from his leg, all but useless. Lai watched him and swallowed hard.

"Should we be worried about him?" Mel asked.

Lai stared at Mel for a long moment before she answered. "He did the same thing when he heard that his mother had died. He needs time to process it."

Lai was surprising herself at her ability to remain outwardly calm. It wasn't that she usually reacted with emotional outbursts, rather that she had never been in such a situation as she had a couple hours before and would have expected a stronger response. Perhaps the scream and the whine at the base was all she had the energy for.

She glanced to Mel sitting next to her. Mel seemed to cope by talking too much.

"Where do you think those officers came from?"

"They were probably dispatched from the academy," Lai told her with a sigh. Though she would rather remain silent, she recognized Mel's need for conversation.

"I thought it was only for training. I didn't know it had active officers."

"It multitasks."

"Do all of the academies have active officers?"

"Not all of them. The ones in major cities are training only. Colonel Parks is isolated from any operations facilities, which is why we have a partial force active at all times. It's supposed to keep the area secure."

"And kill innocent teenagers," Kieran snapped.

Lai and Mel both turned to the girl. She directed her glare to them for a moment before staring out the back of the truck.

Though Kieran had been mostly silent, she had spoken up every so often with a biting remark. Even if she had wanted to, Lai knew better than to argue with Kieran. She figured that one wrong word could set her off.

"How could they have found us?" Mel asked in a quieter voice.

Lai rubbed her eyes with the heel of her good hand, one after the other. "I don't know. Maybe they connected the bombing to a suspected location."

"Well, do you think—"

"Mel!" Lai suddenly shouted. She forced herself to speak more softly. "I don't know. I can't keep talking about this. I'm sorry."

Mel folded into herself and frowned. "So am I." She kicked her legs up onto the bench and rested her head on her hands.

Lai felt bad for shouting at Mel, but she did not have enough patience for a real apology. Her head was pounding, her hand was throbbing, and though it was only half past two, she felt as if she had been awake for days. In the silence, the one she was regretting having asked for, her mind drifted back to the events of the day.

With Romana dead, they were at a loss for a medic. Virginia was the next best thing. Though she was hardly an expert and had little training, she had done two extra rotations at the academy in field medicine. That made her more qualified than anyone else still alive. After five minutes of letting Kieran scream and yell and punch things, Lai had let Virginia through her one-woman barrier to examine Kieran's wounds. She determined that as long as a bandage was applied and pressure was kept constant, Kieran would live without serious medical attention until they reached their first stop in Santa Fe.

After dressing Kieran's shoulder, Virginia made Lai sit down before she fainted from the blood loss of her own injury. Virginia had yelled for someone to get her a med kit and, while repeatedly reminding Lai that she had very little training, cleaned the wound with a stinging liquid Lai could not identify before stuffing it with gauze, wrapping it in bandages, and instructing her to keep pressure on it. Virginia told Lai that she would have liked to come with her on the ride, but she had to focus on Carlton.

When Carlton had taken a shot to his abdomen, Sydney had dragged him back into the storage container where they had been taking refuge with Rylen and Virginia. He was passed off to Virginia for care while Sydney and Rylen returned to the shootout.

Virginia told Jackie that in all likelihood, Carlton would be dead in two hours if he didn't get proper medical treatment, but they all knew that was not an option. Instead he had been loaded into the back of the truck being driven by Sydney, and Virginia had promised to continue working on him for as long as she could.

They hadn't a second to spare before Jackie was shouting orders. They split into two groups and loaded into the trucks for a long drive to Santa Fe.

Lai knew they still had five or six hours to go. That was plenty of time to think about the people she had seen shot down in front of her.

Against her will, the scene of Angella's death played in her mind like a movie. It was different with the others. She hadn't seen Harrison and Anya, the other two *Libertas Publica* members who were at the base, be shot. With Romana, there was no time to sit around and stare, and Lai hardly knew her. Deirdre was at least quick. Angella was something else.

Though Lai had only known the woman for a week, she had grown to admire Angella in a way she couldn't fathom. Since the raid on the transport vehicle, Angella had acted differently around Lai. She'd no longer appeared to be keeping an eye on her as if she might betray them at any moment, as Lai had seen her the day they headed out for Maricopa. Instead she seemed to genuinely enjoy Lai's company and want to talk to her. It was something Lai had not expected, but it was not unwelcome.

Lai idly wondered how much closer they would have grown if Angella was still alive. The thought only brought more pain than was necessary, and Lai forced it from her mind. It was easier than getting the image of her death to clear out.

The death that Lai had been responsible for.

There was a part of her that believed she couldn't have done anything differently, that Angella had made the decision to run across to help them. A more dominant part thought that if she had been more careful and not gotten her hand shot, there would have been no need for Angella to come to their aid.

Lai had yet to voice these thoughts aloud. She could already anticipate some of the results if she did. Mel would sit close by her side and insist she wasn't responsible for the actions of others. Kieran would tell her she was being an idiot. Jaime, however, was a different story. This was his sister. Were Lai to voice her worries, it was possible he would lock on to her as someone to blame.

Her eyes drifted to her friend. The last thing she needed at the moment was someone other than herself to blame her for Angella. She promptly decided she would keep her thoughts to herself.

To her credit, Lai remembered not to use her left hand to steady herself when the truck lurched again.

"Will someone go up there and tell that woman to be careful?" Kieran grumbled.

Lai rose to her feet. Perhaps she would have an easier time sorting through her thoughts in the front seat.

Maneuvering herself around the boxes and bags that were hastily stacked and tied down with rope on the floor of the truck bed, Lai braced her feet firmly against two boxes and pulled the fabric cover aside from the window. She handed it off to Kieran, who took it with only a momentary glare in Lai's direction. Lai slid the window open and gradually pulled herself through feet first into the cab.

Jackie spared her the shortest of glances when Lai lowered herself into the passenger seat and closed the window behind her. Lai pulled the seat belt over her shoulder and clicked it into the buckle on the seat.

"Kieran wants you to drive more carefully," Lai told her.

"Does she now?" Jackie said. Lai could not detect any change in speed or driving pattern, but she did not press it further. "Mind if I keep you company?"

"As long as you don't get blood on the seat."

"This isn't even your truck. You stole it."

Jackie did not respond.

Lai elected to remain silent. She stared out the window and busied herself with admiring the scenery, not that there was much of anything to admire.

Since they had traveled farther north, the desert receded slightly to allow trees to grow. As it was late in the summer, the sun shone blindingly golden in the sky. All Lai could see around them were half-dead trees, piles of rock, sand, and the cracked pavement stretching ahead of them. In the side mirror, the other truck was visible, following closely behind. She hadn't heard any other vehicles since they left the city.

It took a total of three minutes for Lai to grow bored of the desolate landscape. As if Jackie could sense this, she spoke up.

"How's your hand?" she asked.

Lai turned her hand over. "It still hurts like hell," she said with a wince. "At least it stopped bleeding."

"As long as you're okay for another seven hours."

"I'll manage."

They fell back into silence for another ten or so minutes. Lai spent most of it looking in the side mirror.

"How is everybody holding up?" Jackie finally asked.

"You're concerned?"

"Those were my friends too." Jackie's hands tightened on the steering wheel. "I've known Romana since I was seven."

"I'm sorry about her," Lai said softly. Her attention was still on the mirror when Jackie breathed out a loud sigh.

"And about your friend."

Lai gave an almost imperceptible shake of her head. "Kieran has it worse than I do. Those two were inseparable from the moment we all joined the same Beta group."

In fact, Lai could hardly remember a moment when she had seen them apart for more than a few hours. The only time that stuck out in her mind was a training exercise they went on about a year before. They were split into three groups, and Lai had ended up with Deirdre in hers. During even half a minute of downtime, all Deirdre could talk about was her girlfriend.

Lai saw the bullet hit between Deirdre's eyes. "Can I ask you a question?"

Jackie nodded for her to continue.

Lai stared out the front window and watched the faded white lines in the pavement fly past. "Why didn't you and Angella get along?"

Lai felt the truck swerve for a brief moment before Jackie straightened them again. She did not respond right away. Lai wasn't sure if she was going to and decided that she would not ask again. For another several minutes, they drove in silence.

"We were friends when I first joined."

Lai turned to Jackie when she finally answered.

Jackie kept her eyes securely on the road. "I met her when we were both nineteen," she continued. "She had already been a member for nearly two years. My parents kept me from being an official member as long as they could. They weren't sympathetic, but they didn't want me in trouble. When I officially joined, Angella and Salomé showed me the ropes. Salomé was the one who got Angella to join."

"She told me."

"I'm sure she did." Jackie paused to take another deep breath. "The three of us moved up the ranks together. We got our first real assignments all within a week of one another. Other than Romana, they were my closest friends in the *Libertas Publica*.

"Five years ago, there was a raid on one of our bases. We were all there when it happened. Angella was in a small group that went to secure the information we had on hand. Salomé was in another group with me and Romana. We were supposed to be the first line of defense when the officers broke through to the central command rooms. We came under fire.

"Your position in the *Libertas Publica* has nothing to do with how old you are. It only matters how good you are. The commander decided I was a good leader, so she put me in charge of the defense of the base. It was my call for us to stay and fight rather than get to safety. I still believe it was the right decision. We got most of our valuable information onto external drives before we had to wipe the computers. If we had left any earlier, we would have lost a lot more."

Lai was beginning to understand where this story was going. She had already heard the ending.

"Salomé was captured," she said.

Jackie paused for a long moment before she nodded. "She and two others. They were all executed for treason. Angella never forgave me for that."

"But that wasn't your fault," Lai insisted.

"Angella never saw it that way. I made the call for us to stay. She thought if we had fallen back earlier, then Salomé would still be alive.

"After that raid, I continued to receive leadership assignments. Angella switched to covert operations, and we rarely saw each other unless I was in command of her unit. She never gave up a chance to question my decisions. I don't think she kept hating me, but she wouldn't let it go either. Now she gets herself killed under my command. It's funny how things work out."

Lai couldn't even be surprised when Jackie's voice faltered. She realized all of a sudden that the two of them were thinking much the same way in the aftermath. Jackie blamed herself. Lai almost felt silly. Here she was, blaming herself for one death when Jackie was thinking herself responsible for all five, likely six as Carlton wouldn't last much longer.

"This wasn't your fault either," Lai said to her.

Jackie laughed without humor. "You sure about that? It feels like it is."

"I get that," Lai sighed.

Jackie eyed her, and her expression softened. "Why don't we split the blame for her? It might make us both feel better."

Lai stared at her lap and played with a corner of the bandage on her hand. "I can live with that."

Jackie nodded as she pulled them around a corner. From the back came the scraping of boxes as they shifted.

"Do you mind if I leave you alone again?"

Jackie shrugged. "Be my guest."

Lai undid her seat belt and gingerly turned around. She slid open the window again and pulled herself through. She took a hand she was offered on the other side and used it to keep herself steady as she got her footing in the truck bed. When the fabric had fallen out of her face, she checked to see whose hand she had taken and was surprised to see it belonged to Kieran.

"Did you even bother telling her to be careful?" she asked.

Lai sat down next to her and shrugged a shoulder. "Jackie doesn't take orders very well."

Lai noted that Kieran's glare had receded to a less vicious frown.

"How's your shoulder?" Lai asked her.

"Probably about the same as your hand." Kieran nodded to where Mel was lying with her eyes closed. "She somehow managed to fall asleep."

"So you're really talking now?"

Kieran's glare returned. "The quiet was bothering me."

Lai met her gaze evenly. She waited patiently until the glare settled down once again. "I'm sorry."

Kieran took a long moment to respond. "They didn't even stop to see who they were firing on. For all they know, they could have been killing captives. They didn't stop for one second."

Kieran squeezed her eyes shut. Moisture leaked around her eyes, and Lai figured that Kieran didn't want to start crying again. She had already done enough of that back at the base.

Of all the reactions she had seen, and as much as her own confused her, Lai was the most put off by Kieran's outburst. She had seen Kieran get angry enough to scream at a person. A fit of anger would have been nothing new. The anguished screaming and the crying were what truly caused Lai to shudder.

Though both had polar opposite reactions at watching a loved one die, Kieran's and Jaime's reactions were equally disconcerting. The only reason Lai wasn't more concerned for Jaime's lack of reaction was because she had seen it before. With Kieran, it was something entirely new.

Lai knew that she was unlikely to get thanks for keeping anyone from putting Kieran in handcuffs again. That was another thing Lai had thought about over the past two and a half hours. She concluded the reason she had gone into protection mode for a girl who had been nothing but mean to her from the moment they met was because it was something she could actually do. With Jaime she felt helpless. With Kieran, she could provide a shred of help. It made her feel marginally less useless after she had watched her friends die.

Her gaze strayed to Kieran's wrists. She noticed once again the cuts at irregular intervals where the cuffs had dug into her skin when she had slammed them against the ground to get them off. Her hands and arms were still stained with blood, though the cuts had since clotted and dried over. Apparently Kieran had little motivation to clean them up.

Lai reached across the truck bed to where a bag was pushed under the bench. She pulled it over and unzipped it to reveal several folded sheets. Pulling the edge of the top one out, she held one corner in her teeth and used her good hand to tear two squares of material off. Kieran frowned at her as she returned the bag to its place under the bench. Lai reached into her personal bag and grabbed her water bottle. She carefully wetted one of the squares.

"May I?" Lai asked.

Kieran stared for several seconds before she nodded.

Lai took Kieran's left hand and had her rest it on her knee. She washed away the blood as she spoke. "I talked to her."

Kieran frowned. "Talked to her how?"

"The day after you all got here. Mel went to see you and talk about whatever you two talked about. Deirdre came over and asked if I wanted to practice shooting with her."

Kieran's reply was a long time in coming. "She didn't tell me that."

"Who knows? It didn't seem like anything at the time. She told me more about how she grew up. I never knew about her mother."

"She doesn't like to talk about it."

"I can imagine why…. She talked about you too."

The barest hint of a smile ghosted across Kieran's face, though it was quickly overshadowed by her pain.

Lai paused in her cleaning and waited until Kieran met her gaze. "Kieran, I am so sorry for what happened to her. She may have been my friend, but until we talked, I don't think I realized just how much she loved you."

Lai let the silence drag on for a dozen seconds before she went back to cleaning. "I never understood you two."

"You never did like me," Kieran said. "Not that I helped that."

"You really didn't." Lai offered a pained smile. "But I think I understand, at least a little. She was patient, something I never bothered to be."

In fact, no one else but Virginia had ever given Kieran much thought further than how to avoid her foul moods. Deirdre's patience was apparently used for more than combat.

"Do you know what you're going to do now?" Lai asked.

Kieran shook her head and stared at her hand as Lai cleaned it. "I was following her. I only left because she asked me to. Every plan had her in it."

"After this I don't think you could go back to training."

Kieran laughed bitterly. "After what they did to her, you honestly think I could be one of them?" She flinched when Lai pulled the fabric over a cut on her wrist.

"I guess not." Lai gently took hold of Kieran's right hand and brought it forward to replace her left. Kieran sucked in a sharp breath.

"You okay?" Lai asked. She checked Kieran's shoulder but did not see any new blood on her bandages.

Kieran nodded quickly.

"The *Libertas Publica* might let you stay," Lai continued.

"How are you so calm?" Kieran asked.

Lai frowned at the change in conversation. She busied herself with cleaning the blood to give herself time to answer. "I'm not calm," she finally admitted. "I only seem calm."

"You *seem* very calm."

"It's probably a coping mechanism. I'm not used to this sort of thing."

"What, and I am?"

Lai ignored her biting tone. She took extra care not to agitate Kieran's shoulder as she drew the cloth over the girl's wrist. "We all deal with these things in our own way."

"Were you close? With Angella, I mean."

"I barely knew her."

"That's not what I asked you."

Lai sighed heavily. "We were getting there."

"Then I'm sorry too."

Lai tilted her head toward Jaime. "He took it harder."

"He doesn't seem to be doing anything at all," Kieran pointed out.

"Do you remember a year ago, when Jaime got the news that his mother had passed?" Lai asked her.

Kieran thought for a second and nodded. "He was like this."

"Like I said, in our own way."

Lai finished cleaning the blood and used her teeth to rip the other square of fabric in half. "Help me tie these."

With neither having the full use of both of their hands, Lai and Kieran had quite a time getting both strips tied around Kieran's wrists.

When Lai had to use her teeth to secure one, she seriously considered waking Mel to do it for them.

After they successfully secured the strips, Kieran let both wrists fall into her lap. She peered at Lai curiously for a long moment. "You're less annoying than usual."

"I could say the same about you," Lai replied.

A hint of a smile appeared on Kieran's face. It was the first one Lai had seen since she had arrived at the base.

Kieran seemed like she had more to say, but she held her tongue. Lai could tell she was uncomfortable with whatever she was about to say. Kieran looked down and rotated her left wrist several times. Her smile had faded.

"Why are you being nice to me?"

Knowing that Kieran was referring to more than just the work on her wrists, Lai took a moment to find the right answer rather than the quick one. "Despite our differences, you need someone on your side right now. I don't mind being that person."

"But you don't like me," Kieran pointed out. She brought her gaze up to meet Lai's.

"I don't know you very well. You still need a friend."

"So we're friends now?"

Lai allowed herself to smile. "Maybe one day."

The modest smile returned momentarily. "I still don't like the LP," Kieran said in response to Lai's earlier suggestion. "But I suppose now they're a means to an end."

"What end is that?"

Any hint of a smile disappeared just as suddenly at it had appeared. Her eyes burned with the same intensity Lai had seen only moments after she watched her girlfriend die.

"That end is revenge for what they did to her. That end is the Republic being completely destroyed. I am going to tear it apart if I have to shoot the president in the head myself."

CHAPTER TWENTY-THREE

SHORTLY BEFORE the clock on the dash changed to nine o'clock, Jackie turned off the main road and pulled the truck into a small shopping center. Lai stared out the front window as Jackie drove them to the far end of the parking lot, the farthest they could be from the shops while still near an exit. She parked the truck in a row of empty stalls. A moment later, the other truck pulled in two stalls away. Jackie had barely turned the engine off when she launched out of her door and headed to the back of the other truck. Lai followed more slowly.

Sydney reached the back at the same time as she did. By the expression on his face, Lai knew what had happened.

Her worries were confirmed when Jackie let out a choked cry and covered her mouth with a hand. Benjamin, Rylen, and Virginia all jumped out of the back as Jackie went in. Rylen and Virginia approached Lai as Benjamin went to talk with Sydney. Lai noted that while Virginia had changed her shirt, her arms and hands were still stained with blood.

"When did it happen?" Lai asked.

"Not even two hours after we left," Virginia told her solemnly. She shook her head and clenched her fists tight. "I tried, but Carlton needed surgery. I tried."

Rylen put a comforting hand on her shoulder. "We know you did. He wouldn't have lasted even that long without you."

"Then why do I feel like I failed?" she mumbled. She noticed Lai's bandaged hand. "I need to examine that."

With the last hints of sunlight fading from the sky and the dim, flickering lampposts spaced too far apart from one another, it was impossible to see clearly in the parking lot. Virginia led her back to the cab of the truck Lai had ridden in and pulled open the door. She directed Lai to sit in the front seat, pulled on a pair of too big sanitary gloves, and used the light from inside to inspect her hand.

Lai winced as Virginia gently prodded the area around her wound and tugged at the bandages. She bit her lower lip to keep from making a sound.

"There's no need for anything fancy," Virginia announced after a short inspection. "It's not bleeding, so it must have clotted well. I still want to add more dressing and clean it again. I'm riding with you and Kieran tomorrow." She pursed her lips for a moment. "You should have antibiotics to be safe. I don't see any signs of infection, but it can't hurt. Just please remember I am not a doctor."

She glanced to the back of the truck. "How's Kieran?"

"Physically or mentally?"

Virginia sighed. "Both."

"Physically she seems all right, even if she still has two bullets in her shoulder. Mentally, I have no idea," Lai admitted. "She's been angry."

"Did she scream again?"

"No. I guess you weren't expecting that either."

Virginia lowered her voice as she helped Lai out of the truck. "I've never seen her like that."

"How are you holding up?" Lai asked her.

Virginia gave a sad half smile. "Deirdre was one of my best friends. I'll probably start crying again tonight."

Virginia pulled the tailgate down and held her hand out to help everyone out. Kieran was the first out and she let out a pained hiss when she stepped down too hard. Virginia led her back to the front to look at her shoulder. Lai reached into the truck and grabbed her backpack as Mel jumped out on her own. Jaime slept under one of the benches.

"How long has he been like that?" Lai asked.

Mel thought for a moment. "Since half an hour after you went back to the front."

Lai had joined Jackie in the cab of the truck two hours earlier. "Did he say anything?"

"He asked me to find him a blanket."

Lai nodded to herself. It wasn't much, but at least he was talking. Not wanting to wake him, Lai grabbed Mel's arm and pulled her around to the front of the truck. A sudden shout came from the front seat.

"Damn it, Virginia," Kieran complained. She held the seat in a death grip as Virginia inspected her shoulder. When Lai stopped next to the door, new blood was seeping through Kieran's bandages.

"You're lucky these didn't hit any arteries," Virginia said. "I wish I could take them out."

Kieran slapped her hands away and glared. "Over my dead body."

"I'm not going to, but your shoulder is inflamed," Virginia told her. "I do need to clean it with alcohol."

Kieran's glare persisted, but Virginia did not back down. "Your shoulder is starting to swell. I can't just give you antibiotics. It will hurt like nothing else, but I need to clean it."

Kieran held her glare for another several seconds before she rolled her eyes. "Fine."

Virginia nodded, apparently satisfied. "I'll get you some painkillers before I douse it. You, too, Lai. And you're both getting antibiotics anyway."

"Where are we going to get everything?" Lai asked her.

"There's a pharmacy over there," Jackie told them as she approached. She was using a cloth to wipe blood off her hands. Lai figured it was Carlton's. She noted but did not comment on the other redness around Jackie's eyes.

"We're just going to walk in there and buy medical supplies?"

"We've got some money. Lai, you and Virginia come with me." Jackie turned to face the other small group behind her. "I want a full inventory by the time I get back. Anything else we need we can buy tonight. After that the only thing we're buying is gas for the trucks."

"Kieran, I want you to drink a lot of water," Virginia instructed. "When we get to the safe house, I'll deal with your shoulder." She turned her head to Mel. "If she gets any worse, come and get me right away."

When Mel nodded, Virginia accepted a second cloth from Jackie and wiped her own hands and arms clean. Lai pulled her jacket out of her bag and put it on. She let the cuff of her left sleeve hang over her hand. Having the injury out in the open would only cause suspicion. Lai's attention lingered on Kieran for a moment.

Mel put a hand on Lai's shoulder. "I'll keep an eye on her," Mel assured.

Lai put her own hand over Mel's and gave her a thankful smile. Mel returned it before she walked around the front of the truck and hopped into the passenger seat next to Kieran.

Lai fell into step beside Jackie as she led their small group toward the line of stores. Lai pulled her gun out of its holster and tucked it into her waistband instead, then pulled her jacket down to cover it. A gun would attract more attention than an injured hand. Jackie did the same.

"I wish I could do something for Jaime's leg," Virginia told her. Lai pulled her back half a step so they could walk next to one another.

"No one can regrow his leg."

"I know. But I still wish I could somehow fix his prosthetic."

"They'll probably have something for him at the base in St. Louis," Lai reasoned. "Until then all we're doing is driving."

"Do you think it hurt when it was shot?"

"Yeah. It only works because it's connected through thin wires to his nervous system. I don't know exactly how it functions, but he told me that he can feel when things happen to it."

"That must be weird," Virginia mumbled. When they reached the store they were searching for, a brightly lit space with a door marked Howard's Pharmacy, Jackie held the door open for the two girls to enter.

"It probably isn't for him." Lai glanced around the store as she spoke. "He lost his leg when he was four. He's grown up with a prosthetic. He told me they weren't always this high-tech, but he made do."

Virginia hummed an agreement. She too had been looking around at the merchandise. Lai left her wandering around and turned her attention to the man behind the counter. He was watching them closely as he leaned his elbows against the light blue countertop, his mess of brown hair hanging over half of his face.

"Let's be quick," Jackie whispered to Lai. Evidently she had noticed the attention as well. "We've got five minutes."

Lai nodded and headed over to where Virginia was comparing two boxes of painkillers. She held them both up to Lai and frowned.

"These aren't strong enough," she complained. "You and Kieran need hospital-grade drugs."

"We can't get those without a prescription," Lai pointed out.

Virginia huffed and tucked both boxes under her arm. "You two *should* be in a hospital."

Lai ignored her mood. "What do you need me to get?"

Virginia scanned the signs above the aisles and pointed two rows down. "Get me some alcohol. I also need more gloves."

"What kind of alcohol?"

Virginia threw an arm up. "I don't know. I'm not a doctor. The medical kind."

Lai frowned and put her good hand on Virginia's arm. "Are you okay?"

"No, I'm not," she whispered with a glance to the man at the counter. "I watched one of my best friends die in front of me, and now I can't even help you and Kieran the right way."

"You can help us better than anyone else here," Lai insisted. "Come on. I'll let you complain to me later. Right now we have a job to do."

Virginia sighed and shuffled her feet. "I may take you up on that. Now go find me some alcohol."

The three of them spent the next few minutes gathering supplies Virginia asked them for. Lai could tell that Jackie did not like being told what to do, least of all by a teenager, but she bit her tongue and let Virginia order her around. Lai held back a smile. Virginia was more knowledgeable than she gave herself credit for.

When they had gathered everything to Virginia's satisfaction, they brought them all to the counter and placed them before the man. He took a long moment to sift through them before he returned his gaze to the girls.

"There's a hospital a few miles up the road." He pointed behind them and hooked his finger to gesture around the corner. "Whoever this is for would have a better chance there."

"We're getting supplies for a trip," Jackie lied. "You can never be too safe."

The man eyed them skeptically. Lai glanced to his name tag. Apparently he was Howard, the namesake of the pharmacy.

"You've got some interesting supplies for a trip," Howard said. He tapped a finger on the box of antibiotics. "These fight infections. Are you planning on getting an infection?"

Jackie's jaw tightened. Lai could tell she was quickly getting impatient.

"We're in a bit of a hurry," Jackie said. "Can we buy our things?"

"I haven't seen you three around here before," Howard continued. It seemed he had very little intention of selling them their supplies. "Are you with the group that just pulled in? I saw—"

Jackie pulled her gun out and held in loosely at her side. Howard snapped his mouth shut and took a step back. Lai grabbed Jackie's arm to prevent her from raising the gun.

"We really don't have time to answer trivial and invasive questions," Jackie said casually. She didn't react to the hand holding her back. "If you don't mind, we'd like to pay for our supplies now."

"I knew you were LP," Howard exclaimed. "I don't need any of your kind in my store."

"Let's just settle down," Lai said urgently. She kept a firm grip on Jackie's arm and addressed her words to Howard. "I'm sorry. We don't want any trouble. We've had a hard day, and we want to get out of here just as much as you. If you'll just let us buy our things, we'll be out of your hair in a minute."

Howard flicked his gaze between Lai, Jackie, and the gun. No one moved for a dozen seconds. When Howard finally did, it was to carefully grab items off the counter and ring them through his scanner. Lai glared at Jackie until the woman put the gun back into her waistband.

When he was finished checking their items through, Jackie reached in her pocket and threw a handful of bills on the counter. She grabbed the two bags and spun on her heels to walk out the door. Lai and Virginia followed her in a hurry.

"What the hell was that?" Lai hissed when they were walking back across the parking lot.

Jackie kept a quick pace. "I am so sick of being in the field," Jackie replied through clenched teeth. "He already knew we were *Libertas Publica*. I could see it. He just needed some motivation."

"So you threaten him with a gun?"

"I didn't threaten him," Jackie argued coolly. "I just made him aware that I had a gun."

"That was reckless. He could call officers in on us."

"He won't do that. People who don't support us are afraid of us."

"Have you ever considered that you'd get more supporters if you didn't condone violence the same as the Republic?" Lai challenged.

Jackie did not reply.

Lai shook her head to Virginia as they reached the trucks.

"We need to go," Jackie ordered. She handed the bags off to Virginia and opened the front door of one of the trucks. Kieran was still sitting in the front seat. "Out."

"We did an inventory, and there are still a few things we need," Sydney told her when he came around the truck.

"No time. We can get it tomorrow."

"What happened?"

"Jackie decided to show her gun to the man at the pharmacy," Lai told him. She offered a hand to Kieran as she climbed out of the front seat. She winced on her way down.

"That was a smart move," Kieran derided.

"You can question my leadership when we get to the safe house," Jackie said. "Everyone get in a truck now."

Jackie climbed into the front seat and pulled the door closed. Lai sighed in annoyance and walked around back to climb inside. When she, Mel, Kieran, and Virginia had all gotten in and closed the back gate, Lai knocked twice on the window. The truck backed up and turned around, and within seconds they were headed back to the highway.

Chapter Twenty-Four

THE SAFE house they stopped in turned out to be a group of empty shacks off the Dale Ball Trails to the east of the city. Jackie drove the truck along bumpy dirt roads, past a sign that said No Vehicles Past This Point. She was clearly familiar with the area and drove purposefully. From where Lai sat in the passenger seat, she stayed silent and watched the trees fly by alongside the road. She mostly thought about Angella and Deirdre.

When they reached the stone buildings, Jackie pulled the truck in behind the largest one and waited to be sure Sydney did the same before turning off the engine and stepping out. She didn't waste time and ordered anyone who was able to get the supplies they would need for the night and bring them into the building. Lai hopped out and instead circled around the back to her friends. She and Virginia helped a woozy-looking Kieran to the ground. Virginia immediately grabbed the supplies they had bought from the pharmacy and helped Kieran to sit on the door to the truck bed.

Once Lai had helped Mel down, they both worked together to get Jaime out safely. He shuffled along the floor of the truck bed and reached the edge so he could dangle his damaged leg over the edge. Mel let him hook an arm around her neck while Lai took his other hand. He hopped to the ground and clutched them both for support.

"Thanks," he mumbled, the first sound Lai had heard from him since that morning. She squeezed his hand and let him use her for support as he hopped along to the next building and went through the doorway.

Inside, the room was almost completely dark, save for the faint slivers of light coming through the boarded-up windows. The main room was no more than four hundred square feet and had sparse furnishings. There was a large table against the back wall, a lamp in the corner nearest to the door, and two small cots lined up against the wall to the right. She and Mel helped Jaime over to the nearest cot and let him sit down. He sighed loudly and rubbed the spot where his right leg connected to his prosthetic.

"I'll ask Virginia to get you some painkillers too," Mel told him. She turned and quickly walked out of the building.

Lai found her way over to the lamp and flipped the switch a few times. When it was unresponsive, she abandoned it and sat down beside Jaime. He tilted his head slightly to look at her when the cot creaked in protest.

"Are we talking yet?" she asked. "Don't rush it. Wait until you're ready."

"I'm ready," he replied quietly.

Lai instantly wrapped her arms around Jaime and gave him an embrace that took the breath out of his lungs. He returned the embrace after a long moment with about half the force. As he buried his face in her shoulder, Lai brought her good hand up to run it comfortingly through his hair.

"I can't believe she's gone," Jaime whispered into her shoulder.

Lai squeezed him impossibly tighter. "I know. I'm sorry. I would give anything for it not to have happened this way."

"She's kept herself alive for fourteen years. She has been doing this nonstop for almost half of her life. I can't believe this is how it ended."

Lai finally pulled back and saw the shadows splashed across his face. "She fought as hard as she could. You saw that."

"I mean, I guess I always knew it would end like this," he admitted. Through the darkness, Lai thought she saw a tear streak a path down his cheek. "She was a fighter. She wouldn't have wanted to go any other way. But it happened too soon."

Lai put her hand on his shoulder and let him continue speaking.

"All that stuff I told you about Cuba, you remember it? I told you when we fled Havana that she stayed behind. What I never told you is that she called every week for the three months before the bombings to check on us. Elisa, my other sister, she told me that our big sister was off keeping us safe. Angella always made sure we were safe. What am I supposed to tell Elisa and my father now? When it was my turn to keep her safe, I couldn't even do that simple task."

"Hey, this is not your fault," Lai insisted. She waited until Jaime met her eyes before she continued. "I feel guilty, too, but she knew what she was doing today. Angella made her own calls, right? You said that to me once. In the end she was still protecting you. She didn't die for nothing."

"That doesn't make me feel better," he said.

"I know. I don't expect you to rationalize this tonight. I know I won't be able to yet. Right now you're allowed to feel whatever you want. If you want to be sad, you want to scream, you want to go back to being quiet, it's all fine."

Jaime nodded a few times and lowered his eyes. "Right now I want to lie down. My leg is hurting."

"How is it?" she asked.

Jaime rubbed it a few more times. "It feels weird."

"But how are you feeling about it?"

"It seems like a silly thing to worry about right now."

Lai nodded and scooted to the edge of the cot as Jaime lowered himself down onto it. He shuffled around to settle himself in as Mel walked through the door. In her hand were two small pills. She had a bottle of water in the other hand.

"Two painkillers, courtesy of Virginia," she said.

Jaime lifted himself up on an elbow and took the two pills from her, then tossed them in his mouth and threw back his head to dry swallow the pills. He immediately lay back down and closed his eyes.

"Thanks," he said.

Lai gave a half smile to Mel. "How's Kieran? Did you see her?"

"Kieran is ready to rip her arm off," Kieran growled as Virginia helped her into the building. They went to the cot farther up the wall, and Kieran collapsed onto it without delay.

"She needs those wounds cleaned now," Virginia told them. She turned to Kieran. "Shirt off."

"Excuse me?" Kieran snapped.

"I need a sterile area to work with." Virginia's voice softened back to the gentler tone Lai was familiar with. "You don't need the infection to get worse."

Kieran grudgingly complied. She stripped off her jacket and threw it at Lai. Lai caught it and put it aside, and did the same when Kieran tossed over her shirt. Kieran leaned back against the wall and closed her eyes as Virginia pulled aside her bra strap.

"Mel, get the antibiotics and the painkillers," Virginia instructed. "She needs three of each." She glanced to Lai. "Give her the same."

"Isn't three a lot?" Mel asked, though she did as she was told.

"It won't be a lot when I'm pouring alcohol on her bullet wounds," Virginia replied.

"Who's hungry?" Jackie inquired as she stepped into the room. She dropped the two cloth bags she was holding on to the floor near the door and leaned against the doorframe. Jaime held up one arm from where he was lying. Mel and Lai both hummed in reply as Lai was handed her six pills. She took the water bottle Mel had previously offered to Jaime and swallowed the pills in three rounds.

"There's a decently working gas stove in the next building," Jackie told them. "Sydney's going to make soup. We'll be close if you kids need anything."

Lai nodded her thanks as Jackie left the building.

"Can someone give Lai more dressing?" Virginia asked as she pulled gloves onto her hands. She frowned in obvious concern when Kieran groaned as she swallowed her pills. "I don't have time."

"I got it," Jaime said. He sat up and stretched his arms above his head. Lai glanced back to the bags by the door. One of their med kits stuck out the top. She retrieved it and unzipped it to pull out the bandages. When she got what they needed, she zipped the bag up and left it next to Virginia. Lai noted that Mel had moved to the other cot to sit next to Kieran and hold on to her good hand.

"Salamat," Lai thanked Jaime as he cut off a long strip of dressing. As he wrapped it around her hand, Lai's gaze strayed to where he worked. She knew that under the bandages there was still gauze stuffed into her hand. If she could feel anything properly it would probably bother her.

She didn't dare move it. Her entire hand was inflamed into a bright red that spread out from under the bandages and wavered at her fingertips.

"Damn, *asere*, you really got hit."

"Thanks for pointing out the obvious," she breathed. Lai let him work in silence for a long moment. Only when he was tying off the bandage did he speak.

"Lailani?"

With the use of her full name, Lai knew he was about to get serious. "Yeah?"

"Have you thought about your family recently?"

Lai's gaze shot up to her friend's face. She had not expected that question from him. She let out a lengthy breath to stall for a few seconds.

"Of course I think about them," she replied. She grimaced as the bandage tightened around her hand.

"You didn't answer my question."

"I don't know how to answer your question. Of course I think about them," she repeated.

Jaime sighed and fixed her with a curious stare. She met his eyes with some reluctance and forced herself to hold his gaze.

"I think about my family differently," he said. He fell back onto the bed before he continued and stared at the ceiling. "My mother is gone. My father is in hiding. Angella…." He took a moment to swallow before continuing. "And then there's Elisa. I never know where she is. But you know what your family is doing."

"I don't talk to them that much. You know that."

"I know your mother didn't want you to become a protection officer."

"She was worried about me."

"And two years ago, you told me that she doesn't sympathize with the Republic."

Lai squeezed her eyes shut tight and pressed the palm of her good hand against one of her eyelids. She could feel the fog of the painkillers clouding her thoughts and making it difficult to concentrate for too long.

"My mother fell in love and left everything behind to come to this country. She didn't think about what she was going to, what she was taking us to. She only knew that she loved my stepfather."

"Your stepfather who doesn't like you."

Lai sighed heavily. "He likes Imee. She's his little angel. She was barely a year old when our father died. Ethan is the only father she ever knew. I remember my father, and I didn't welcome this new man with my mother. To say it caused tension in our family would be an understatement. He only likes that I joined an academy."

"Even so, aren't you worried about them now?" Jaime asked. "What we're doing could fall back on them."

Lai laughed without humor. "My stepfather the ambassador. I'm sure."

"I'm thinking about Imee," Jaime said softly.

Lai opened her eyes and pulled her lower lip through her teeth before speaking. "Maybe I can find a way to see her again when things have settled down."

"You really believe that?"

She shrugged and turned her gaze to her friend.

"God fucking damn it, Virginia!"

Lai started at the sudden outburst and quickly turned toward the commotion. Her attention fell on Kieran, who was holding Mel's hand in a death grip as a stream of alcohol was poured over her bandages.

"You could have given me some fucking warning!" she yelled.

"It's better when you don't expect it," Virginia argued. She let more liquid flow over Kieran's shoulder.

"Oh mother—if you don't cut it out, I am going to rip your fucking head off!"

Virginia tilted the bottle back and the stream of alcohol ceased. As Kieran growled angrily through her teeth, Virginia capped the bottle and placed it in the med kit. She then grabbed the bandages and cut off several long strips.

"When that dries, I'm covering it again," she told Kieran. "How are you feeling?"

"Fuck off," Kieran groaned. She placed her left hand over her eyes. She flinched when Mel placed a comforting hand on her good arm but did not protest.

"I didn't know Kieran was quite that colorful," Jaime whispered to Lai.

"You never shared a dorm with her," she whispered back.

"ARE WE going to talk about why you pulled a gun in that pharmacy?"

Jackie glanced up from her bowl and turned her attention to Sydney when he spoke.

"I didn't know it was something we needed to talk about," she said coolly.

Sydney's gaze flicked between the pot of soup he was working on and Jackie, sitting a few feet away on a bench. He stirred as she ate the first bowl.

"That's not like you, Jack," he went on. "That was reckless."

"Says the man who just last week convinced me to steal two Republic trucks," she shot back.

"Come on. I'm trying to be serious." Sydney turned the dial on the stove to lower the heat and sat down next to Jackie. "Run me through what happened."

"Nothing happened! That guy was pushing me. All he needed to do was give us our damn supplies. It wasn't like I actually shot him."

"You threatened to."

"I made him aware that I had a gun," she retorted.

"Jackie, it's me you're talking to. No need for all this."

Jackie sucked in a deep breath and let it out through her teeth. Her fingers clenched tightly around her spoon until her knuckles turned white.

"I lost her," she whispered. "Damn it, I lost her."

There was no doubt as to whom she was referring.

"When I met Romana, I spent weeks learning sign language because I wanted to be her friend. Imagine that, seven-year-old me spending all her free time at the library teaching herself to sign."

"She told me about that," Sydney said quietly. When he looked up to his friend's face, he found tears in Jackie's eyes.

"I just keep losing people. I'm supposed to be responsible for everyone. The commander trusts me and I get everyone killed. Romana, Carlton, even Angella."

"Hey, I'm still here," Sydney consoled. "We're both still here. That means you didn't fail. I'm alive, Benjamin's alive, and all those kids are alive. That counts for something."

"Tell me again tomorrow. Maybe I'll believe you then." Jackie leaned forward until her forehead rested on her knees. "I knew what I was getting into." It seemed she was speaking to herself more than to him. "I have always known these things happen. I knew it."

"That doesn't make it any easier when it does happen," Sydney said.

Jackie refused to look up.

"I think you could use some time off," he decided.

At that she did turn her head to peer at him. "Time off?" she echoed incredulously. "We don't have a job that gives us time off. The past week may as well have been time off."

"I think Cara would understand if some of us needed a break, especially after this morning. Our commander understands losing people better than any of us."

After a moment Jackie pulled herself back upright. "I'm not asking Cara for time off."

"Then ask her for a safer assignment," he suggested.

"Why are you so sure I need a break?"

Sydney smiled sadly. "Because I do. And I'm not the one in charge."

Jackie let out a frustrated sigh and gave Sydney a light punch on the shoulder. "Then you ask for yourself."

When she made to stand up, Sydney put a hand on her arm to stop her. She gave him a questioning expression.

"At least consider asking for an on-site assignment once we get back to base," he pressed.

A corner of Jackie's mouth twitched upward. "I will consider asking," she conceded. "That's all I'll do." She stood up and stretched her arms above her head before heading toward the door.

"You're so stubborn," he said.

She glanced back over her shoulder and winked at him before exiting the building.

CHAPTER TWENTY-FIVE

LAI STARED out the back of the truck as they rolled down the dusty concrete road. Several meters behind them, the other truck followed with Sydney in the driver seat. All around them, the dry fields spread out until the ground shot up to form a mountain range Lai couldn't name. The sun beat down on them as if they weren't driving north into what should be less sweltering heat.

She turned her attention from the road to her friends inside the truck. Across from her sat Virginia, who was currently going through their med kits once again. By Lai's count it was the fifth time in the four hours since they had left their safe house. Virginia seemed to realize she was being watched and glanced up. When she saw it was Lai, she offered her friend a quick smile before going back to her work.

Jaime sat on the other end of the bench across from her. He was occupying his time by moving his leg to get a feel for the makeshift splint now securing his prosthetic.

After they had finished eating the previous night, Jackie had noticed how bothered Jaime seemed by his sudden lack of mobility. When she offered to build him a temporary splint, he hadn't believed she could do it with their limited resources, but she admitted to the group that she had always been rather good at working with her hands. An hour and a half later, she had built a somewhat crude yet functioning wooden splint from scraps of wood and a sling from one of the med kits. While he could never run a marathon in it, it was better than no working leg at all for the time being.

Across from Jaime on the far side of the bench where Lai sat, and past a precariously stacked set of boxes, Mel and Kieran were leaning against one another as they slept. How they managed to with all the bumps on the road, Lai couldn't fathom.

Once Virginia had finished rebandaging her shoulder the previous night, Kieran had been in a sour mood and remained mostly silent until she eventually fell asleep. Lai had to admit she didn't mind the silence. Once they had set off that morning, Kieran had noticeably improved in both her mood and her physical state. Any signs of infection seemed to have been washed away with the alcohol. Though Kieran was not up for a lively group conversation, she had pulled Mel aside, and the two had talked for most of the first three hours of the trip before they both decided to get some more sleep.

Lai found their fast friendship quite peculiar. She figured it had to do with whatever the two of them talked about when Mel visited Kieran in lockup. Though Lai had asked, Mel wouldn't reveal what that was. She would only say that Kieran had confided in her and she wasn't going to break that confidence. Lai didn't think it was worth pushing for the time being.

"I really need a shower," Jaime suddenly announced.

Lai turned her attention to him and gave him an amused smirk. "That's what you're thinking about right now?"

"Yes," he confirmed. He ran a hand through his greasy black hair for emphasis. "At least in Maricopa we could have sink showers."

"It's only two or three more days," Virginia spoke up. She glanced over to him and tucked a loose strand of her own braided black hair behind her ears. "I'm sure our hair can survive for that long."

"It's not just that," he insisted. "We're all covered in dust, and to be entirely honest, everyone in this truck smells."

"Wow." Lai laughed. "That's very nice of you to say."

"He does have a point," Virginia agreed with an amused smile of her own.

"Maybe there's hot water at the next safe house. We only have another six hours to go."

"You think those two will sleep through it?" Jaime asked with a nod toward Mel and Kieran.

Lai shrugged. "Kieran might. I don't think she slept at all last night."

"I'm surprised any of us could," Virginia said, much more quietly than she had before.

Lai's smile fell, and she leaned back against the cover. "Yeah. I haven't slept a full night since the truck ambush."

All three fell silent, their words replaced by the sounds of the wheels rolling over the cracked concrete. Lai returned her attention to the vast sweep of road behind them.

The first mine went off only seconds after their conversation ended. Lai didn't see it as it went off on the side of the road several meters ahead of them, but everyone could hear and feel it. The road shook with the sudden detonation. and the truck swerved violently to the other side of the road to avoid it. Lai would have toppled over had she not grabbed one of the ropes that secured the cover to the truck bed.

Her ears rang at being so close to the explosion. Her thoughts were in a jumble, and she didn't have a chance to straighten them before a second explosion rocked the air.

The truck swerved again. Already wide-awake from the first explosion, Mel had gone crashing onto the floor and was now clutching the edge of the bench for dear life, her face completely white. Kieran braced herself against the corner and gritted her teeth as she was forced to use her injured shoulder for support. Virginia had also fallen from the bench into a pile of boxes that did little to soften the blow. Jaime managed to stay upright, his hands clutching the bench as Jackie swerved the truck wildly to avoid any debris.

"What the hell was that!" Kieran shouted.

"Jackie would have seen if anyone was around," Lai replied. "We must have set off some kind of mines."

Lai waited and forced herself not to loosen her hold on the rope. She strained to hear anything but could only hear the roar of the engine and the heavy breathing of her friends. Once she was reasonably sure they weren't going to hit any more explosives, she picked her way toward the window between the truck bed and the cab. She got down on her knees and braced them against two boxes while using her good hand to slide the window open.

"What's going on?" she demanded.

Jackie suddenly veered to the left onto a side road that Lai knew wasn't heading east.

"We triggered proximity mines," Jackie hissed. She didn't spare a glance back to Lai. "There must be trigger plates in the road. I'm taking us to a safe house near Pueblo West. We can plan a new route when we're not surrounded by bombs."

The window remained open as Lai collapsed back onto the bench next to Kieran. She eyed the girl with great unease. Kieran returned her expression with a hard stare. Lai squeezed her eyes shut and made herself think.

For there to be proximity mines set up in the roads, the Republic would need to be sure that *Libertas Publica* members would be driving by. Any uncertainty would almost definitely result in civilian casualties or injuries. A roadside bomb planted by the government wasn't as easy to cover up as false convictions. Of course, there was no way to be sure it was the government that had planted the mines, but Lai couldn't think of another explanation.

She could, however, think of an explanation as to how their location was revealed.

"Jackie," she called through the window without opening her eyes. She waited a moment to ensure Jackie had heard her. "Are you sure that man at the pharmacy didn't call officers?"

"Of course I'm not sure!" Jackie exclaimed as she took another sharp left. "It doesn't matter. We'll go the long way once it's cooled down."

Lai opened her eyes and looked through the open window out in front of the truck. The second left had taken them into what seemed to be a sparsely populated rural community. Houses were clumped in small groups near one another with the groups all about two hundred meters apart lining both sides of the road. A few of the clusters were stores rather than houses. It was not unlike the compound where Jaime's family lived.

After passing six groups of buildings, Jackie slowed the trucks and pulled into a smaller unit with a two-car garage in the center connected to the largest house. The truck screeched to a halt a few feet short of the entrance before she carefully eased it into one side. A few seconds later, Sydney came up on the other side. Without even turning off the ignition, Jackie shot out of the driver seat to the door with Sydney hot on her heels. They both grabbed a lever on either side of the opening and pulled hard until the garage door continued lowering itself. Only when it touched the ground and left no way to see into the garage did they relax.

Lai took a deep breath and finally loosened her grip on the rope. Her friends did the same and allowed themselves to relax. Lai took a moment to flex her sore fingers as Jackie came back to turn off the engine. She gestured through the open window for them to come out the back.

Before Lai did as she was told, she took a moment to make sure her traveling companions were all right. Virginia had already stood up, and she rubbed her head with a grimace. Lai gave her a questioning look, which Virginia waved off.

Mel fussed over Kieran, who glowered at her injured shoulder as if she could intimidate the pain away. Mel appeared unharmed, if a bit shaken up. She gave Lai an unconvincing smile when she saw her cousin watching her.

Jaime was clearly on edge and wasn't hiding it nearly as well as everyone else. He shakily stood up and headed for the back of the truck. Lai caught his eye, and he gave her a troubled look, which she returned. He crouched down and hopped out of the truck before he turned to offer a hand to Lai. She took it and landed on the floor of the garage with the thud.

The garage was lit by a series of shoddy lamps that illuminated the interior. It was only just big enough to hold the two trucks, which fit snugly, as there was little else in the room. A few tools lay scattered on the ground, and a small pile of scrap wood was in a heap in the far corner. To the right was a single door that led in the direction of the connected house.

Jackie headed for said door and swung it inward. "Angella used this safe house a lot when she was active." She glanced back to Lai and Jaime. "She insisted on this house because it has a two-car garage."

"I'm glad she did," Lai said with a twinge of sadness at the mention of Angella.

Jaime mutely followed Jackie when she walked into the house.

Virginia jumped out of the truck next, with Mel and Kieran close on her heels. Rylen was just getting out of the other truck, and he instantly rushed to Virginia's side. She stayed back with him while Mel and Kieran caught up with Lai.

"You okay?" Mel asked when Kieran fell into step beside her.

"I'm fine," she lied.

Mel side-eyed her but said nothing. Lai shook her head at the familiar Kieran appearing again.

They walked through the door into a narrow hallway that branched out into several rooms. The doors were all closed, with the only opening being the turn in the hall at the end. There were no pictures on the walls or anything to indicate anyone lived in the house. Lai knew no one did, at least not full-time.

Lai led Mel and Kieran down the hall and turned right into a large living space. As it was, the room was mostly empty, save for a dining table and three chairs. A single shaded window was set in the back wall. Jackie sat on the table next to Jaime, who rested in one of the chairs. They glanced up when the three entered and stopped in the center of the room.

"We should lay low here for an hour or two," Jackie decided. "Sydney is just getting some food for us." Lai turned her head at the sound of footsteps behind her. Virginia, Rylen, and Benjamin entered the room.

"Is there a safer way around the main roads?" Jaime asked.

"It will add another half day of travel, but it's better than being blown up."

It was then that the floorboards creaked behind her. She looked around. Everyone was accounted for and no one was moving. That left only one possibility.

Her hand crept to her gun in its holster, and she held up her injured hand to the others. They all fell silent at her signal. Jackie got down from the table and pulled out her own gun, keeping it pointed at an angle to the ground. Virginia and Rylen put their hands on the guns they had been lent, as did Jaime and Benjamin with their own. Mel pressed herself up behind Lai as she turned to check the way they had come in.

All at once the room erupted in a flurry of noise and movement. Officers poured into the room with their guns raised as they shouted commands to stand down. Lai's companions fell in beside her. Lai reacted in an instant as she pulled her gun from the holster and raised it to fire.

As her finger curled around the trigger, Lai's hand froze before she could fire a single shot. Her muscles locked up all through her arm. They barred her from moving it at all. Officers continued to arrive and shout orders, but Lai was paralyzed.

Her mind flashed back to the previous morning. She saw Angella being shot, once in the calf, once in the hand, in her throat, through her eye. She saw it again.

She saw the aftermath of the fragmentation grenade she threw that killed eleven officers and maimed the twelfth so Jackie could finish him. The blood stained the road and created a pool around the carnage that she was responsible for.

They were under fire. The panic flared inside her as she recounted the bullets raining down on the paneling she gripped as a shield, her only protection from the barrage of bullets being thrown at her.

The pain in her hand blossomed anew as she saw the bullet streak through her hand and leave a trail of blood and gore across the ground.

All of this took place within the span of three seconds. The grip on her gun loosened. Her breathing quickened, and her heart felt as if it would beat out of her chest.

Lai couldn't even blink. She knew she had a clear shot. She was the front line. She could hit any officer in front of her. Her accuracy was unparalleled at her age. If she shot, she would hit her target.

She did not shoot.

Even if she had wanted to, after her initial hesitation there was no chance. Before she even knew what was happening, something slammed into the crook behind her right knee. She lurched back and felt a hand grab her gun before an elbow hit the side of her face. She gasped at the sudden shock of pain and doubled over for a moment. In a rush of clarity, her mind screamed at her to right herself. She did, only to find herself face-to-face with her own gun and Kieran behind the trigger.

Lai froze again, only this time it was in identifiable shock.

"Well, isn't this interesting," Kieran said, a wicked smile growing.

Lai couldn't find the words she wanted. The officers came around behind her and disarmed her friends. There was no way to fight back now. The space was too small, the odds too unbalanced.

"Rylen," Kieran said as her gaze shifted to him.

Lai glanced back to see him standing beside Virginia with his gun half out of its holster. He glared at her until she gave him a pointed look. After a short hesitation, he pulled out his gun and turned it on Virginia. She let out a gasp of betrayal. Lai thought Virginia might cry.

"Virginia, come on," Kieran said.

"I can't believe you two," Virginia cried.

Kieran stared for a moment longer before she turned her attention back to Lai.

Sergeant Washington came through the doorway last and seemed pleasantly surprised at seeing Kieran with a gun pointed at Lai. Kieran flicked the gun up. Lai knew she couldn't fight and held up her hands as instructed.

"Harris, how nice to see you again," the sergeant said. She walked with an obvious limp. Her own gun was held ready, but she didn't aim it at anyone. There was no need; the officers walked back to join the others with everyone's weapons in their hands.

Lai turned her head ever so slightly as Jackie was shoved up next to her. Jackie glared daggers at the sergeant as she held her own hands up in surrender.

"How did you find us?" she spat.

"We've been watching this house for over a month," the sergeant explained. "A concerned citizen pointed us in this direction."

"Kieran?" Mel whispered from just behind Lai.

"I'm sorry it had to come to this," Kieran said. She didn't look terribly sorry. "But this is what happens when you break the law."

"You left just to report back to them?" Lai kept her expression neutral to mask her fury and hurt.

"Actually no. Someone else did that part for me. I was deluding myself for a while, but I came to my senses."

"I knew you couldn't be a part of these traitors, Reynolds," the sergeant said proudly. She eyed Rylen. "Mr. Porter, I'm glad to see you agree with her."

"What about everything you said yesterday about Deirdre?" Lai asked. An officer came around behind her and forced her hands into cuffs. She let out a brief cry when he touched her injured hand.

"I've been doing some thinking." Kieran lowered the gun as the rest of them were cuffed. She stuffed it into her waistband before she continued. "Do I really want to throw my life away for some lost cause? One that actively tries to destroy an institution that protects us if we follow the law?"

"You know that isn't true!" Lai shouted. "You saw those files."

"I saw people who got what they deserved."

"And Deirdre?"

Kieran seemed to falter for a moment before she steeled herself. "Deirdre didn't realize what she was getting into. This could have been avoided altogether."

"Screw you, Kieran," Lai spat. She narrowed her eyes as Kieran only smiled.

"I don't think I'm the one who's screwed," she taunted.

"She's right," the sergeant spoke up. "An example needs to be made of each of you. In accordance with the laws of the Republic, you have all been found guilty of treason against the country and you are to be executed under these laws. You will be taken to the nearest training facility to be executed tonight."

"Sergeant?" Kieran said. Sergeant Washington looked down at her and nodded for her to speak. "You should let Beta Five do it."

Lai let out her breath in a gasp. Tears stung her eyes, but she forced them back. She would not let these people see her cry.

Her cheek throbbed, and she was sure a bruise was forming, as if it mattered. Lai clenched her teeth together and only struggled minimally as an officer grabbed her arm and shoved her forward. She wordlessly trudged back down the hallway to the garage. Footsteps behind her told her that the others were following. She tripped through the door, and the officer pushed her back against the wall.

"Wait here," he ordered.

Lai scowled up at him before he headed toward two Republic trucks that were just pulling in next to the house.

Her attention was diverted when Jackie was shoved into the wall next to her.

"Damn it," Jackie breathed. Her face betrayed her fear through the mask she attempted to put on. She glanced around the garage once and frowned.

"Where's Sydney?" she whispered to Lai.

Lai realized for the first time that Sydney was nowhere to be seen. She shrugged a shoulder. "Hell if I know."

They both bit their tongues when the sergeant limped through the door. She eyed Lai purposefully. "Don't worry, Harris, you'll be joining your friend soon enough."

Lai frowned in confusion. "My friend?"

"Oscar. He was executed yesterday for treason."

Lai's breath caught in her throat, and she found there were no words. She didn't want to believe it. She couldn't believe it.

And yet it made sense. Taking Oscar to a hospital would never have gotten him to stop talking. He was determined to have people know the truth. The only surefire way to shut him up....

"You're lying," Lai argued, her throat feeling suddenly dry.

The sergeant shook her head, a hard glint in her eyes. "I wish I was. He was a good student. If only he hadn't lost his way, he might still be alive. I could say the same for you."

"You stood there and shouted at me to execute my own cousin, and you honestly expected me to do it?"

"I expect every student to do what is required of them."

Lai shook her head, once again at a loss for words.

Jackie took over for her. "It's not as simple as that. None of this is simple. You don't give us a choice. It's either follow a corrupt system or take a stand and get screwed over."

"Like your parents did?" the sergeant asked.

Jackie's mouth hung open.

The sergeant continued. "Yes, I know all about your parents, Jackie Anton. They were found with an entire house full of explosives. They would have been executed either way."

"You people didn't need to set the house on fire," Jackie whispered.

"I'm not here to argue with a criminal. I'm only here to bring you all to justice."

Jackie scoffed and fell silent. Lai looked back up just as Kieran walked into the garage. She held Lai's gun in her hand.

"Can I ride back with her?" Kieran asked as she nodded to Lai.

Lai fixed her with an even glare, which Kieran promptly ignored.

"Are you sure you haven't had enough of her over the last few days?" the sergeant asked.

Kieran shrugged.

The sergeant thought for a moment before she nodded. "Let's load them up!" she called out to her officers. Lai bit her lip to hold back another cry of pain when an officer hit her injured hand. He led her back outside into the glaring sunlight, followed by the rest of her companions.

Lai didn't know right away what she was feeling. Her stomach clenched and her heart continued to beat like a hummingbird's. She was angry and betrayed.

She realized all at once the particular kind of fear that had a vise grip on her. It was different than in the warehouse the previous day. That fear had been fueled by adrenaline. The danger had been immediate, and there was a clear solution as to what could be done.

This was different. There was no obvious answer, no identifiable way out of the situation. It somehow seemed more final.

Lai didn't just feel scared. She felt hopeless.

CHAPTER TWENTY-SIX

THE CHAINS clanked against the side of the truck, the metal links swaying with the movement as they rolled along the road. Lai sat with her legs crossed on the floor of the truck and her arms held above her head by handcuffs connecting to a chain that hung from a series of bolts along the side. On her right Mel sat with her knees at her chest and looked alternately between Kieran and Lai.

For the past ten minutes, Lai had comforted Mel when she could and bit her tongue when the two other officers told her to shut it. When they both complained about how tired they were, however, Kieran offered to keep an eye on their prisoners while they slept. They had taken her up on her offer and were asleep in minutes.

Lai watched Kieran sitting on the bench against the back of the truck bed, her own gun still in the girl's hands. She seemed to be amusing herself by removing and replacing the clip.

Lai couldn't believe her. In fact, she wasn't sure she did. Kieran was a lot of things. She could be stubborn, rude, and incredibly egotistical, among other things that Lai had never liked her for. But if there was one thing Lai knew about her, it was that she had not been acting when she said she wanted to destroy the Republic.

So the real question was why Kieran was doing it.

"I don't believe you," Lai said.

Kieran met Lai's eyes evenly. "Oh you don't?" she replied in a flat voice.

Lai narrowed her eyes. "I heard you before. You meant what you said about getting revenge for Deirdre. I don't believe you."

Kieran stared at Lai for a long moment. She opened her mouth as if to speak, but before she did her eyes flicked to the officers resting next to her. She sighed and fixed Lai with a scowl.

"I had to put on a convincing show for the sergeant. What was I supposed to say, that the reason I was betraying you was only to keep myself safe? She would never have gone for that."

"How could you do that?" Mel spoke up in a choked whisper. Both sets of eyes shifted to her tearstained face. "If you're not sympathetic, how could you go back to them?"

Kieran's expression lost some of its fire. "This isn't about you. This isn't about anything but keeping myself alive. Forget revenge for Deirdre. She wouldn't want me to throw my life away for a lost cause. I had to make a decision. Do I stay with you people and get myself killed, or do I forget this useless fight and stay alive?"

"You didn't have to disarm me," Lai growled. She clenched her good hand into a fist. "We had a shot to get out of there."

"Come on, Lani, you know better than that. You didn't even fire."

Lai sucked in a long breath and turned so she looked just past Kieran's head. That was the last thing she wanted to talk about.

At the mention of it, however, her mind refused to stay away. She couldn't fathom what had happened earlier. She simply froze. Her hands locked up, and she couldn't make them move to pull the trigger.

But it wasn't that simple. If the flashbacks were any indication, she would say she had a strange sort of panic attack. She could think of no other explanation, even if a panic attack hardly fit like a glove.

"What did happen to you back there, Lani?" Kieran inquired. She twirled Lai's gun around, her attention shifting to focus on it. "Couldn't get a clear shot?"

"How's your shoulder, Kieran?" Lai deflected. She let her attention fall back onto Kieran's face and kept her expression neutral.

Kieran placed the gun on the bench next to her and eyed her right shoulder. "It hurts less than it did yesterday. Virginia would have made a good field medic."

"She still might."

"All right, I had nothing to do with them showing up. If I had tried to fight my way out of there, I would have a bullet in my head like Deirdre, and where would that get me? We were screwed the moment we went into that house. Everything after is only a result of that, not a cause."

"Does it matter to you at all that we're going to die?" Mel spoke up. "That I'm going to die?"

Kieran's brow creased. As she spoke, she wouldn't meet Mel's eyes. "You were already going to die."

"And now I definitely am, and you don't even seem to care."

For a long moment, Kieran did not respond. She ran a hand through her unruly curls and slowly dragged her hand down the side of her face until it fell back in her lap. Finally she looked at Mel. The muscles around her eyes twitched as she attempted to hold her expression still.

"I'm not going to be sorry for your mistakes," she said monotonously. She averted her gaze again when a cry caught in Mel's throat.

"Ikaw malupit maliit na…," Lai mumbled. "That's too far, even for you."

"You know me, Lani. I've never been the sensitive type. I won't apologize for her murdering someone and you breaking her out. You shouldn't have done it if you didn't want to face the consequences."

"So I was supposed to let her die? Is that what you would have done?"

Before Kieran said anything, Mel knocked her knee against Lai's. "This isn't worth it," she muttered. "We obviously misjudged her."

"I just want to know what she really has against us," Lai said as she stared openly at Kieran.

Kieran sighed once again. "I already said, this isn't about you."

"Then explain to me why the hell you volunteered to execute us."

"What better way to get the sergeant to trust me and Rylen again?" Though Lai doubted it, Kieran actually looked sorry. "If you're going to die, it doesn't matter who does it. This way we'll make it quick, and he and I go back to normal."

"And you never thought to make this work for Jaime too?" Lai asked. "He was my hostage. Everyone saw it."

"No one actually thought Jaime was your hostage. Rylen, Virginia, and I are the only ones who this could work for. We throw it back on any of us who don't go back. They never saw what we did when we broke out; they only know that we did it. It's easy enough to say Virginia and Deirdre planned the whole thing and dragged us along with them, and we only went to make sure they didn't do anything to harm the Republic."

"So you're throwing your girlfriend under the bus," Lai said. "I see. I didn't expect that from you, Kieran."

"She's dead." Kieran's voice faltered, and she had to take a moment to compose herself. "If I have to say those things about her to keep myself alive, then she would want me to. I'm sorry about this. I really am. I may not like you, Lai, but I never wanted you to die."

"That's exactly what's happening now."

"That part isn't my fault."

Apparently unable to take any more, Mel squeezed her eyes shut and lowered her head to her chest. Lai knew she and Kieran had gotten close over the past few days. Her betrayal had to hurt Mel more than Lai.

"If you're worried about being safe, we could have fought our way out of there, and then you could have stayed with the LP, or left," Lai pointed out. "These aren't the only two options."

At that Kieran laughed. Lai frowned and stared at her until she stopped.

"You're naive if you think there's any other options for people like us," she countered bitterly.

"People like us?" Lai echoed.

Kieran shook her head and picked up the gun again. Her face had adopted an incredulous expression. "You can't be this clueless."

"What do you mean?" Lai demanded.

"People who aren't white. Anyone who doesn't have light enough skin. We don't have options. We can join an academy and become one of them, or we can kiss a good life goodbye."

"It isn't that black and white," Lai argued. "I'm not denying it's harder for us, but you can't oversimplify it that much."

"You never saw it, did you?" Kieran scoffed. "Of course you didn't. You may be a nonwhite immigrant, but your stepfather has connections. Mr. Ethan Harris, the ambassador who fell in love with a widowed Filipina woman and brought her and her two daughters to the Republic. The white man who used his connections to keep his stepchildren from knowing what real racism is like. You don't know anything, Lailani. Not a damn thing."

"I'm sorry about what's happened to you, Kieran, but you can't blame me for it," Lai insisted.

Kieran laughed bitterly. "Of course I can. I can blame you for everything. If you hadn't saved your cousin, this never would have happened. She would still be alive."

Lai suddenly understood. It wasn't about her social status at all.

"This is all about Deirdre," Lai realized.

"Oh, she gets it now. Of course it's about her."

"She was my friend. I never wanted her to get hurt."

"You should have thought of that before you joined a revolution!"

"I didn't force her to leave!" Lai shouted. "Sometimes people die. I'm sorry she had to die, but she knew what she was getting into when she left the academy. And in case you forgot, another friend of mine died in there too. Jaime had to watch his sister die. Deirdre made her choice."

For once, Kieran didn't glare. She didn't appear angry at all. She looked at Lai with such neutrality that Lai felt even more terrified.

Kieran leaned forward to rest her arms on her knees and meet Lai's eyes evenly. The gun hung from her hands, inches from Lai's face. "If you don't shut up, I am going to put a bullet in your other hand."

Lai bit her tongue and forced herself to remain silent.

CHAPTER TWENTY-SEVEN

THE DRIVE lasted for fifteen hours, with two short stops to refill the tanks and switch drivers. Lai knew it was standard procedure to drive without any unnecessary stops when transporting prisoners. Too many stops offered chances for escape, and that was the last thing Sergeant Washington wanted to happen.

Lai managed to drift off a few times on the drive, only to be suddenly awoken when the truck hit a bump in the road or took a hard turn. She counted the time in her head, and was only off by an hour when they arrived and were made aware of the early hour of four in the morning. When the chain securing Lai's hands above her head was finally disconnected from her handcuffs, her arms were sore and aching from having them suspended above her the whole time, which was to say nothing of the burning sensation flowing through her hand.

If Lai had to give Kieran any credit, she did nothing to disturb the injury when she transported Lai from the truck into the academy. Lai supposed she should accept it as a small consolation, though she was hard pressed to do even that.

The familiar walls brought no comfort to Lai as she was marched through the halls, around corners she knew, and past rooms she had spent her days in. The place she had come to call home now felt very much like a tomb. The comparison was apt, as bodies were taken to the basement after execution to be incinerated. Burials were reserved for the just in life, as the sergeant often said.

At the early hour, Lai did not expect to see many people in the halls, save the guards that patrolled regularly. She was correct, as they passed only half a dozen officers, who all offered dirty glares or smug sneers of disdain. Lai kept her face blank and marched at the head of their line with Kieran only a step behind her to guide her along the path, not that she needed to be led. Lai knew where to find the cells.

They turned the final corner, and Lai was faced with the padlocked and key-code-accessed double doors that led to the secondary wing of cells. Kieran stopped them in front of the doors. The sergeant came forward and tapped out a combination on the keypad, followed by pressing her hand to the pad to be scanned. The lights next to the pad changed to green with a quiet ping, and the lock clicked open. The guard next to the door then pulled a ring of keys from his pocket and unlocked the padlock to let the doors swing open.

Kieran gave Lai a shove to get her moving. Lai held her head high and walked straight through the doors. The sergeant took the lead and headed for the second row of cells down the hall. With a gesture of her head, officers came from behind to open the heavy doors. Lai started walking before she could be pushed again and marched herself right into the first cell. She turned around in time to see Mel and Jaime entering behind her.

She met the door as it was slammed in their faces.

"Hands," an officer said through the small barred window. Lai pushed her arms through the narrow slot and felt the cuffs loosen around her wrists. She pulled them back in and cradled her injured hand to her chest as the others went to have their restraints removed.

When the officer left, Kieran stepped up to the door. She opened her mouth to speak, but before she could get one word out, Lai cut in.

"None of us care what you have to say, Kieran," she said in the most neutral voice she could manage. She was done letting Kieran get a rise out of her.

Kieran drew her lips closed and shook her head. Without saying one word, she walked away. Lai stayed where she was and listened until the main doors slammed shut.

The silence dragged on. Lai figured most of the cells in the secondary wing were out of use at the moment. No doubt they were waiting for a new shipment of prisoners.

"It's interesting that it ends like this."

Lai turned her head to look back at Jaime. He had moved to a far corner of the room and sat with his legs sprawled in front of him.

"Interesting," Lai echoed.

Jaime nodded and stared at the wall. "The three of us, in here together. The way we started this whole mess."

"Interesting isn't the word I would use," Mel said from where she leaned against the right wall.

Lai met her gaze, and her brows drew together. "I messed up." Lai squeezed her eyes shut and faced away from her companions. "I messed up, and now we're here."

"You didn't mess up, *asere*," Jaime insisted. "We fell for a trap."

"I froze out there."

When Jaime did not respond, Lai turned fully around and opened her eyes.

"I froze," she repeated. "And we got caught."

"There were too many of them," Jaime argued. "Even if you had fired, they would have still caught us."

"I had a chance there. I know I did. I'm a good shot. I'm a fast shot. I could have gotten a few in and caused a distraction and some more of us might have gotten away."

"Lai, it wouldn't have—"

"Stop trying to make me feel better!" Lai sank down to her knees and fell back against the door with a thud. "Please. I froze. I never freeze."

"Maybe you had a reaction to something," he suggested.

Lai shook her head. Maybe he was right, but she didn't want to think about it anymore. She had already run through the scenario a million times on their drive over. A panic attack had since been ruled out. In the state she was in, she couldn't think up a better option.

Not that she had time to. By her best guess, they had half a day more to live. The sergeant wouldn't risk keeping them alive past then. They needed to be dealt with quickly or else they could have time to cause more problems.

This time, Lai didn't see a way out. Rescuing Mel was spontaneous, with no chance of anyone foreseeing the escape. The raid on the base was a firefight, something Lai was highly trained for. Being locked up with the entire academy on high alert, with only six of them versus hundreds of fully trained officers, plus at least two hundred trainees, was something entirely of its own.

"Hey, Lani."

Mel's words broke Lai out of her thoughts. She met her cousin's eyes again. Mel's gaze displayed the fear she was facing, but she also seemed to be trying to hold it back.

"Thank you for saving me." Mel blinked several times as wetness overtook her eyes. "But I'm sorry you ended up here. I can never forgive myself for that."

Tears threatened Lai as well, though she did not blink them back. She was never one to cry in front of others if she could help it, but it hardly mattered anymore.

"This isn't your fault," Lai insisted. She couldn't bear it if Mel blamed herself for what was happening.

"I keep thinking that it is," Mel choked. She sank down to the ground and threw her arms in the air helplessly. "I'm going to die anyway. I was always going to die. You two weren't. I dragged you into this."

"Hey. We got ourselves into this. I chose to save you. Jaime asked me to take him hostage." Lai shook her head and looked down at her lap. "If anything, I screwed things up for us the moment I said yes to joining the LP."

In a moment, Lai was on her feet again. She rapidly paced around the room in irregular patterns, her boots thumping on the concrete floor.

"This all started when I decided to get you out. I don't regret that decision, Mel. I could never regret that decision. You got a death sentence for defending a person you love, and it took it happening to you for me to realize how wrong this all is. Whatever is going to happen, until the moment I die, which is going to be very soon, I will never regret saving your life.

"But I got us in over our heads. Our plan was to get out of the country. My only priority was to get you out and keep you safe. The *Libertas Publica* helped us, but that was all it was supposed to be: help. I never wanted to get into a rebellion. I never wanted to be a part of a revolution, yet here we are. Here we are in a cell about to die, and it could have been prevented if I hadn't said yes to joining a group labeled a terrorist organization."

"Lai," Jaime tried to cut in, but he was quickly silenced.

"No," Lai said firmly. "I need to say this."

Jaime shut his mouth and let her continue.

"After the raid on the base, we should never have stayed. That only proved how dangerous it is to stay with them. Maybe if the situation wasn't so hot, it would have worked. I wouldn't have minded it working. But we killed fifteen officers during that raid, and twelve a few days before with the truck raid. I should have realized it then. We could still have gotten out. Gone north, found a way across the border. Started new lives. But I kept us in a war we could have avoided."

"We all decided to stay," Mel interrupted.

Lai stopped her pacing for a moment.

"You didn't force us," Mel continued. "I could have insisted we leave. Jaime could have. Neither of us did."

"But you took my lead," Lai said. "Don't pretend you weren't following me. You both have been the whole time. I would have if I were you. I was set to be a squad leader when I finished training."

"But I made the wrong call. The membership offer was given to me. I accepted and joined their fight when I should have been focused on keeping you safe."

"I am not your responsibility," Mel insisted. Her glare surprised Lai enough to stop walking again. "You may have training, but I'm not some helpless child that needs decisions made for her. I knew the risks of joining the LP. I could have said no. This is my fight as much as anyone else's. I'm the one who was supposed to be executed. If I don't have a reason to fight this system, nobody does."

Lai wanted to disagree, but she couldn't. At the very least, she knew Mel was right about one thing. They all decided to stay and fight rather than leave with the possibility of a better life. But it wasn't enough to assuage all her guilt.

"What does it even matter now? We're all about to die anyway, including you." Lai waved a hand toward Mel. "That's what I can't accept. You're right. You're not my responsibility. But you are my cousin and I love you. Everything started because of that. I can accept losing the flash drives and the information not getting to the LP. I can even accept myself dying for a cause I believe in. What I cannot accept is that you are still going to die. After everything I messed up, after how hard I tried, I couldn't even help you survive."

Lai put her hands to her head and squeezed them painfully against her temples. She gritted her teeth against the added agony of her injured hand but did not stop until she felt a wetness against her left temple she was sure was blood.

"Stop it," Mel ordered. She stood up and hurried over to where Lai stood. "Lani, stop it."

Lai listened and lowered her hands. Her attention fell to the red that colored her bandaged hand. She couldn't bring herself to care.

Ignoring the pain, Lai stalked over to the wall opposite her companions and leaned her forehead against the cool stone. She rested her left wrist on her head and ignored the blood that dripped down to mat her hair.

"I couldn't even do that," she whispered. "*Letse*. You're still going to die."

In a flash, Lai lifted her head and had her left arm raised with her hand in an excruciating fist. She brought her fist forward to make contact with the wall, but before she could, a pair of hands grabbed her arm and held her back. They tightened as she fought momentarily, but she quickly lost her resolve.

She turned around as Mel loosened her grip and pulled Lai into a tight hug. Lai let her arms hang limply at her sides as Mel held her.

"Come on, don't do this," Mel pressed. She brought a hand up to give the back of Lai's head comforting strokes. "Don't give them the satisfaction. You want to cry? Fine. But don't hurt yourself on purpose. It's not worth it."

"How are you so calm?" Lai mumbled into Mel's shoulder.

Mel finally pulled back and gave a heartbroken smile. "I did this whole thing a week ago. I don't have another breakdown in me."

It was possible that the anxiety was making Lai's perception shaky, or perhaps she really did find it amusing. Either way, at Mel's words, Lai found herself letting out a nervous giggle that swiftly evolved into a genuine laugh. Mel gave her a funny look for a moment, but it wasn't long before she too was swept up in the laughter. When chuckles were heard from behind them, both girls turned to see Jaime had joined in their laughter.

In a sight you would have to see to believe, three teenagers set for execution shared a brief lighthearted moment that gave Lai just what she needed to pull herself together. The laughter went on for another few seconds before it died. Lai grabbed Mel's hand and pulled her over to the wall and down next to Jaime. Everyone settled into their spots, with Mel on Lai's left and Jaime on her right. There they sat with remnants of their smiles still visible.

"So this is really it." Jaime sighed.

Lai rested her head back against the wall and stared at the ceiling. "This is it."

"I never thought it would end up how it did," he admitted.

"Me neither."

"I wonder what would have happened with you two if I hadn't gotten arrested," Mel said.

Lai glanced over to Mel and brushed a long blonde hair back from her face with her good hand. "Jaime and I would still be students. We wouldn't know just how screwed up the Republic is. We would be on the other side of a base raid."

"We'd all be alive," Mel pointed out.

"We'd be sheep," Jaime argued. "We would follow our commanders because we were never taught differently."

Lai reached over to grab her friend's hand and hold it in her lap. "We would be every other student in this academy."

Mel reached her own hand over and placed it on top of Lai and Jaime's. "If I'm dying, at least it's with you two."

Jaime squeezed Lai's hand as he spoke. "I can see my sister soon."

"And we can see Oscar," Mel added.

Lai breathed out a heavy sigh and the corners of her mouth rose into a cheeky smile. "I'll still be stuck with you two."

Jaime elbowed her lightly while sporting his own slight smile.

If it was possible for Lai to be thankful for anything at the time, and even if she felt wrong for thinking it, she was truly thankful to not be alone in her last few hours. Of course she would rather have no one else executed alongside her, but if it were to happen, at least she could spend the time with her best friend and her cousin.

If company was all she could have, then she was damn well going to be happy about it.

"Hey," Mel said softly with a gentle bump against Lai's shoulder to get her attention. Lai faced her and Mel's grip tightened on her hand.

"If we're getting all philosophical and spiritual here, you'll get to see your dad again."

Yes, there was also that small solace for Lai to consider. Her father, who had died in a fishing accident ten years before, whose face she could only recall through photographs. If she were somehow in the good graces of whatever awaited after her execution, her father would be the first person to see. It was that thought that for the next twelve hours allowed her to keep her mind.

CHAPTER TWENTY-EIGHT

BY LAI'S internal clock, she figured it was around four in the afternoon when they were finally removed from their cells and led to the training area. With the bag over her head, she could see nothing of the halls they were being led down, but that mattered little. She knew every turn they made, and she knew exactly when they reached the prisoners' entrance to the training room. It was a quick walk; the guards hurried them along as if eager to see traitors executed. For a moment, Lai idly wondered if there would be a video camera set up in the room.

She heard the ever-familiar sound of the doors opening in front of her and stepped forward when she received a shove from the officer holding her arm. They walked another short distance before she was stopped and turned around to face what she knew was the main area. She took shallow breaths and stared ahead at nothing. The cloth bag made it difficult to breathe. Whenever she tried to take in a deep gulp of air, the bag would mold itself to her face until she blew it away. After trying that a handful of times, she settled for the short breaths. They would be fine until the bag was taken off in a moment.

Lai let her arms go limp as someone grabbed her wrists and undid her handcuffs. Before she had a chance to move, her arms were pulled up to each side of her, and she felt her wrists being fastened into the wall restraints.

A good choice, she noted. The wall restraints were two curves of metal bolted into the wall to either side of the prisoner. They could not be adjusted and so were only used if the prisoner fit the width of the space. Evidently, she did. She assumed Jaime and Virginia did as well. Mel, being half a head taller than the three of them, would likely have her arms above her head. She was less of a risk anyway without training. Wall bolts were harder to break free from.

At the sound of heavy footsteps approaching, Lai closed her eyes and waited. A few seconds later, the bag was pulled off her head, and she was grateful for the darkness behind her eyelids against the glare of fluorescent lights beating down from above. She allowed her eyes to open gradually to adjust to the brightness. Half a dozen seconds later, when her eyes were fully opened, she was finally able to see the room that spread out in front of her.

The remaining members of Beta Five, minus Rylen, were all standing about in the training room with their focus on the six now shackled to the wall. Lai spared a glance to each side of her. She was in the middle of the group, with Jaime to her far right and Mel in between them. To her left were Virginia, Jackie, and Benjamin, all restrained in the way she had assumed.

Lai took a deep breath and found that her chest shook as she did so. She couldn't decide whether or not that surprised her. Of course she would be fearful in the face of death. It was only natural. Still, even in a situation unlike any she had been in before, she thought she could hold it together. If for nothing else, doing so would surely help the others stay calm.

Lai turned her head forward again and caught the eye of Kieran, who was standing at Lai's station and twirling a gun in her left hand. Lai was less put out to see it was Kieran's own gun, though upon further inspection she could see her gun at Kieran's waist. It seemed even in her last moments, Kieran wouldn't give Lai a break.

Kieran caught Lai staring and tilted her head ever so slightly. "Your hand looks like hell, Lani." The expression on her face was indecipherable. "What did you do, punch a wall?"

"Something like that," Lai replied coolly with a slight flex of her left hand. Her eyes flicked to Kieran's right shoulder. "Your shoulder looks better."

Kieran shrugged on her good side and ceased the handwork with her gun. "I got the bullets removed while you were locked up. It pays to have a real medical facility."

"I'm so glad," Lai said with a sardonic smile.

Try as she might, Lai somehow found herself unable to be angry with Kieran any further. The girl did have a sliver of a point. For someone with her background, safety was the most important thing. If this was the only way, who was Lai to fault her for taking whatever chance she may get?

It didn't stop Lai from being bitter, but anyone about to die would be bitter at the person who did not bother trying to stop it. Perhaps her anger had dissipated, not because she didn't want to be angry but because there was little point to it anymore.

Regardless, Lai didn't want to spend her last few minutes conversing with Kieran. She let her gaze wander around the room to the nine other members of her former training group. A few of them were talking in the back, their guns holstered. Five others, Siobhan, Tamsin, Vineet, Chinua, and Naja, stood at stations next to Kieran where one of the six was held against the wall. The sergeant stood off to the far left having a hushed conversation with one of the lieutenants of a Delta group.

"Where's Rylen?" Virginia asked.

A few turned to her. Everyone seemed reluctant to answer. After a long silence, it was Siobhan who broke it and answered.

"He didn't want to see this," she replied with a hard look in her eyes, harder than Lai was used to seeing on her. "He was dehydrated anyway. He's in medical, resting."

"Somehow you're all okay with doing this," Jaime remarked.

This time it was Kieran who spoke up first. "We do this all the time. It's our job."

"You've never had to execute friends before," he pointed out.

"Friends don't betray us," Vineet called.

"Friends don't join a terrorist group," Claudia agreed from the back.

"You see?" Kieran said. "It's easier this way."

"Is it easier for you too?" Mel asked.

Kieran turned her gaze to Mel and kept her mouth shut. Mel took the opportunity to continue. "You're the one who's been with us for four days."

"At least Rylen could admit it's hard," Virginia said.

Before anyone else could speak up, the sergeant marched forward and took up her usual position at the side of the firing stations.

"Enough talk," she called in her authoritative voice. She planted her fists on her hips and swept her gaze over the students in the room.

Rather than watch the sergeant as she issued orders, Lai turned her attention to her cousin and attempted a comforting expression. When Mel returned it with her own hardened look, Lai wasn't at all surprised. Mel had changed a great deal since Lai had rescued her from this very room, and even more since she'd left for training. Uncertainty could bring out the strangest things in people.

"I am setting no parameters for this execution," the sergeant told them. "Shoot to maim. Shoot to kill. I don't care. As long as they're all dead in the end, what you do to them first is no concern of mine. There won't be any ethics committee to hear about it and breathe down our necks."

Lai felt a brief twinge of worry before the feelings settled in her stomach. She didn't believe any of them would want to hurt them more than they had to. Betrayed or not, hurting a friend, even a former one, was never an easy task.

"You all have fully loaded weapons," Sergeant Washington continued. "Use the entire clip if you want."

"It doesn't matter what you do," Jackie snapped all of a sudden. She waited until all eyes had turned to her before she continued. "You children can make us suffer before we die. The *Libertas Publica* doesn't end with us. It only ends when this government has fallen to rubble beneath your feet. When that happens, you'll be the sorry ones. I can die knowing we'll still win in the end."

"That was an amusing little outbreak." The sergeant smirked. "You won't be so brave when you're bleeding out."

"We'll see," Jackie growled.

As Sergeant Washington ordered the six students to ready their weapons, Lai turned her head to the right and stared over at her cousin and her best friend.

"Thank you," she whispered in a remarkably steady voice.

"For what?" Jaime asked.

Lai allowed the barest hint of a smile. "For helping me do the right thing."

"Even if it ends like this," Mel added with a slight nod.

Lai let out another deep breath and closed her eyes. "Even like this."

When the sergeant called for the students to aim, Lai opened her eyes, gave Mel and Jaime one last smile, and faced forward to accept her fate. She made herself stare straight at Kieran as the girl held her gun steady in her left hand. Lai traced the line of fire to her forehead and allowed herself to be grateful for that at the very least. A quick death was better than what Kieran could feel entitled to.

There was a transient moment of silence in the room, a brief window where everyone seemed to hold their breath before the coming fire. Lai reveled in it, embraced it, accepted it as her last moment on the earth. If for nothing else, she was going to be grateful for that moment.

"Fire."

In a motion that seemed too swift to comprehend after the everlasting few seconds of quiet, Lai saw Kieran spin around and aim her gun at the sergeant.

"On your knees," Kieran ordered.

The room burst into a flurry of movement as the other five Beta Five students turned their guns away from their targets on the line and pointed them at the nearest of the six officers around the room. In the back, the remaining four students pulled out their own weapons and made sure at least one gun was on each officer. They all shouted commands to the officers, ordering them not to touch their guns and stay where they were.

"I said on your knees," Kieran growled. After the shortest of glances to the six on the line, the sergeant ever so carefully did as she was told.

"Anyone who so much as lifts a finger is getting a bullet through their skull," Kieran threatened.

Any confusion spiraling throughout the room was lost on Lai. In any other state, she might have been completely baffled. As it was, with her mind already decided upon understanding, it didn't take a second to see what was happening.

One smirk from Kieran confirmed it.

Out of the corner of her eye, Lai could see one of the officers reach for the gun at his waist. Before she could so much as open her mouth to utter a cry of warning, Naja fired a bullet into his forehead. Kieran barely spared a glance, her attention divided between Lai and the sergeant.

"Siobhan, help me with them," Kieran instructed. With one last hard glare to the sergeant, she holstered her weapon, hopped over the safety line, and hurried to where Lai stood restrained to the wall.

"You are one sneaky girl," Lai marveled.

Kieran held out her hand for the keys Siobhan had procured and flashed a cheeky smile. "I try," she said as she unlocked the bolt on Lai's left wrist.

"This whole time?" Lai asked.

Kieran nodded while unlocking the bolt on the other side. "You doubted me."

When both restraints were undone, Lai carefully massaged her left wrist. "Believe me. I won't do that again."

Kieran offered her one more smile before she handed the keys to Lai. As Lai went to work unlocking the others, who were either sporting expressions of unmitigated disbelief or profound gratitude, Kieran took hold of her gun again and walked over to stand not a meter away from the sergeant.

"Oh my God," Mel breathed when Lai unlocked her handcuffs. She allowed Mel to throw her arms around her for a brief moment before Lai gently pushed her off and went to free Jaime. There would be time enough for rejoicing when they were truly free.

Not that she could blame her after what she had been through twice.

"Yo pensaba que estábamos muertos de seguro," Jaime laughed as he was freed. "Kieran is very convincing."

Lai let out a relieved smile and gave her friend a clap on the shoulder before moving on.

As she freed the others, Lai allowed herself a moment to catch her breath. It was only her intensive training to stay in the moment and keep focused on the task at hand that kept her from crying out with the pure joy of still being alive when she thought she would be dead a minute ago. It was as if she was somehow living on extra time now. She figured she would be feeling that for quite a while.

That is, if they were even alive for more than another few minutes. They were, after all, still very much inside the academy walls.

"You got everyone to do this," Lai said in genuine awe as she came to stand beside Kieran. The others behind her were all free and now finding their way into the main area, where the students were providing them with firearms of their own.

"I called a group meeting," Kieran explained, her gun still on the sergeant and her eyes on Lai. "None of them were very happy with the idea of shooting you, especially not after I told them about the falsely convicted prisoners. Not to mention what happened to Deirdre. It took surprisingly little convincing. Here."

Kieran reached down to her waistband and pulled out Lai's gun. She went to hand it to Lai, but Lai immediately snatched her hand back at the sight of it.

"I can't," she admitted, memories of the base raid flashing in her mind once again.

A second later, Mel came up next to them and took the gun. "I got it."

At Lai's raised eyebrow, she continued. "I got a few lessons from Jaime."

"You got four," he corrected from a few feet away.

"Be careful," Lai warned.

Mel nodded once and fidgeted with the safety.

"I hope you have a plan now," Lai said to Kieran.

Kieran took a deep breath before she spoke. "You could say that." Without another word she did a one-eighty and aimed her gun at the wall at the back of the room. Lai turned just in time to see her shoot at the fire alarm.

Just as Lai remembered from thrice yearly drills, the cacophony of the alarm bells rang out. They were accompanied by the blinking red emergency lights in each corner of the room that flashed in time with the incessant ringing.

"Time to move out!" Kieran shouted over the alarm.

Like clockwork, Beta Five fell into a standard retreat formation with Kieran, their apparent leader, Mel, and Lai in the center.

"Kieran?" Lai said.

"I got this, Lani," Kieran insisted as the group moved back toward the exit.

"Can you cut out the Lani now that you're not acting?" Lai stepped backward with Kieran, a half step behind the girl in case things went south sooner than expected.

Kieran let out a shaky laugh. "Not a chance."

They moved swiftly toward the door, their backs never turned from the sergeant and the five remaining officers in the room. Lai knew that soon enough there would be more than six people to deal with. She couldn't imagine what Kieran hoped to accomplish by setting off the fire alarm. That essentially begged additional officers to make their way to the training room to discern the source of the disturbance and whether or not it really was a fire.

The door clicked open behind them, the same door she had escaped through not two weeks before. She glanced over her shoulder and placed a hand on Kieran's back to guide her through the door.

Outside, the sun was blinding, as Lai expected it to be. She noted that the four students, or rather former students, taking up the back had turned to face the desert as they made their way farther from the academy walls.

Lai quickly glanced to either side. Jaime flanked them on the right. He held his gun in a tight two-handed grip. The splint was still attached to his prosthetic and caused disruptions in his stride as he walked unevenly backward.

"You doing all right, Jaime?" Lai called over to him.

Jaime met her gaze and flashed her an optimistic smile. "You kidding, *asere*?" I did it for eleven years without a fancy prosthetic. I can do it now."

Lai returned his smile and focused ahead. Their retreat was slow, but it was cautious. While turning and running might seem to be an enticing option, it offered no protection and would likely end in them all being dead due to lack of warning to an attack.

Even as they were proceeding, Lai wasn't sure what they were hoping to accomplish. The first time Lai had broken out, she had a hostage, albeit a fake one, but a perceived one nonetheless.

"Kieran—" Lai began.

"I said I got this," Kieran cut her off.

Lai scowled and attributed Kieran's shorter than usual temper to their less than pleasant situation. "Please tell me there's a real plan here."

"The plan is escape," came the reply. "I had to work on short notice."

"That's it?"

Kieran sighed loudly. "We can circle around the side of the building and jack two of the trucks."

"You think that will—"

As Lai had expected, two squads of officers poured through the open door with firearms at the ready. Half a second later, they started their barrage.

With nowhere to hide, the group all dropped to the ground. Without a weapon of her own, Lai ducked behind Kieran as the girl returned fire. Mel fell in beside Kieran and fired her own string of bullets, albeit less accurately.

Lai didn't have to check to know that more officers would be joining those already outside in a moment. Surprise had been their only advantage, and that disappeared the moment Kieran shot the fire alarm.

"*Letse*, Kieran!" Lai shouted over the sound of gunfire. "You know why they built the academy here? There's nothing around it for miles! That makes it very difficult to escape!"

"You did it!" Kieran shot back as she continued to fire. From Lai's vantage point, an officer grasped a hand to his throat and blood spurted from between his fingers.

A sudden choked cry brought Lai's attention to her left. Through the rain of bullets, Benjamin fell forward into the sand. His gun dropped from his hand, and he slumped to the ground into an unmoving heap.

Not five seconds later, Devlin's body hit the ground. As he went down, he was hit with another three bullets in quick succession.

A rush of dread hit Lai in an instant. This wasn't working.

"We need to move," she called, hopefully just loud enough for those around her to hear. "If we stay here, they'll take us out one by one."

Without a formal order, everyone rose to their feet and the members of Beta Five fell into an evasion pattern of quick, erratic movements to take away any hope of an easy target from their assailants. Lai did the same in an unpredictable dance that edged them closer to the eastern side of the building where they would find the supply trucks. It was looking like that was their only option.

Barely two meters in front of her, Lai watched helpless as Siobhan was hit squarely in the abdomen. The girl doubled over and collapsed to her knees as she let out an irregular, high-pitched wheezing.

The image of Deirdre going down flashed in Lai's mind as she sidestepped around a patch of brush.

"Siobhan!" Tamsin screamed as she ran forward to her friend. Lai snapped to attention and pulled her back just as a second bullet went sailing into Siobhan's forehead.

"No!" Tamsin cried in a choked whisper.

Siobhan went down in a cloud of dust and sand as the blood seeped from her head wound to paint the ground crimson.

Lai desperately attempted to partition her flashes of memory from the task at hand. "Tamsin!" she said with great urgency. Tamsin gradually shifted her attention to Lai as tears traced lines down her face. "Siobhan is gone. We need to keep moving."

As if to prove her point, a bullet grazed Lai's left calf. She hissed and took a few uneven steps back.

Escaping from the north side of the academy had one clear advantage. Officers deployed from the east near the trucks and supply storages. There was nothing to the north but dry and desolate sand, at least not until the compounds where they had escaped the first time.

Their escape plan had another clear flaw. Officers deployed from the east near the trucks they wanted to reach.

Another squad of officers deployed from the east side of the building. They were fully armed with bulletproof shields and assault rifles that outmatched their handguns by tenfold. The officers took up a defensive position and set themselves up to shoot.

Jaime stumbled over to Lai and followed her pattern of steps. He wiped a mixture of blood and sweat from his forehead and fired at the swiftly assembling group of officers.

"Tell me we have a better plan than this, *asere*," he said.

Before Lai could answer, he shoved her to one side and fired several bullets in quick succession. Two officers holding assault rifles went down before they could return fire.

"I think this is some last-ditch effort," Mel called as she circled around behind them.

"So we're screwed," Jaime growled.

Lai was about to agree when she heard the one thing that could make her change her mind.

"Vivat populus!"

In all the chaos, Lai hadn't heard the trucks approaching.

They came roaring over a sand dune, two trucks with metal plating secured to the sides and front. They were bigger than the stolen supply trucks, and a head stuck up from each with an assault rifle mounted to the roof just in front. On the front metal plate of each truck was the symbol of the *Libertas Publica*.

The trucks skidded to a halt next to one another in a V shape. An instant later, fully armed and protected LP members poured out with heavier weapons than Beta Five had been able to grab. They took up positions behind the trucks with their firearms pointed at the officers advancing to either side.

The shock wore off as soon as a familiar face stuck his head out of the driver seat of the closest truck.

"Someone call for some backup?" Sydney asked with a cheeky smile.

Lai wasted no time in sprinting for the cover of the trucks. She ducked her head as bullets peppered the metal plates and dove the final few feet to safety. Several more thuds sounded behind her and she turned to see the rest of her friends joining her. Jackie circled around the other side and laughed with elation as she fired openly.

"You're a few minutes late," Kieran shouted from behind the other truck. Sydney hopped out of the truck with his own M4 and shrugged a shoulder.

"It took some convincing," he explained before he let loose a storm of bullets.

"How the hell did you pull this off?" Lai called over to Kieran.

"Rylen can hack anything," came the reply. Kieran accepted a new handgun from an LP member and answered the academy officers' fire with her own.

Lai flattened herself to the ground and peered under the truck. She focused her attention on the door from the training room, as she expected more officers to come out any moment. When they did, they would be further outnumbered until there were a hundred to one. Even with the help, Lai didn't know how they hoped to accomplish their escape with so few numbers against the entire academy.

All of a sudden, the door slammed shut as if a huge gust of wind had blown against it, though there was hardly a breeze to be felt.

It took Lai half a moment before she saw the flashing red light above the doorway.

"I said one minute, damn it," Kieran grumbled.

Lai jumped. She hadn't heard Kieran come up next to her. "What are you talking about? How is the academy locked down?"

"I told you. Rylen can hack anything," Kieran said with a wink.

As if drawn by the sound of her friend's name, Virginia joined them in their crouched positions behind the front of the truck.

"What do you mean?" she asked breathlessly. Lai noted with concern the blood that dripped from Virginia's right side. Virginia herself hardly seemed to notice it.

"I told him to wait for my signal and lock down the academy," Kieran elaborated. She paused for a moment to fire half a dozen bullets and then ducked back down. "No one is getting out of there anytime soon."

"He's stuck inside?" Virginia gasped.

Lai didn't think she could admire her team members more than in that moment.

As Virginia grappled with the fate of her friend, Lai forced herself to take several deep breaths. She had done a quick count of LP members when they arrived. Sixteen. Add to that the eleven armed and alive teenagers in the mix, they were more than a match for the thirty or so officers that remained. Less in fact, as Lai watched Sydney toss a grenade in the direction of the officers with their now-useless shields.

Shouts came from the officers as they realized what was happening and that they would not be receiving any more backup. The gunfire gradually diminished until no weapons were being discharged. In an instant the LP members were moving out from their blockade and shouting orders.

With a smug grin on his face, Sydney tossed bulletproof vests down to the Beta Five members. Lai caught one and pulled it on over her jacket. As she did, she became painfully aware of the aches and bruises covering her body. A glance at her forearms revealed shredded sleeves and arms, thanks to her dive behind the truck. The wound on her left leg stung like all hell, and her head was filled with an excruciating ringing.

But she was alive. They were alive.

She stood up cautiously. A peek over the hood of the truck revealed the officers convening into one group with their weapons laid on the ground and their hands on their heads. By a quick count, there were only sixteen of them left.

A hand grabbed hers as she started forward. She looked over to see Mel offer her a shaky smile that matched the quivering in her hand. Lai squeezed it tightly and pulled Mel along toward the surrendering officers. The sergeant was among them, and she sported a death glare that normally would have had the students quaking in their training gear.

"You're going to regret this one day, Harris," the sergeant promised. "All of you. This country won't ever be safe for you again."

"This country has never been safe for us," Jackie said as she strolled up next to Lai with an M4 over her shoulder. The corners of her mouth twitched up, though her eyes showed nothing but contempt. "It starts here. We will continue getting our small victories, and they will continue to grow."

"Once we've released the information on the wrongfully executed prisoners, you'll have bigger problems than us," Sydney added. He stuck his hands into his pockets and pulled out half a dozen flash drives. At his companions shocked expressions, he gave them a wink. "I managed to grab these before I slipped away from the house."

"You're nothing but filthy terrorists," Sergeant Washington spat, "and you'll get what you deserve."

"We don't need to waste our time with them," Jaime said with a wave of his hand. He stood next to Lai and shoved his gun into his waistband.

"He's right," Sydney agreed. "We need to get moving."

He leaned over to Jackie and whispered something to her. She nodded and crossed her arms. Sydney turned to the teens scattered around behind them.

"All of you can follow Lilian," he said with a gesture to one of the LP members standing by, "and she'll take you to a secure facility."

He turned his attention to Lai and pointed out her, Mel, Jaime, Kieran, and Virginia. "You five can come with me and Jackie. No time to waste."

The members of Beta Five all huddled together uncertainly.

"It's all right," Lai reassured them. "I know we can trust them."

A hand landed on her shoulder and Lai turned as Tamsin pulled her into a tight hug. She returned it with equal force until Tamsin pulled away half a dozen seconds later.

"Stay safe," Tamsin said.

Lai gave her a comforting smile. "You too."

Jaime and Mel rejoined Lai as she followed Jackie toward one of the trucks. She looked back. Sydney followed behind. She gestured her head to him, and he jogged up beside them.

"Where are we going?" Lai asked.

Sydney grinned wide. "The commander wants to meet our newest recruits," he told them with a wink. "Assuming you five have accepted our offer."

"Hell yes we have," Mel laughed.

Lai nodded her agreement along with the others around them.

They pulled themselves into the back of the truck as Sydney climbed into the driver seat. Two other *Libertas Publica* members joined him in the cab of the truck while Jackie came to make six members in the back. Before she climbed in, she whistled once to the remaining members around the officers. When one looked back, she crossed her arms in front of her with her fists balled tight and nodded. The man then relayed orders Lai couldn't hear.

"What are they doing?" she asked.

Rather than receiving a verbal answer, she got her reply as the thirteen *Libertas Publica* members discharged their weapons into the kneeling officers.

Lai couldn't even get out a gasp as the truck roared to life and peeled away from the slaughter to take them deeper into the desert.

CHAPTER TWENTY-NINE

THE *LIBERTAS Publica* doesn't leave loose ends.

That was what Jackie told Lai when she asked why they had to kill the officers rather than leave them unarmed outside the academy.

"It's a matter of security," Jackie said with a slight shrug of her shoulder. "Leaving highly trained officers alive poses a risk to our safety."

Under normal circumstances Lai would have been inclined to probe further, but as it was, she was utterly exhausted after a sleepless night and the improvised escape. Arguing with Jackie about execution was the last thing she needed.

The first three hours of the drive brought them north through the desert, in the same direction Lai, Jaime, and Mel had gone after their first escape. Rather than stay north, however, the trucks cut a path to the west, skirting just south of Yuma, enough so that Lai was surprised they stayed north of the border. In a tiny village Lai never caught the name of, they swapped the conspicuous logoed trucks for a moving van. A strange choice, Lai thought, though it would certainly draw little attention. Much to her delight, the van had been outfitted with seats in the back that proved comfier than the military trucks she had grown accustomed to. She even managed to steal a few hours of sleep here and there as they headed north before they could hit the coast.

As she was intermittently sleeping, Lai would have missed much of their journey, even if they hadn't been in the back of the moving van. During a brief rest stop to refill the gas tank, Lai managed to talk Jackie into letting her ride in the front cab with her for the remainder of the trip after Jackie claimed the driver seat. Jackie relented once Lai reminded her how she could be quiet when she wanted to, proven by their drive to the safe house a few days earlier.

The front seats were even more comfortable than the seats in the rear, and Lai managed another couple hours of sleep as Jackie led them closer to the base and to safety. The road they took that ran parallel to the highway was mostly deserted, a fact Jackie seemed grateful for.

If she was being honest with herself, Lai was grateful for it as well. The fewer people they passed, she figured, the less chance they had of being caught again. Escaping from the academy for the third time was not a challenge Lai was eager to attempt.

Especially not if it ends in another mass execution, she thought, and then almost laughed at the irony. Mass executions in the name of security.

The sun had only just breached the horizon when Jackie turned them west to skirt the city of Sacramento. Lai expected her to continue past it as she had every other city they had passed, but instead she stuck close to the outskirts as she once again turned them to the north.

Lai felt one corner of her mouth turn up. "So the base is here."

Jackie eyed her without turning her head from the road. "I didn't say that."

"You also didn't drive this close to any other city we weren't stopping in. The base is here."

By the way Jackie pressed her lips tightly together, Lai thought she was holding back a smile. "I guess you are a member now," she conceded, a hint of her smile breaking through, "even if you are just a kid."

"Hey, it was a bunch of kids that saved your ass back there," Lai reminded her with a growing smile.

Jackie only grunted. Lai repressed a laugh and turned her gaze forward again.

They continued along the edge of the city for another twenty or so miles. As they drove, Lai noticed buildings in the distance, though the sun shining through the gaps made it difficult to focus her attention on them for too long. The view to the west was less interesting, hardly more than an expanse of desert over a shallow river. Lai knew precious little about this area, though she supposed she would be getting to know it if the base was located in the city.

Just when Lai thought they couldn't possibly drive any farther without passing the city limits, Jackie pulled onto a road that snaked its way into the northern part of the city.

"Almost there," Jackie said, quietly enough that it was almost to herself.

Lai looked over to her. "When was the last time you were at this base?"

Jackie thought for a moment. "Two months. I don't technically operate out of any one base. I just go where Cara tells me. I'll be glad to be somewhere with actual security." Jackie let out a loud, annoyed huff. "I don't ever want a field assignment again."

Lai smiled to herself and followed Jackie's line of sight to the sign on the left side of the road. Behind it, another stretch of dried grassland spread out as far as the eye could see.

"Natomas Park," Lai read aloud as she peered out the front window. "It doesn't look like much of a park."

"It used to," Jackie chimed in, "at least before the government added three times as many water pipes to leach water from the west coast. After that, the watering of parks stopped being terribly important."

Lai hummed an acknowledgment and leaned back into her seat. "So how does the nation's most notorious terrorist organization manage to hide its main base?"

Jackie let out a quick chuckle under her breath. "In plain sight."

Lai raised her eyebrows and waited for Jackie to explain further.

Jackie offered her a sly grin. "You'll see" was all she added.

Lai huffed and let herself sink a few inches in the seat. She winced as her pant leg brushed the wound she had there and reached across to pull it back from her skin with her good hand. When she looked back up, they were pulling into the parking lot of what seemed to be a school, though it was crumbling and blackened as if by a blaze.

"This is the base?" Lai asked doubtfully.

Her attention strayed to the multitude of empty window frames, where a flash of movement caught her eye.

"Was that a guard?" she asked with a frown.

Jackie shrugged. "Probably."

"Are they going to shoot us?"

Jackie didn't answer right away. Instead, she brought the van to a stop and opened her door. She jumped out of her seat before Lai could ask what she was doing.

She walked a few paces in front of the van and raised her right arm in the air. She made a fist and pumped it twice before bring it to her chest.

"Vivat populus!" she called out. Lai recognized the saying when Sydney had first revealed him and his companions as friends.

Jackie remained still for a long moment, a bit too long for Lai's comfort. Worry crept into her mind for a second before the call was returned. She breathed out a sigh of relief.

Jackie quickly turned around and made her way back into the van. "Now they won't shoot us."

Lai kept her focus ahead as they pulled toward the building. After Jackie's announcement of arrival, Lai could see at least another half dozen people moving around inside or surrounding the building.

A sudden grating noise filled Lai's ears, like something being dragged harshly across stone. Her estimation turned out to be correct when a large metal door pulled back along the concrete, allowing the van to pull into the building. Their van stopped, and Jackie pulled the keys from the ignition and stepped out again. Lai followed suit and walked around the front of the van to meet her. She was quickly joined by the others, with Mel immediately moving to her side.

"This is weird," Mel said simply.

Lai nodded her agreement. The small room was empty save for the moving van, its nine previous occupants, four armed guards, and a large metal double doorway with a keypad next to it. Jackie nodded to the guards and made her way over to the keypad. With a flick of her wrist, everyone followed her over to the back of the dimly lit room.

The guard closest to the doors turned as they approached and punched a series of numbers into the keypad. When he finished, he pressed the large green button on the bottom. There was a minute pause before the doors shuddered open to reveal a spacious cargo elevator.

Mel seemed concerned. "This thing looks a hundred years old."

Lai had to admit she too had concerns about getting into it. Rust climbed up the walls, and the thing groaned before anyone had even set foot in it.

Jackie waved off their worries. "It's safe." She stepped in first, followed shortly after by Sydney and the other two *Libertas Publica* members.

It groaned ever louder under their weight.

"I'm sure," Kieran grumbled from where she stood a step behind Lai.

Lai glanced back at her and shrugged helplessly. Without another word she stepped in, joined a few seconds later by the rest of her companions.

Jackie shook her head as the doors closed in front of them.

"What?" Lai asked.

"Oh, nothing." Jackie chuckled as the elevator began its descent. "You pull off a rescue and escape from a heavily armed facility, and a creaky elevator makes you nervous."

"Esa cosa se ve sospechosa…," Jaime mumbled.

Lai chose to ignore the comments as her mind buzzed with questions. "How is this even possible?" she asked. Her gaze darted around the rusted lift, and she took further note of the dated engineering.

Jackie glanced to her briefly before she replied. "This area used to be an underground storage facility. There were originally seven elevators to the lower levels from the surface. Five were completely sealed off when it was decommissioned in the late twenty-eighties to build an elementary school above ground. When the school was wrecked in a fire ten years later, the property was abandoned entirely."

"One of our early members stumbled on this place by accident," Sydney added.

Jackie nodded and tapped the side of the lift with her knuckles. "We sealed off the other one. This is the only way in or out of the base that leads directly to the surface, other than the labyrinth of tunnels out east. Makes guarding it a lot simpler."

Lai hummed shortly. Any further questions she might have had died in her throat as the lift shuddered to a halt. The younger occupants stumbled for a moment as the elevator creaked out its last protests before settling into place. Not a second later, the doors slid open.

She hadn't exactly expected a welcome committee.

Guards, sure, but the three people who stood in front of her were minimally armed, and the woman in the center sported a wide grin on her face.

Lai stepped aside as Jackie swept out of the elevator and planted herself in front of the woman.

"Commander," she greeted formally, a hand flying to her forehead in a salute. Rather than return it, the woman Lai could reasonably identify as Commander Cara Vandere grabbed Jackie's arm and pulled her into a tight embrace.

"Shut up, Jacqueline," she laughed. Lai stared at Cara with great interest. Cara winked to her. "Always so formal, even when she nearly died."

Cara pulled back and allowed Jackie to free herself from the commander's arms. Jackie coughed once and turned back to face the group as they stepped out of the elevator after her.

"Jacqueline?" Lai whispered to Jackie with a poorly hidden grin as the woman fell back next to her.

Jackie rolled her eyes. "Only she gets away with it."

Lai felt herself bite her tongue as the elevator doors groaned shut behind them. The seven of them now stood in a messy line in front of the commander and the two members who flanked her.

Cara placed her hands on her hips, fingers tapping rhythmically, and nodded to Lai. "Lailani Harris, I presume?"

"Yes, ma'am," Lai confirmed with a nod of her own.

Cara emulated Jackie's eye roll from a moment before. "You'd think with how everyone addresses me that we were in the Protection Force."

As Cara appraised her, Lai took a moment to do the same to the people in front of her and the surrounding area.

They had exited the elevator into an intersection of wide halls leading out in three directions. Two armed guards stood off to the side near the hall to their left, their eyes trained on the new arrivals. Before them, a multitude of people bustled around and across the halls and skirted the group in the center. Few paid them any mind, all clearly consumed with their respective tasks, though one or two stopped to salute the commander, which earned each a good-natured eye roll and wave of her wrist.

Her attention returned to the commander. She was a rather small woman, perhaps only an inch taller than Lai herself, and no more than forty. She wore an oversized black T-shirt, tan cargo pants held up by a packed utility belt, and black combat boots. Her jet-black hair was pulled back in a loose ponytail that let a few strands fall in front of her eyes. Lai made note of her ethnicity, apparently Southeast Asian, though her lack of an accent implied she was not first generation, or at least not a recent immigrant. How could she be, anyway, if she was the commander?

Her relaxed demeanor was what caught Lai off guard. She had expected the leader of the *Libertas Publica* to be more imposing, if not in stature then in disposition. The open grin on her face, coupled with her probing gaze, left Lai wondering what could possibly make this woman tick.

Though it felt like much longer, Cara stuck her hand out to Lai only a handful of seconds later. "Cara Vandere," she said, her grin growing impossibly larger. "I have heard some great things about you."

Lai grasped her hand and returned the smile, albeit more reserved than Cara's.

Cara's attention shifted to Kieran. She clicked her tongue, and her eyes narrowed ever so slightly as she took in the girl. "You organized the big escape?"

Kieran nodded and kept her expression polite but neutral.

"I have to say, I approve." Cara chuckled. She took a step back and pointed to her two companions. "Sorry. This is Maurice Tao." She wagged a finger to the man standing to her left. "Oversees security of the base. He'd have an aneurysm if I didn't bring him to meet outsiders."

She placed a hand on the back of the wheelchair of the dark-skinned woman sitting to her right. "Annie Jones, logistics. I couldn't survive without either of them."

Without missing a beat, Cara made a wide gesture to the group in front of her. "Those all look painful."

Lai glanced down at her bandaged left hand, and further at the wound left when a bullet sliced the side of her leg open. The rest of her companions were faring about as well.

"Come," Cara said simply. She turned on her heels and started down the long hall in front of them, not waiting to see if they were following.

Jackie shook her head and shrugged when Lai shot her a questioning look. "Just go with it," she advised, and fell into step behind Cara.

Lai waited until everyone had started walking before she took up the rear. Kieran, who was only a few steps ahead of her, slowed until she was at the same pace.

"She's certainly...." Kieran's last syllable dragged out as she searched for words.

"Different?" Lai suggested.

Kieran let out a noisy breath. "I was going to say weird."

Lai hummed her agreement. "Weird works."

"You trust her?"

Lai shrugged and offered a faint smile. "I think I will."

"HOW MUCH do you know about how we started?"

Lai opened her eyes, her vision momentarily assailed by the fluorescent lights beating down from the ceiling. She took a moment to regain her senses, her focus greatly distracted by the stinging in her left hand, and turned her attention to the woman who had spoken.

Cara sat on the bed across from Lai with her legs dangling over the edge, her feet clearing the floor by no more than an inch. She would resemble an excited child, were it not for the weapon at her hip and the experience etched into her features behind the smiling face. She fixed Lai with a questioning look.

Glad for the distraction from the medic working on her injured hand, Lai answered her question. "Most of what I know is rumors, and chances are half of it isn't true."

Cara nodded once, and one side of her grin came higher on her face. "Tell me."

The others in the infirmary either seemed to be completely ignoring their conversation or giving the pair their full attention. The medics, including the one working on Lai's hand, ignored them for the most part, except to give an instruction. A few beds away, Kieran and Mel sat close together, their hushed conversation falling away as they tuned into Lai and Cara's. The next bed over from them, Jaime turned his head to listen as well while two medics poked and prodded at his prosthetic. Virginia, standing across the room covered in bandages, moved a few steps closer.

Lai thought for a moment. "From what I've heard, the *Libertas Publica* started as two separate groups that merged about seven years after the forming of the Republic. One group stood for the reinstatement of the States. The other, I'm not sure of. They were more loosely organized, I think."

Cara shrugged a shoulder. "That's more or less true. The original State Freedom just wanted the States back. They had a leader who swore he could be elected if President Emilia bothered to hold an election."

"I've also heard they formed to create anarchy," Lai continued. "The people who joined only wanted an excuse to create chaos. Any violence they cause only proves it. That's why you were designated a terrorist organization. At least, that's what they tend to say in school."

A high-pitched laugh burst from Cara's throat. "They would say that, wouldn't they? Violence instantly equals terrorists."

"To be fair, you *are* trying to dismantle the government," Kieran pitched in. When Mel gave her a light elbow to her ribs, she only rolled her eyes. "Well, they are."

"She isn't wrong," Cara said, her grin turning mischievous for a moment. "That is our main objective." Her face fell back into the same ever-present curious smile. "But it's a lot more than that.

"When the Republic formed, there was quite a bit of backlash, even if our new president did pull the country from the brink of political collapse. The State Freedom formed very fast, within a year. They had one goal: put things back the way they were. Understandably, they didn't gain a lot of traction at first. Despite the criticisms of the Republic, the United States had been chaotic in the years leading up to the formation. Even with an uncertain future, most people didn't want to go back to that.

"Fast forward five years. An already racist system has just gone to a whole new level. The new immigration laws target people of color exponentially more than white people. Full-time militarized police are basically given a free pass to harass whomever they please."

"Sounds just like home," Kieran mumbled.

Cara glanced to her briefly before she continued. "Another group formed in response to this. They called themselves the POC Liberation Front. They were more loosely organized, yes, but they had a purpose. Fight back against a system that oppresses people of color legally and without a thought.

"While I will be the first to admit the United States did a horrible job for its nonwhite citizens, the Republic legalized whole new forms of oppression. Racial profiling wasn't just used. It was encouraged in a much more public way. The hoops you'd have to jump through to immigrate only got higher off the ground. Grandchildren of illegal immigrants could be deported to a country whose language they didn't even speak. You think this happened to European immigrants too? Let me tell you now, it didn't.

"Less than two years after this group formed, people started to realize that State Freedom had a lot in common with them. Leaders from both groups met and agreed that combining their efforts into an official opposition group would serve their best interests. They joined, and with a play on words, changed their name to the *Libertas Publica*. Which, yes, does translate to State Freedom.

"Over the years, we evolved from protests and information spreading to sanctioned raids. Violence was never, and has never been, our philosophy, but nobody ever changed anything by asking nicely.

We don't condone violence; we just understand its usefulness and its inevitability. It's easy to see how that can be misconstrued to the masses as advocation."

"That sounds about how our supervising officers talked about you," Lai agreed.

"If you don't condone violence, why did Jackie order over a dozen unarmed officers executed?" Jaime asked. All eyes turned to him, though he kept his own gaze unwavering on the ceiling.

Cara tilted her head. "Did she? I'm sure she had a good reason."

"When you guys showed up, we managed to get the weapons away from the officers at the academy," Mel explained. "I thought we'd just leave them there."

"But instead they were all shot," Jaime finished. "They didn't need to be shot like that."

"To be fair, they would have seen which way we went," Virginia pointed out. She had a mildly uncomfortable air about her. "Leaving them without doing anything would have been a risk."

Lai declined to comment on the matter. She was still a mess of conflicting emotions and attitudes about the event in question.

"Jackie isn't a rookie," Cara said. "She gets to make those calls in the field. I trust her."

"We could have just knocked them out," Jaime countered.

"You're very vocal about this," Kieran commented, frowning. "I'd think after everything you wouldn't care what happened to Republic officers."

Jaime shrugged a shoulder. He was a silent for a long moment before he replied. "It just felt unnecessary," he said softly.

He fell silent after that, and the room quieted with him. The only sounds were the beeps coming from various medical devices and gauze being unwrapped by one of the medics.

Of course he had a point. They could have done any number of things to avoid killing those officers. Restrain them, blindfold them, leave them until the other officers managed to get out of the building. Even knock them unconscious.

But that would have taken time, time they might not have had. There was no way to know when the lockdown would end and officers would pour out of the academy and kill on sight.

Besides, didn't Lai know what she was getting into? Didn't they all? After the last two weeks, they'd be fools to expect a nice, quiet sanctuary waiting for them. No, they all knew that there would have to be more deaths before they could succeed.

The silence stretched out before them, everyone seemingly unwilling to break it. Thankfully, one of the medics did it for them, the man who had been working on Lai's hand for the past half hour.

"Can you move your fingers one at a time for me?" he asked.

Lai shook herself out of her thoughts and did as she was told. She carefully bent her pinkie finger to a forty-five-degree angle. She nearly let out a sigh of relief. "It hurts, but it's manageable."

As she moved the rest of her fingers to the medic's instructions, the change of topic noticeably defused the atmosphere in the room.

Mel jumped up from her seat and made her way over to Lai. She bent and examined Lai's hand. "That looks better."

"She's lucky she didn't get an infection," the medic said. He jerked his head back to where Virginia stood. "That one did a pretty good job, considering the circumstances."

Virginia smiled and shrugged a shoulder.

"All right, he's done for now," came another voice from across the room. All eyes turned to Jaime's bed. His prosthetic was patched and reconnected where previously wires stuck out.

"Whoa," Mel breathed. "It looks exactly like it did before."

"It'll work the same too," Cara said, "or close enough to it until it's tweaked to fit your old specifications."

Jaime pulled himself into a sitting position and tentatively tapped a finger against the prosthetic. A moment later, he bent it at the knee. He frowned and let out a soft hum.

"Feels weird." He turned so he was sitting with his legs over the side of the bed. He experimentally rolled the ankle and shrugged. "But it works."

His gaze met Lai's from across the room, and he shot her quick smile. She promptly returned it. She knew the repaired prosthetic meant more to him than he was letting on.

"Think you can walk on it?" Cara inquired.

Rather than give her an answer, Jaime stepped lightly onto the ground and let his legs support his weight. With one hand against the bed for balance, he shifted his weight around for a few seconds before taking a step forward with the prosthetic.

He let his full weight rest on the metallic leg. He took another step and balanced there for a long moment. Finally, he looked back up to Lai and nodded.

"Fantastic!" Cara exclaimed. She jumped off the bed, her combat boots causing her to land with a heavy thud. "Time for the grand tour. Follow me."

With a wave of her hand to punctuate her words, Cara headed toward the same door they had entered through. She had a noticeable skip in her step, as if the disagreement earlier had not fazed her in the slightest.

Jaime was staring after Cara with an undecipherable expression on his face. After a second he noticed Lai's gaze and met it with a raised eyebrow that reminded Lai far too much of his sister.

A quick shake of her head told him there was nothing to worry about. The exchange having taken place in only a few seconds, they fell into step alongside one another and followed behind the others.

As they entered the hall, Lai took another opportunity to look around. She continued to do so as the others spoke.

"Do you really have time to be showing us around?" Virginia asked. "Aren't you the commander?"

Cara glanced back over her shoulder and shrugged, her nose scrunching up as she did so. "I like to get to know new recruits. Besides, you're an interesting bunch."

Lai couldn't help but wonder how often that constant smile of hers was genuine.

Their small group continued down the corridor back the way they previously came. When they reached the intersection, rather than turn right and head to the elevator, Cara led them to the left, deeper into the facility.

The short walk down the hall led them into an expansive room at least three times the size of their training rooms. Metal tables and dated computers filled the room in a messy arrangement, with papers strewn across tabletops. Clusters of people stood around, their voices echoing throughout the space. As Cara delved into an explanation of the function of the room, Lai partially tuned her out, only listening with one ear, and focused on what she was seeing.

There were about thirty people in the room, excluding their group. Nearly half of them stood around the largest table, where a detailed map was laid out. A stocky man in the center gestured to something on the map, which earned him nods from the majority of the group. Lai couldn't make out what it was from the distance. A few of them gave Cara salutes when they noticed her. She promptly waved them off.

The others were split into smaller groups and spoke in hushed voices. Cara mentioned the word "logistics." Though she expected to identify none, Lai nonetheless took a moment to search for any discernible marker of rank among the people. When she found none, she figured she wouldn't have known what they meant anyway, hardly being familiar with the structure of the group.

Her friends stood just in front of her, and they appeared to be paying closer attention to what Cara was saying. Mel, to Lai's immediate right, listened with rapt attention as Cara detailed their procedures for storing valuable information. Kieran, who stood on the other side of Mel, seemed to be listening, though her face betrayed her skepticism. Virginia gazed around the room, her gaze darting between the various groups of people. Jaime stood motionless, his face a mask that did nothing to hint at his emotions.

Cara began walking again, and everyone quickly fell into step. She led them down another hallway and continued with her commentary. Lai made a mental map as they wound through the halls and past dozens of doorways. Cara gestured around her.

"These are the living quarters. You four girls can share. You," she said with a pointed finger to Jaime, "need roommates. I'll ask Sydney if he'll take you in."

Jaime was being unusually quiet. Lai tried unsuccessfully to catch his eye. He seemed to be avoiding all eye contact for the time being.

He could just be nervous, Lai reasoned. She was still apprehensive about their new situation. It was a big, and quite frankly sudden, shift of circumstances. It was bound to be a bit jarring for the former students.

Despite her fears, however, Lai did feel that they were finally in a place where she could be comfortable. At the very least, it was better than the academy. Here, they could fight for something they believed in.

Lai's attention strayed to her cousin again. Mel would also be safe. That was what started the whole thing. That had been her goal all along. Everything else came second to that.

They all pressed to one side of the hall as a line of a dozen or so members streamed past in a quick jog. One of them handed Cara a piece of folded paper on the way past. She stopped and opened it, scanning the words Lai was too far away to read.

Cara clicked her tongue and folded the paper again. Her brows had drawn together in something akin to a frown. It looked wildly out of place on her.

A moment later she seemed to notice she was being stared at. Her smile returned, and she waved off their concern.

"Possible Republic transports to the east," she said. "We'll have to draw back security to avoid being seen."

She went back to her casual pace.

A few minutes later, they came across Jackie as they left a weapons supply room. She spoke to Cara briefly in a hushed tone before the commander nodded. With a quick wink to Lai at her curious glance, Jackie fell into step beside Cara as they continued their tour.

After about twenty minutes of touring, they ended up back at the elevator where they had come down. Lai was glad to stop. Her wounded leg was starting to give her trouble.

Cara turned to face them. "All right, I think that's it for the first day of school tour," she announced with a clap of her hands. "If you'll excuse me, I have to do some real work now. I'll get someone to show you to your rooms." She made to turn away but was stopped when Jaime finally spoke up after nearly half an hour of silence.

"I'm not staying."

Whatever words Lai might have said stuck in her throat and choked back her breath. The words sent a wave of alarm through her. She whipped her head to the side to look at Jaime.

Jaime was standing calmly, his eyes set firmly on the commander. The only betrayal of emotion was a slight shaking in his right hand. Lai didn't think she had ever seen him so serious.

Not that she was thinking very clearly. Not staying. *Leaving.* No. He couldn't. Jaime couldn't leave them. He couldn't leave her. Not now. Not after everything—

"You're not staying," Cara echoed with a subtle edge to her voice. Her smile wasn't entirely gone, but it had tensed a great deal and her eyes no longer matched it.

"I can't stay," he said. "I can't do what you do."

"Jaime, what are you talking about?" Mel asked, her voice a myriad of conflicting feelings. She took a step toward him, a hand outstretched as if to grab his arm, but Kieran held her back with a gentle touch on her shoulder.

"I may not think the Republic is right, but I don't think you're handling it the right way." His words were still directed only at Cara. "You didn't have to kill those officers. *You* didn't have to condone it. But you did. I don't want to do that. I've been doing that for three years. I'm tired of murdering people being the answer to every problem."

"It isn't the answer to every problem," Cara countered smoothly. Her smile gradually faded until it was completely absent. Her eyes narrowed. In that moment, she looked dangerous.

"Even if it isn't, it's the answer more than I'd like. I won't make myself do this anymore."

For nearly a minute, no one spoke. Jaime and Cara continued to stare each other down. Jaime's face was pure determination. Lai knew then that he had already made up his mind. He was really going to leave.

Cara seemed to be studying him as if she couldn't decide whether or not he was serious, or whether or not she wanted him to be.

Concern overwhelmed Mel's features. Kieran's hand was still on her shoulder, a hard frown painting her face. Virginia, a few steps behind the two, swayed back and forth as her gaze flicked between everyone's faces.

Next to Cara, Jackie seemed surprisingly uncomfortable. She kept glancing back to the commander as if waiting for a verdict from a judge.

All at once, Cara seemed to have made up her mind. She crossed her arms over her chest, and the questioning left her eyes.

"Someone get the kid a travel bag," Cara ordered, her face still an unreadable mask.

"Cara, don't you think—" Jackie started.

"It's fine," Cara interrupted. "Just get him a bag. We'll escort you outside, Jaime, and point you in the right direction."

Jackie frowned, though she did as she was told. She turned on her heels and walked swiftly back down the hallway.

"Jaime." Lai locked eyes with him.

He gave her a sorry smile, the first real emotion she had seen on him since he first spoke. "I can't stay here. This isn't the way I want to do things."

"Then how do you want to do things?"

"I'm not sure, but it's not this," he answered honestly. His voice lowered before he continued. "They executed sixteen people right in front of us. I thought we were done with that. If they're not, then I am."

Lai was speechless. Though it didn't compare to what happened to Oscar, the effect wasn't too far off. She was losing her best friend. Even if he would still be alive, if he left....

"What are you going to do?" she asked, her voice dangerously close to breaking.

Jaime let out a heavy sigh. "I'm going to find my sister."

Lai frowned. "Do you even know where Elisa is?"

"No. But I'll find her. I'll find her, and then I'm leaving this country for good. I could go back home. At least Cuba is relatively stable right now."

A wave of intense emotions washed over Lai. "I may never see you again," she whispered.

Jaime squeezed his eyes shut tight. "I know. I don't want that. But if I stay here, I'll be fighting in a way I don't agree with. I can't make myself do that."

"And I wouldn't want to make you do that. But I'll still miss you."

A faint smile found its way onto Jaime's face. "I'll miss you, too, *asere*."

Unable to hold herself back any longer, Lai stepped forward and pulled her friend into a hug that caused him to stumble back a step.

"We started this together," she whispered into his shoulder. "You didn't even have to do this."

"I wasn't going to leave my best friend," he replied with an unconvincing laugh. His arms wrapped around her, and he squeezed her tight. "Thanks for taking me hostage."

A laugh burst from Lai's lips despite herself. The two of them stayed that way in each other's arms, neither of them saying another word. Without her even noticing, their friends had taken a few steps back to give them space. Lai squeezed him harder and ignored the slight sting from her left hand. It was hardly worse than what she was feeling elsewhere.

Jaime turned his face so he could speak quietly in her ear. "You could come with me," he whispered.

Lai shook her head. Part of her wanted to. It wanted to so badly she was ready to abandon their newfound security.

"I couldn't," she said. "This is a fight I want to be in."

He sighed, as if he knew she would say that. He probably did. "You and Mel watch out for each other."

He finally pulled out of their hug, though he kept one arm around her. His attention turned to Mel. "Don't let her get into any trouble."

Mel giggled despite herself. "Don't you get into any trouble."

He went around to say his goodbyes to the rest of their friends. Mel pulled him into a fierce hug. He whispered something to her that Lai couldn't hear. It made them both laugh. Mel gave him a gentle shove and moved back to Lai's side. She brought her hand down and clasped Lai's right hand in her own. Lai smiled to her thankfully.

Kieran wouldn't hug Jaime, but she offered him her hand. He rolled his eyes and took it.

"You're not as annoying as I used to think you were," she told him. "I hope you find your sister."

He gave her a one-sided smile. "I hope everyone here doesn't drive you crazy."

Virginia hugged him, albeit less forcefully than Lai or Mel had. They shared a few words about Rylen, with Virginia giving a deep sigh and Jaime casting his gaze down.

Just as Jackie and another woman returned with a backpack, Jaime stopped in front of Cara. He met her gaze evenly and spoke politely. "Don't let anything happen to my friends." He held out a hand for Cara to shake.

She paused for a long moment before she took it. "Are you sure you want to do this?"

Jaime nodded immediately. "I know you want to do the right thing, but it isn't how I'd do it. You'll be better off without me here."

Cara said nothing as Jaime extracted his hand from her grip. He thanked Jackie as he took the pack from her. She said nothing, only nodded and glanced over to Cara.

Jaime took a moment to rummage through the pack. When he was satisfied, he hummed his approval and zipped it back up.

Finally he circled back around to Lai. "All right. This is it."

"This is it." She leaned forward and placed a single kiss on his cheek. "Good luck."

He glanced to the ground and gave a wistful smile. "What would Oscar think of us now?"

A heavy sigh and a shrug was all Lai could reply with. Jaime chuckled lightly. "I know what he'd think. He'd think we were out of our minds, but he'd end up right where we are now."

Lai mirrored his smile. "I think you're right."

Jaime hefted the pack higher on his back and took several deep breaths. He glanced over his shoulder at the elevator for a long moment, as if steeling himself for what he was about to do.

"All right," he said, barely loud enough for Lai to catch, "*aquí voy.*"

He turned around and took a few steps toward the elevator.

"Hey," Lai called out.

Jaime turned back halfway, his face looking very much like he was holding the bulk of his emotions under control.

"Mahal kita," she said with a smile.

Jaime smiled in return, having recognized the Tagalog phrase she had used in the past, even if only a half dozen times.

"*Te quiero*, Lailani," he replied in his own language.

She kept her focus on Jaime's back as he stepped forward to the elevator. Though she wished she could deny it, she knew it was the last time she would ever see her best friend.

Cara, Jackie, and three other LP members loaded in behind him. He gave Lai one final smile before the doors closed.

"That's that, then," Mel said.

Lai put her good hand on Mel's shoulder and squeezed. "He'll be okay. He's always been strong."

She couldn't tell whether she was trying to convince Mel or herself.

"Let's get you four to your room," the woman who had arrived with Jackie said from behind them. She gestured down the hall and waited for them to follow.

"Ugh," Virginia groaned.

"You all right?" Mel asked.

Virginia waved a hand and nodded, though she continued to grimace. "Headache."

"You should go see a medic," Lai advised. "We've been through a lot."

"I'm fine," Virginia said. "Just—ouch."

"Me. Dic," Mel said purposefully. "Go. Shoo."

"You're the boss, I guess." Virginia squeezed her eyes shut and gave a single nod. "Fine."

Another LP member offered to take Virginia back to the infirmary. She left the others with as best a smile as she could manage. Lai, Mel, and Kieran followed behind the woman down a series of twisting halls. A sign marked Dormitories pointed them to the left, but the woman continued forward.

"Aren't we going to our room?" Kieran asked.

The woman turned her head a fraction. "Keep walking."

"Lai?" Mel whispered. She raised her eyebrows helplessly.

"What's going on here?" Lai asked. She stopped walking and crossed her arms. Mel and Kieran did the same. "Cara said to take us to—"

"You need to see something first," the woman snapped. "Follow me."

She didn't wait for them. She continued her purposeful walk until they were left with no choice but to follow.

"This isn't right," Kieran mumbled.

"We'll see," Lai responded.

Another minute and the woman stopped them outside a closed door marked Security. Through a window, they could see Maurice sitting in front of a computer terminal. A dozen screens showed the outside of the base.

"What is—" Lai began.

The woman raised a finger to her lips. She nodded to the door. "Not a word."

She turned and walked back the way they had come. Lai watched her go until Kieran grabbed her shoulder.

"Look," Kieran said.

Lai peered through the window, watching for any movement on the screens. On the upper right monitor, Lai recognized the elevator they had entered in. The doors slid open, and Jaime stepped out, with Cara, Jackie, and the others close behind.

"Why do we need to see this?" Mel whispered.

Ignoring her question, Lai frowned. There was no sound, but Jaime appeared to be talking to Cara. The commander gestured off-screen. Jackie stood with her arms crossed and her gaze down.

Jaime turned back to face the commander. Lai couldn't see his face.

In a movement too quick for him to react, Cara pulled the gun from her holster and fired.

Lai fell back a step and shut her eyes tight, her hands automatically going up to protect her face. For a blissful moment, she couldn't see, and she thanked God she hadn't been able to hear.

When she opened her eyes, she confirmed that a bullet had just torn through her best friend.

For a moment time seemed to stand still. She closed her eyes again, as if not moving and not seeing would....

No. Not happening. It isn't happening. It didn't—

Her eyes shot open. She watched in slow motion as Jaime fell forward onto his knees. Her mind shut down, not allowing her to react or think properly.

Blood. There was blood soaking through the back of his shirt. Too much blood. Too good of a shot.

Another followed. It hit not an inch from the first, through his left side. A clean shot. An accurate shot.

A trained shot.

It wasn't until his body fell forward, unmoving, onto the floor, that Lai was able to draw in a single rational thought.

No.

She heard Mel choke out a cry. From the corner of her eye, Mel stepped forward. Kieran grabbed her and pulled her back, her arms around Mel's torso to keep her from going into the room.

She was denying it. That was why she wasn't feeling it. She wanted to run outside, go to him, do something, anything. But there was nothing she could do. He wasn't moving on the screen. Cara and Jackie were already going back inside, leaving the others to pick up his body. She didn't need to check. She already knew.

He was gone.

She had seen people die. She had seen numerous people she cared about die in front of her with a bullet through their body. She remembered the emotions well. Anguish. Rage. Heartache.

Denial when she heard about her father.

Now she felt numb. It was almost curious.

That thought was the key to opening the gateway of her emotions. Unbridled fury rushed through her and left her in a state of shock and outrage.

This was different. This was a cold-blooded execution.

This couldn't be justified.

CHAPTER THIRTY

LAI SPENT the rest of the day talking herself out of snapping Cara's neck.

Con: Killing her won't solve anything.

Con: The LP will kill you.

Pro: It would feel really damn satisfying.

What was one more dead body, right? That was what they had ahead of them again. Nothing really changes. The circumstances might change, the exact situation surrounding the actions, but as far as she was concerned, there was hardly a difference between one execution and another.

The hours immediately following Jaime's death passed very quickly.

Kieran wouldn't let Lai go to find Cara. She grabbed Lai and Mel's wrists with gentle force and pulled them back toward the dorms. The woman who had led them to the security office was waiting outside for them.

"Why," Kieran growled.

"The *Libertas Publica* doesn't leave loose ends."

"Why show us?"

"You deserve to know. Go get cleaned up."

"You think after that we can—"

The woman stepped forward. "I think you can. Forget it. Take room four and don't say a word." She turned and started to walk away.

"What's your name?" Kieran asked.

"Forget you know me." She stopped at corner to the next hall. "I'm sorry."

WITH NOTHING else to do, the three girls took showers and changed out of their dirty clothing. Lai stayed under the scalding water for an hour, as if it would burn away the sight of all the death.

Jackie stopped in with dinner a few hours later. The food was amazingly appetizing after the past two weeks of stale bagels and endless apples, but none of them had the stomach to eat.

"Everything okay?" Jackie seemed uncomfortable standing there, shuffling her feet and only meeting Lai's gaze once.

"It's fine," Kieran said in a steady voice. "We're just tired."

"All right. Cara wants you all in top shape for tomorrow. If you're up for it, we'll start on training exercises right away. Your injuries permitting, of course."

"No problem." Kieran took the trays of food, an array of vegetarian lasagna and cucumber salads.

Jackie glanced between the three girls and nodded. "I'm in room six if you need anything." The softness in Jackie's voice would have been surprising if Lai didn't know why it was there.

Lai wished she didn't seem guilty. It would have made it that much easier to hate her.

The silence stretched out until Jackie cleared her throat and walked away without a word.

Left to their own devices, Mel and Kieran began to talk.

"I can't even believe this," Kieran scoffed. "She's acting like nothing happened."

"I bet they've done this before," Mel said, as if to herself. She sat beside Lai on one of the beds, the covers bunched into her fists. Lai had her hands in her lap, her left flexing regularly, her stare glued to the bandage wrapped around it. The sting hardly registered.

"It's all excuses," Kieran continued. "This is what we wanted to get away from. This type of thing, courtesy of the Republic, is why I'm even here. They killed whoever they wanted, even people who didn't deserve it. I could live with executing criminals, even now. But what they're doing is different. They're executing innocent people because it serves them.

"That is exactly what the LP is doing. It was convenient to kill Jaime, just like it was convenient for those officers to kill Deirdre. No one cares. No one gives a single thought to the people that are affected by this. Even these self-righteous bastards care more about their greater ideas than they do about the actual living people they're doing it all for.

"They say they want the citizens of this country to be able to live in safety, without fear. But what happens if they get that? Hmmm? What happens then if a person does something they don't like? Will they just kill them because it's convenient? Do they execute them for the slightest possibility of rebellion? Is that the country we'll always deserve? One where you either fall in line to the leaders or you die?

"Damn it, this isn't what I left for." Finished with her rant, Kieran fell back heavily onto the bed opposite where Lai and Mel sat. She let her head rest against the wall and closed her eyes, apparently exhausted.

"So what do we do?" Mel whispered.

Lai's head shot up. "We leave."

Both girls gave her incredulous stares.

"Leave," Kieran echoed.

"Yes." Lai nodded, her face a hardened mask. "Leave. Now. Leave and never come back. Leave this group, leave this area, leave this damn country. Either way, I'm done."

"But we can't leave," Mel protested, albeit weakly. "They're not going to let us."

"You want to stay?" Lai asked coolly.

A shake of Mel's head was her reply.

"Then—" Lai paused for a moment to pull in a shuddering breath. "—we leave."

Kieran sat up straight and set her face into a hard frown. "Lai's right. We need to get out of here."

"But what'll we do then?" Mel asked. "We don't have any money, and the government wants to kill us."

"I don't care," Lai said simply. "I don't care who wants me dead or how powerful they are. All I know is nobody here is doing things the right way, and I refuse to be a part of that. There's no 'lesser of two evils' here. They're all just wrong."

"It won't just be the government that wants to kill us," Mel pointed out. "The *Libertas Publica* will want our heads on spikes for leaving, especially now. For all they know, we could be running back to the academy to betray them. I wouldn't put it past us if I didn't know better."

"To hell with that," Kieran snapped. "We've survived this long."

"I'd rather die out there than stay and pretend I'm okay with what they're doing," Lai agreed.

"But we'll have nothing," Mel protested loudly.

"Why are you fighting me on this?" Lai demanded in a sharper tone than she typically used with her cousin.

Mel didn't react to her tone. She only clenched her fists together and stared down at them in her lap. "For five minutes I felt safe. Ever since I killed Violet's dad, I haven't felt safe for a single second. Today, when we first got here, I felt safe. Even if it didn't last, it happened. I can't... I mean, I don't know how to shake that. I don't know how to reconcile that with their leader, when she...." Her voice trailed to an indecipherable whisper.

Lai could relate to the feeling. Since the moment she shot Sergeant Washington—no, since the moment she saw Mel on the firing line, Lai hadn't had a real moment to rest, to feel even the slightest bit safe. Every second she was looking over her shoulder, scared to death that something would happen to her or Mel or Jaime. That it would all be for nothing.

In the end, when they finally reached a place they could say was secure, even if it would only be for a time, Cara only proved to her that there was no safety, at least none that she could expect from others. No matter what happened, there was always something, always one more defeat, one more shot fired.

It was never going to end.

Jaime had been with her since the very beginning. Aside from Oscar, he was the first friend she'd had at the academy. She had been a scared fifteen-year-old girl, way in over her head, hoping to prove that she could take care of herself, hoping she could one day protect her country. Serve her country. Prove to herself she could handle her own life.

And then what did she know, there was Jaime, thinking the exact same things as her. A boy from a hard background hoping to rise above it and work to the greater good.

A boy who had sacrificed it all to help her save her cousin, someone Jaime had never even met. That hardly mattered. He only knew he was watching out for his best friend. Lai knew that if Jaime had been in her position, she or Oscar would have done the same without a second thought.

Now she had lost both of them, one to the Republic and one to the group sworn to take them down. Two corrupt organizations with a sickening disregard for life, whatever they might preach.

Lai had had quite enough of it all. It was clear now. She would get no real help from some institution that had to look out for the group before anything or anyone. Who was to say she wouldn't be next? There were other shooters out there without questionable loyalty and even more questionable trauma. It would be the smart thing to do.

At the end of the day, Lai could trust her friends. She could trust Mel, she could trust Virginia, and now she could trust Kieran. She would trust any of them more than she'd trust herself in her current state. Even her family back in Baltimore couldn't compare. As far as she was concerned, her list ended there. The *Libertas Publica* couldn't even come close.

In a way, she supposed she'd made up her mind the moment she could get in a clear thought after Jaime's death. There was no place for her with more killers.

Better on the run, with the constant threat of being found and executed, than that.

A prolonged sigh from Mel brought Lai out of her thoughts. She blinked several times and became suddenly aware of the sharp sting in her left hand. She had clenched it into a fist without noticing. Thankfully, there didn't appear to be any ripped stitches.

"Mel," Lai said softly. She placed her good hand over Mel's. "I understand you're afraid. You aren't used to this. You never needed to be. At least Kieran and I trained for dangerous situations, for times when we might get hurt or die. As new as the reality is for us, it has to be even more shocking for you.

"But we all have to get over it. There's nothing for us here. I can't stay here knowing they…." Lai allowed herself a moment to swallow the lump building in her throat and steady her voice, for Mel's sake as much as her own.

"I don't feel safe here, and neither do you. That moment of security is gone, and it isn't going to come back any time soon. Either we accept that, or we sacrifice the very reason we decided to fight. There's no in between.

"I know what Jaime would do. He wouldn't sacrifice an inch."

For a time, no one said a word. The only sounds that permeated their modest room were the continuous hum of the ceiling lights and their own breathing.

Mel looked to Kieran first. The two shared a long look that to Lai spoke every word of their loss, their anxiety, and their newfound comfort in one another. Kieran understood how Lai felt in losing Jaime, but Lai could see there was even more to it she couldn't begin to understand.

When their gaze finally broke, Mel turned to Lai. Her brow scrunched and her face morphed to pure determination. Lai did her best to match it with an added half smile for support.

"All right." Mel took a deep breath and let it out in a long exhale. "We're leaving."

"All right," Lai echoed. "Then we'd better start packing."

The three girls sprang into motion. Lai and Mel yanked open the doors to the two small closets in the room and grabbed the clothing that was neatly folded on the shelves. Kieran crouched down to pull the backpacks they had been provided with from under the bed. In the drawer of the table between two of the beds, Lai took their small stash of pain meds she and Kieran had been given in case they needed some in the night.

Thank you, LP.

The backpacks could hold close to a week's worth of clothing, but that would only weigh them down. Each of them packed only one pair of pants, a T-shirt, a tank top, a bandana, and a few changes of socks and underclothes, in addition to the set of clothes and the shoes and jackets they were already wearing.

They also had Kieran and Lai's guns, though Lai's was currently tucked into Mel's waistband. She didn't want it back anytime soon.

There was no food in the room, but they didn't have time to worry about that. It wasn't like they could walk up to Cara and ask her for provisions for their long trip ahead. At the very least, they did have full water bottles. There were also two flashlights in the room and four sets of hygiene products. Lai grabbed all of them and divided them into the bags.

"What do we do when we leave?" Mel asked.

The question caused Lai to pause in her task. She shot a questioning look across the room. Kieran tilted her head and shoved a hand in her pocket.

"Well," she said with a hint of a smirk, "we could always find our own way to take out the government."

"How do you suggest we go about doing that?" Lai inquired with a frown, not entirely sure whether Kieran was serious. "We don't have anything but our word."

Kieran removed her hand from her pocket and revealed a handful of flash drives. "That's not entirely true," she said with a shrug.

Lai's eyes widened. "Why do you have those?"

"Sydney almost left them in the back of the van. He was tired. I grabbed them before we got out. No one asked for them. I was going to give them back before…."

She let the rest of her sentence fall away and turned her attention to the wall. She replaced the drives in her pocket and smirked. "At the very least, it's our safety net."

"Kieran, I could kiss you," Lai said with a genuine smile on her face, the first she'd had in half a day.

"I didn't think you were into that sort of thing," Kieran teased.

Lai smirked. "Mel can do it for me."

Less than a minute later, they each had a decent amount of supplies tucked into their bags. There was no food and no money, but that was something they were simply going to have to find on the outside.

When the bags were zipped up, Lai hoisted one onto her back and tightened the straps to fit her. She waited until the others had done the same before she stepped toward the door.

Kieran grabbed Lai's arm and forced her to turn back.

"What about Virginia?" Kieran asked. Her voice betrayed her concern for her friend. "We can't leave her here. She'd want to leave with us if she knew."

"We don't have time," Lai replied. She didn't want to leave Virginia behind. "We have an hour at best before the night patrol starts, and Cara said earlier that they have a group meeting planned for tonight. The halls will be all but empty. If we don't leave this second, they'll have the flash drives tomorrow, and then we'll have nothing, even if we manage to get out another night. This is our one and only shot. Virginia is smart. She'll be fine."

The hopeless expression on Kieran's face showed that she knew the truth of Lai's words. "I hate this."

"I know."

Lai extracted her arm from Kieran's grip and turned back to the door. "We should go east," she decided. "Cara said they were pulling back their security."

"Yes, because they saw a Republic patrol," Kieran added.

"We can't risk the LP catching us. At least we'll stand a chance if we get outside."

Kieran voiced no further objections. Without another argument, Lai took a deep breath and opened the door.

At first she opened it only enough to peek her head out and check the hall. Though there was no one in sight, Lai waited an extra half dozen seconds, her ears tuned to any indicator of activity. When she heard none nearby, she opened the door all the way and motioned for Mel and Kieran to follow.

Lai led them down the hall to the left, a mental map of the layout of the base in her mind. She was suddenly even more grateful that she had been paying closer attention to her surroundings than to what Cara was saying.

They paused at the end of the hall where it branched off in either direction. Stepping lightly, Lai peered around to the right. All clear.

They made their way through the maze of halls at a cautious yet swift pace, pausing at every corner and whenever they heard movement. A few times, when Lai was sure someone was about to round the corridor and see them, she shoved her companions back around the corner or through the nearest doorway, praying that the room was empty. It seemed luck was somehow on their side that night; they all were.

When they came to the hall that housed the med bay, Lai made sure to lead them in a wide sweep around it. Lights flickered from under the doorway. She ignored the pang of sadness that struck her at the thought of Virginia.

As they rounded the corner into the hall that led to the logistics room, Lai held her arm out to stop her companions. There were definitely people in the room.

Lai stepped as lightly as possible and made her way closer to the corner. When she was a few steps away, she leaned over to catch a brief glimpse around into the room. A group of half a dozen people stood around the center table while they pored over maps and argued among themselves. A thought suddenly struck Lai, and she gestured the others forward.

"We don't have a map of the tunnel system," she whispered. She had been so preoccupied with the idea of escape that she hadn't even considered it. That, and Jaime's death was surely clouding her awareness.

"They'll have maps of the whole base and all the tunnels," Mel replied just as softly. "Cara said they do."

"Well, how the hell are we supposed to get one?" Kieran hissed.

Lai flinched at her rising voice. "We could try to steal one," Lai reasoned, "but we're not going to get in there without them seeing us."

"I could create a diversion," Kieran suggested. "Circle around to the other side and get them to follow before coming back around here."

"Then they'll know something is wrong...."

"Oh for the love of...," Mel mumbled. Before either of them could stop her, Mel shouldered off her pack, shoved it into Kieran's arms, and strode confidently around the corner into plain view of the half dozen people in the room.

"What the hell is she doing?" Kieran hissed.

Lai didn't reply. She was frozen where she stood, convinced that Mel had just ruined their entire escape plan. What did she hope to accomplish by getting them caught?

"Hey there!" Mel greeted cheerfully. The woman closest to her turned at her voice.

"Can I help you with something?" she asked.

"As a matter of fact, you can! Can I have a map? This place is confusing, and I already got lost, like, six times looking for the bathroom."

Another man, one Lai recognized from their earlier tour, turned and tilted his head to Mel. "You're one of the new recruits, right?"

"That's right," Mel confirmed. "First day on the job."

The man smiled to her. "Of course. I think we have an extra one.... Leila! Can I get a base map?"

A woman across the table took a moment to riffle through a messy pile at least twenty pages deep. No more than a dozen seconds later, she pulled out a folded piece of paper and handed it to the man.

"Here you are," he said as he gave Mel the map. "This should help you find your way. The bathrooms are marked in blue, believe it or not."

"Thank you!" Mel pulled two pages apart and glanced at the map. "This is perfect."

"Good night, then."

With a grin and wave back over her shoulder, Mel calmly walked back around the corner to where Lai and Kieran waited. Both eyed her with equally incredulous expressions.

"You two have to stop thinking like officers sometimes," Mel said. "People respond better when you're nice."

Lai stared blankly at Mel for a moment before snatching the maps from her hand and heading back the way they had come.

With a wide berth taken around the central command center, Lai continued on to where she remembered the tunnels connected to the base. She consulted the map to be sure, and sure enough, she had them headed in the right direction.

It took no more than four minutes for them to reach the doors leading to the east tunnels. As Lai suspected, there was no one guarding the inner doors. There was hardly any need, especially before night. Lai had seen the tunnels on the map. Without a map such as theirs, there was little, if any, hope of ever navigating the labyrinth successfully.

One last glance around confirmed that there was no one in sight, though if they didn't hurry, the night guard was sure to come to their posts. They would not take kindly to three teenagers trying to escape.

Lai paused for a moment to fish around in her pack for a flashlight. She opened the map and folded it back until only the tunnels were showing.

"You have a pen?" she asked.

Kieran nodded and reached into the side pocket of her bag.

Lai took the pen and uncapped it. After a deliberate study of the tunnels, she used the red ink to draw a path from where they now stood to the tunnel exit she deemed the safest.

"All right," she said, "we're following this route exactly. Stay close behind me and don't slow down. If you get lost in there, you probably won't get back out."

"Whereas if we all get lost, at least we're together?" Kieran thought out loud, almost too quietly for Lai to hear.

She rolled her eyes and handed the pen back. Though her hand stung, even from simply holding the map, Lai forced herself to concentrate. She nodded her head toward the center door. Kieran took the cue and stepped forward to grasp the circular handle. With a grunt of effort, she spun the wheel around until it emitted an echoing click. Kieran pulled the door open to the seemingly endless darkness beyond.

Lai didn't want to waste a second. After a look behind to ensure they were both following, Lai stepped into the black maw armed with only a map and her flashlight.

They followed the winding tunnels for nearly an hour. None of them spoke very much. Lai was too busy concentrating on their course and dared not risk being distracted. Mel and Kieran both seemed equally unsettled by the creeping blackness that surrounded them. The tunnels smelled of damp clay, and particles of dust floated by in the beam of Lai's flashlight.

Even so, their surroundings couldn't sway her. She was singularly determined to have them out.

With everything they had been through, it seemed a strange departure to be trekking through gloomy underground tunnels. After all the action, all the noise, the clanking of their footsteps echoing off the walls was almost welcome.

Lai stopped every so often to mark where she thought they were on the map. In that way, it recorded their escape in a way no others would be aware of. When the ground beneath them began to steadily climb upward, she knew they were getting closer to the surface.

Despite her confidence in their location, it was quite a relief to all three girls when they reached the large steel door at the end of a particularly lengthy branch of tunnel. Mel let out an exaggerated sigh and rushed ahead of Lai.

"I hate these tunnels. I love this door."

Lai allowed herself a slight smile as she folded the map until it could fit in her pocket. She handed the flashlight off to Kieran and stepped ahead of Mel to the door.

Before her fingers closed around the latch, she felt a hand on her back. She turned and met Mel's eyes.

Mel offered an unconvincing smirk. "You know, I wasn't built for this life."

Lai held her gaze and mirrored the expression. "I think you handle it very well."

With one last encouraging smile to her companions, Lai turned and, with a slight grunt at the effort of forcing the latch down, pushed open the door to the dry night air.

Lai stepped out first into the cramped room. Mel came to stand beside her as Kieran forced the door shut behind them. She handed the flashlight back to Lai and frowned.

"This looks like an old shed," she commented.

Kieran was right. The tunnel had let them out into a small wooden structure no more than two meters wide. An assortment of tools littered the ground around them. Starlight filtered in through thin gaps in the ceiling planks.

A padlocked door was the only thing that stood between them and the outside.

Kieran stepped forward to it and grasped the lock in her left hand. With a hard tug, the wood that held the lock and metal clasp in the door broke away.

"You'd never expect the entrance to a top-secret base to be in here," she said as she dropped the padlock to the ground.

She cautiously pushed the door open and stepped out into a stone courtyard with a dried-up garden covering half of the ground. Vines snaked up walls that rose two stories over their heads on all sides. To the left, there was a path leading around a corner of the building. Kieran went on ahead to scout it out while Lai took a moment to breathe in the air, however hot and dry it might be. After the old damp of the tunnels, it was quite welcome.

"We're in a residential area," Kieran announced when she came back into the courtyard. "I don't see anyone or anything except more buildings like this one. We're clear."

"We're clear," Lai echoed under her breath. A thought returning to her, she reached into her pocket where she had slipped the map and then into the side pocket of her bag. She pulled out a lighter and wasted no time in setting the folded paper ablaze.

"What did you do that for?" Kieran questioned.

Lai let the smoldering map fall to the ground. "We wouldn't want any Republic officers getting a hold of this. Besides, we hardly need it now."

"Speaking of now," Mel cut in as she rocked on her heels, "now we're out. We're clear, like Kieran said."

"We need somewhere to go," Kieran agreed with a nod.

"Lani?" Mel said.

Lai brought her gaze up from the map as it turned to a pile of ash. "The way I see it, we have limited options.

"We can't fly. Going west means hitting water. South takes us back into Republic controlled land, or farther to Mexico. East takes us farther into the interior of the country, which is the last thing we want."

"Mexico is a bad idea," Kieran said. "Even if we made it through to the border, they're the last country that would want to help fugitives."

"It sounds like we have one real option," Mel pointed out.

Lai nodded once. "If we head north, we'll eventually come to Canada. The borders may be closed, but with what we have, they may let us in. If not, smugglers would take us over for the right price."

"We were thinking of going north before, back when we were at Jaime's house."

Kieran planted her hands on her hips and looked up at the clear, star-filled sky. "Then we've made up our minds. We're going north."

Lai closed her eyes and made herself take several deep breaths.

This was it. They had passed the point of no return, and now they were completely on their own. The government wanted them dead. The *Libertas Publica* wanted them dead. They had nobody but each other and nothing but the bags on their backs.

That, and a handful of flash drives with incriminating information against the government.

With the flash drives, they could start the destruction of a corrupt institution that had cost countless innocent citizens their lives. One that had cost Lai the life of her two best friends. One that regularly imposed on the lives of whomever it pleased. One where even the resistance would kill an innocent boy for daring to disagree with them.

Oscar was gone. Angella was gone. Jaime was gone. She had long since thrown out any hope of seeing her family again. This was the life she had now.

If they were to have any hope of safety, any chance of staying alive and putting an end to the Republic once and for all, there was only one way to go for now.

Lai met their eyes with a look of pure determination.

"All right. North it is."

JORDAN GILLESPIE is a young author living in British Columbia, Canada. She is enrolled at the University of Victoria in Greek and Roman Studies with the hopes of eventually becoming a librarian. She has been writing since she was too young to hold a pencil and had to dictate stories to her mother. When she isn't writing, Jordan enjoys rock climbing, baking, playing with her pets, spending time with her girlfriend, and losing to her girlfriend's little brother at Mario Kart. She is a lover of tea, coffee, and any local café where she can buy a good vegan muffin.

Including LGBT characters in her writing is hugely important to her. Young people especially deserve to see themselves represented in a diverse range of genres, and Jordan hopes to add to this body of work with her own writing. She has published three short stories with Harmony Ink Press in their *Harmonious Hearts* collections, and won the pride month short story contest in June 2019 at the locally owned bookstore Bolen Books. Her favorite genres to read are science fiction, fantasy, and speculative fiction, and her favorite authors are Ursula K. Le Guin, Madeline Miller, and Neal Shusterman. Jordan can be found on Twitter @JordanGillespie and on Tumblr @vicbcwriter. *Accuracy* is her first published novel.

www.harmonyinkpress.com

Also from Harmony Ink Press

FELICITAS IVEY

I'M NOT
WHO YOU
THINK I AM

www.harmonyinkpress.com

www.ingramcontent.com/pod-product-compliance
Lightning Source LLC
Chambersburg PA
CBHW051631260626
47170CB00004B/1131